LUCKY DOG

The Moonstone Chronicles

Book 2

Carol R. Ward

Lucky Dog
Copyright 2016 by Carol R. Ward
Published by Brazen Snake Books

This book is for Bishop, the real lucky dog. And for Sheila Herrington, who kept the faith.

Acknowledgments

This book would not have been possible without the wondrous Jamie DeBree, a magical woman in her own right. And special thanks to Ciara Ward-Baker for all her hard work on the cover.

Chapter 1

The small camp fire was nothing more than a pile of glowing embers within a ragged ring of stones. In the distance, a wolf howled mournfully at the quarter moon that glimmered faintly through the trees. There was no wind, but small rustlings filled the night air. Oblivious, the cloak-wrapped figure beside what was left of the fire snored gently.

The chestnut mare, tethered nearby, whickered and pawed the ground as a shadow stole into the camp. Ghosting from tree to tree, the shadow made its way carefully to where a travel pack had been left haphazardly near to where the sleeper lay. With infinite care and a delicate touch that belied his size, he searched the pack thoroughly.

What he was looking for was not there. Biting back a frustrated sigh he sat back on his heels and looked around the small camp. There, the tree the horse was tied to. There was a pair of saddle bags lying at its base. The would-be thief cautiously moved in that direction and swore softly as he stumbled over the saddle left carelessly near the horse.

He froze as his intended victim stirred. The sleeper muttered incoherently and one slim arm freed itself from the cloak long enough to gesture in the air. There was a crackle of static, a flash of blue light, and the sleeper slept on.

It was morning. There were birds chirping their fool heads off and a shaft of sunlight hitting her in the face. Even before opening her eyes, Jessica O'Connell felt the keen edge of disappointment that the last several weeks had not been just a bad dream. Instead of a nice, soft bed, she was waking up on the damp, hard ground. And she was cold, the bone deep cold that came from sleeping outside.

This whole situation was so not fair!

It was one thing to see the amount of space the Darkwood Forest took up on a map, it was another thing altogether to be actually traveling through it, witnessing its vastness first hand. Every day it was trees and more trees beyond. She was even beginning to dream about trees, although dreaming about trees was preferable to the reality of waking up surrounded by them.

Before she could get too caught up in feeling sorry for herself, the mare neighed at her and pawed the at ground."All right, all right. I'm getting up."

Groaning, she stood and stretched. The fire was dead, no big surprise there. Just another one of the many inconveniences she was learning to live with. No matter how well she thought she had it banked it was never enough. There must be some trick to it she hadn't discovered yet.

"What the devil's this?" She tripped over a pile of clothing near the saddle. "And where'd you come from?"

This was directed at a large, shaggy black dog, peering at her from the underbrush. The dog whined and came into the open, wagging his tail hopefully.

"That's just what I need, company for breakfast."

Yawning hugely, she opened the pack and rummaged around inside it. "Sorry, horse," she said. "You're on your own. I'm out of grain. You though, dog, are in luck." She held out a chunk of moldy-looking cheese and a half a loaf of hard bread.

The dog whined in the back of his throat.

"Hey, beggars can't be choosers."

She tossed most of the cheese and a generous portion of the bread towards him. They vanished almost instantly.

Jessica nibbled at her bread, trying to imagine it was a breakfast bagel, or even a biscuit spread with jam. It didn't work. She took the last swig of water from her water skin. The water had a funky taste to it that she made a concentrated effort to ignore.

This was it. The last of her supplies. If she didn't find a town or a village or even a farmhouse today, she'd be in serious trouble. Who was she kidding? She was already in serious trouble. But if she didn't find some food today she'd be both hungry *and* in serious trouble.

With a sigh she reached inside her shirt and pulled out a milk-white amulet.

"Howard?"

There was no answer.

"This is what happens when you try to help out a friend," she muttered. "They teleport you into a different dimension and forget about you."

Several weeks ago, Howard, Jessica's oldest friend, was experimenting with magic and accidentally sent her to this magical realm. The moonstone pendent she'd found in a box of her mother's things was their only means of communication. It came in two parts - Jessica had one half and Howard held the other.

"Wakey, wakey, Howard. Rise and shine."

Since she'd arrived in this realm she'd been rescued from a cliff by a bona fide prince, attacked by a giant bird, made friends with a squire and an honest to goodness bard, vanquished an army of illusions, and then was framed for murdering a king. Oh, and there was the little matter of her being in the possession of a natural talent for magic, which at this point was more trouble than it was worth.

The dog cocked his head and yipped at her; Jessica ignored him and shook the amulet. "Damn it, Howard. Where are you?"

"Do you have any idea what time it is?" a very grumpy, disembodied voice asked.

"At least you got to sleep in a real bed." She let the amulet hang outside of her shirt and began to saddle the horse. "Tell me again why I have to go all the way to the southern continent to get help? Aren't there any wizards up here in the north?"

"Lots of them," he replied with a yawn. "But first you'd have to find one powerful enough to help, and then you'd have to persuade them to help . . ."

"It was kind of a rhetorical question, Howard."

"Oh. Are you still lost?" A trace of amusement replaced the grumpiness.

"I am not lost. I'm taking a shortcut."

"You can't take a short cut when you don't know where you're headed," Howard pointed out. "Your signal's weak this morning, Jess. What have you been up to?"

"Nothing!" she said indignantly. "I've been very careful to preserve my power."

Nothing short of self-preservation would induce her to squander her power. She still harbored the belief that Howard could figure out a way to bring her back home making the trip to the southern wizards unnecessary. But to do that he'd need an energy boost, hence the hoarding of her natural power.

"Are you sure?" Howard asked.

"Yes I'm sure. There hasn't been a reason to. I haven't run into any people; I haven't even seen any wildlife around, unless you want to count the dog that's hanging around the camp this morning. One that likes to steal clothes, apparently." She toed the pile of clothing near her pack.

"A dog? Clothes?"

"He probably just strayed from some farm. He seems friendly enough."

"Hmmm," Howard said. "Do me a favor Jess and don't go anywhere just yet. I want to check on your power loss."

"Well hurry up. I would really like to try and find an inn or even a barn to sleep in tonight. And I'm out of food - I'll need to find some place to resupply."

She leaned back against the tree and yawned again. Maybe she could have a quick nap while she waited. A shadow passed overhead and she glanced upwards, frowning.

"Oh great, this is just what I need to cap off this miserable week."

The sun was slowly being smothered by grey, ominous looking clouds. Rain gear had not occurred to her when she'd packed for this trip. So far she'd been lucky to find shelter close by whenever the weather turned against her. It looked like today was the day her luck, such as it was, was going to run out.

"How'd you sleep last night Jess?" Howard asked suddenly.

"What?"

"You heard me, how'd you sleep?"

"How do you think? It was cold, the ground was hard and some animal started rooting around the campsite. Probably that dog." She glared at the animal in question, as though he were to blame for the change in the weather.

There was a canine grin on his face as he sat there with his tongue lolling out of his mouth.

"You mentioned a pile of clothing . . . could you check them for me?"

"I think you've slipped a cog Howard."

"Just humor me."

Jessica stooped to rifle through the pile of clothes. "Black shirt, feels like cotton or linen or whatever they make clothes out of, black leather pants that have seen better days, and very nice, well worn leather boots, sized big. Someone's going to be real ticked off. The dog must have robbed them while they were skinning dipping or something. But why bring the clothes here?"

"Keep digging Jess."

Jessica folded the clothes neatly and set them aside. "The boots have knife sheaths, fully loaded. And . . ." she paused. "Howard, there's a couple of really big knives and a huge sword here. What's going on? I can see the dog carrying off clothes, but not weapons." She looked around nervously. "Who left all this stuff here and why?"

"Jess, I—" Howard paused, then restarted. "Did you notice anything special when you heard that animal rooting around in your camp last night?"

Her brow furrowed. "There might have been some lightning, but I was too tired to worry about it. I might have uttered a profanity or two."

"Would one of those profanities have been something along the lines of son-of-a-bitch?"

She shrugged. "Could have—no!" Jessica swiveled around and stared at the dog, who backed away from the look on her face. "You're not suggesting . . ."

"It's consistent with your loss of power Jess."

"How could this happen?"

"This kind of spell takes more instinct than concentration."

She rubbed a hand tiredly over her forehead. "I don't have time for this."

Howard maintained a prudent silence.

"Well it serves you right," she told the dog. "Who do you think you are, sneaking up on me in the middle of the night? You're probably a thief and the world's better off with you as a dog."

The dog simply sat, watching her.

"At this rate I'll never build up enough power to get back home," she muttered angrily. "All right Howard. Tell me how to change him back."

"Well, the thing is Jess . . ."

"Holy Saint Christopher! What now?"

Howard spoke quickly. "The thing is, you'll have to wait until the next quarter of a waning moon to reverse the spell because it appears to be tied to the lunar cycle."

"You mean I'm stuck with this dog for a month?"

"That about sums it up, Jess."

Jessica glared at the dog. His tail thumped the ground.

"Look at the bright side. For the next month you'll have someone besides your horse to talk to."

"Not funny Howard."

How had things become so complicated, Jessica wondered. After she'd been accused of murdering the king and her friends had rescued her from the dungeon of Ghren, the plan had been to meet up at the Rusty Lion in Vargon's Reach. From there Jessica, Sebastian the bard, and Gareth the former squire, were going to continue on to the southern lands in search of a wizard named Thackery who was her best hope of getting home again.

The escape plan went pretty well. Wendel, a wizard of very minor abilities, was able to cast a glamour causing Eleanor the former lady's maid, Meren the tanner's wife, and Gareth, much to his chagrin, to appear just similar enough to Jessica to cause those chasing her confusion. They rendezvoused at Vargon's Reach on schedule, but just as they were about to part ways one of Meren's sons spied two of the new king's special guards, the ones impervious to magic, lurking in the market.

Obviously there was more to these magic-proof guards than they realized and a new plan for getting south was needed. Jessica was adamant that she'd imposed on her new friends above and beyond what could reasonably be expected of them. They'd uprooted their lives enough for her already. Meren and her husband Reece had two children to think of - she insisted they continue on to the mountains as they'd planned, although Meren insisted on keeping her red hair for the journey.

Eleanor, too, insisted on keeping her red hair, and she and Wendel opted for taking a more scenic route to meet up with Reece and Meren later. After much soul searching, Gareth decided to go with them, this time in the guise of the bard Sebastian. It was to be hoped that they'd draw the witchguards away.

To further muddy the waters, Jessica and Sebastian decided to split up. Sebastian chose a route that skirted the Darkwood Forest while Jessica decided to take the last route anyone would expect her to take, through the forest itself. They would meet up on the other side at an inn in Eglion belonging to a friend of Sebastian's.

The novelty of being on her own had lasted for all of one day. Jessica wasn't much of a horseperson, and she was definitely not the outdoorsy type. Sebastian had tried to give her a few pointers on choosing a suitable campsite but really, wasn't one area of woods much like another? She learned differently her first night alone when she spread her bedroll beside a picturesque pond and was up all night slapping mosquitoes. The next night she found a nice spot on a slight rise, and was kept awake by the cold wind sweeping over it.

There were countless trails threading their way through the Darkwood Forest. A handful of these were well travelled and fairly safe, but many were well hidden and with good reason. Darkwood was also known as the Thieves Forest, the destination of many a thief trying to escape justice.

The trail Jessica had chosen was not one of the most frequented, but she was still a little surprised she hadn't seen anyone else. What she didn't realize was that while the trail she was on would have eventually taken her to where she wanted to go, it was taking her in a roundabout way and every mile she traveled took her further into danger. And that was before she'd gotten herself lost.

Chapter 2

"I have a question Howard," Jessica said. "If I don't know how I turned this guy into a dog, how am I supposed to turn him human again?"

"We'll cross that bridge when we come to it, I guess."

The dog gave an unhappy whine.

"I've got a better idea," she countered. "You should start teaching me how to use my magic."

"Jessica . . ." Howard paused while he tried to come up with a reasonable excuse. Though Jessica was unaware of it, magic came to her honestly. The fact was, she had been born in the magical realm, sent through the veil as an infant to hide her from a powerful blood mage. The southern wizards were in fact her father and grandfather, who were working with Howard to guide her.

They wished to remain anonymous and had been adamant that she wait until reaching them before attempting any more magic. Something about not wanting her to attract the wrong kind of attention. While Howard agreed on principle, it nettled, just a little, that they didn't think he was capable of teaching her the basics. "Remember what happened the time you tried to light a fire?"

"But I did light one," she pointed out with a grin. The incident in question took place shortly after her arrival in the kingdom of Ghren, when she inadvertently scorched an entire clearing while attempting to light a small fire. "And I've been practicing, check this out," she said, forgetting that the moonstone was audio only.

Howard moved over to his scrying bowl so he could see her. During her first few days in the magical realm he could only talk to her. But Thackery, her father, and Paran, her grandfather, taught him to use a scrying bowl and now he had visual as well as audio. She didn't know this of course, and she tended to forget he couldn't see her. But for some odd reason, something to do with the magical properties of the moonstone itself, she never seemed to question it when he commented on something he would have had to be able to see her do.

Now he watched as she held out her hand and concentrated. A small ball of fire appeared, hovering over her palm. Her brow furrowed slightly and it began to spin, then she began gently tossing it from hand to hand. Jessica grinned. "How's that for learning control?"

"It's great Jess, but I wouldn't recommend tossing and spinning at the same time. It might—"

As if it had a mind of its own, the ball of fire suddenly spun away from her. It zipped through the clearing, ricocheted off of several trees, then exploded in a shower of sparks. The dog yelped and ducked into the bushes; the mare neighed, pulling at her lead as she tried to bolt.

"—get away from you," Howard finished. "I suppose it might be a good idea to teach you some basic control so you don't have any more accidents." He tried, and failed, to stifle a large yawn.

Jessica smiled. "You're a peach, Howard. What time is it there?" she asked suddenly.

"It's just after four a.m. But don't worry about it," he added hastily. "You know me, my hours are all over the place." The truth was he hadn't been sleeping well since she'd entered the forest, but he kept that to himself. No sense in her worrying over his worry.

"Sorry. I wish there was some way of figuring out the time difference."

"I think the days there are longer than the days here, although I still haven't quite figured out by how much."

"It's too bad you couldn't use that voodoo of yours to make a watch that would translate the time for us."

"Yeah, too bad," he said with another yawn.

"Never mind," she said with a chuckle. "Go back to bed, Howard. I'll talk to you later."

"Later, Jess." He turned away from the scrying bowl and tried to muster the energy to go back to his bedroom. Maybe he'd just rest his head on the work table and nap instead. It wouldn't be the first time.

The soft glow enveloping the moonstone winked out.

Jessica picked up the saddle bags and slung them over the mare's back. "I can't believe how quickly I've gotten used to this," she muttered. The mare ignored her. The dog, who'd crept back out of the bushes after the fireball exploded, tilted its head. "Make camp, break camp, saddle the horse, unsaddle the horse—Lord what I wouldn't give for a nice, hot bath."

She gave one last tug to the saddle before preparing to mount. The dog made a noise, and pawed at the pile of clothing on the ground.

"Seriously? You expect me to cart your crap around too?"

He whined, giving her a very impressive dose of puppy-dog eyes, and wagged the tip of his tail hopefully.

Jessica sighed and pulled the travel pack down. She managed to fit the clothing and knives inside, but the sword posed a problem.

"I don't suppose I could leave this behind?" she asked.

The dog barked and shook his head.

It was too heavy for her to wear, even if she hadn't already been wearing a sword of her own, and she couldn't just hang it from the saddle because the mare flinched every time it touched her. At last she pulled out her spare blanket, wrapped the sword and sheath in it, and tied the whole thing to the back of the saddle.

"There, happy now?"

The dog thumped his tail and grinned that canine grin of his. She climbed into the saddle, something else she was starting to get good at.

"I don't suppose you know where the nearest inn is, do you?"

The dog woofed at her and trotted down the trail. Jessica arched an eyebrow and nudged the mare in that direction.

By mid-morning it was drizzling. Not wet enough to impede vision or progress, but enough to seep into Jessica's clothing.

Later the drizzle turned into a steady rain and she hunched down into the saddle. Only the thought of a soft bed and a hot meal kept her going.

Late in the afternoon, if time could be told in the dismal grey, they halted at a river bank. The river was swollen from the rain, the remains of a bridge could be seen on either bank. Jessica stood up in the stirrups, then sat back with a sigh.

"Let me guess, the inn is on the other side of that river."

The dog barked, a somewhat forlorn sound. He was looking rather bedraggled himself. Jessica was too discouraged to offer him any comforting words. She sat for a long while watching the river boil past. At last she pulled out the amulet.

"Howard, I need your help."

He was there instantly. "What's up Jess?"

"We need some shelter, this side of the river. At this point I'll even settle for an overhang, as long as it's dry."

"I'll get right on it Jess, just hang tight."

Howard turned to his scrying bowl and started scanning the area. It never failed to amaze him that this one spell worked every time. Sure it was using magic borrowed from the two wizards in Jessica's world, but it was still magic, and he was using it. Waving his hand and muttering an incantation in a foreign tongue, he managed to get the picture in the bowl to pull back to give him a better view.

"Well this isn't going to work," he muttered after a few minutes. With the area in the bowl pulled back for a more panoramic view, it made the details harder to see. Not that he could really see anything except trees. He could see the silver thread of the river Jessica was beside, but he couldn't pinpoint her exact position. All he could tell is that she was nowhere near the trail she'd been following in the beginning, she really was lost. He was going to need some help.

Howard waved his hand over the bowl to clear the image and then whispered a single word. The oil filling the bowl shimmered and then cleared, revealing the inside of a stone room high in a wizard's tower. There was a rustle of movement and then a freckled face appeared, looking down into the bowl on the other side of the spell.

"Master Howard, how may I be of service?"

"Ah, Ithcal. Would you be so kind as to fetch either Master Paran or Master Thackery. Please assure them it is not an emergency, but it is rather important."

"Right away master." The face disappeared and receding footsteps could be heard.

Howard couldn't help the grin that crossed his face at being called "Master", especially since Ithcal had probably worked more magic in his life than he had.

Jessica's father and grandfather ran a wizard's school in the southern continent. When she'd first arrived in their world, the students had been on a break so they'd been able to spend most of their time in the scrying room talking to Howard and watching Jessica. But school was back in session and Paran and Thackery had classes to teach.

Since they preferred to keep their presence a secret from Jessica, Howard was their only means of helping her on her journey. They relied on him to watch over her and had five of their best students take turns sitting in the scrying room in case he needed anything.

"Friend Howard, is aught well with my granddaughter?" Paran's face filled the scrying bowl.

"She's still in the Darkwood Forest—"

"Yes," Paran nodded. "The forest is quite vast. She will be traversing it for many days yet."

"I think she's a little lost. She's run out of supplies and she could use some place to shelter for the night - it's raining. My scrying skill is still pretty new. I can't see the forest for the trees, so to speak."

"Ahh." Paran nodded sagely. "What's needed is a locator spell in conjunction with the scrying. This is something we should have thought of teaching you earlier."

"Teach me?" Howard repeated, trying to be cool and not too eager.

"'It is not much more difficult to master than the scrying and you have managed that with ease."

Howard waged an inner war with himself before speaking again. "While I appreciate the offer and would love to learn a new spell, it's going to take time and Jessica can't wait."

"You are a good friend, Howard. 'Twill take only a moment."

Howard nodded and Paran's face disappeared from view. It was back again in under a minute.

"There is an inn within a day's ride, but it is on the other side of the river and I fear the bridge is washed out. With the rain the river is too dangerous to ford. There is a farm to the south about half a day's ride, and a wayfarer's station about a candlemark to the west. From the look of it it's been abandoned, but the structure is sound."

"I don't think she's going to want to ride for another half a day, so the wayfarer's station it is. Thank you Paran."

"It is my pleasure. And Howard?"

Howard stopped with his hand in the air, ready to dismiss the image.

"When my granddaughter is situated, contact me again for that spell."

"Thank you!" Howard said with a grin.

Chapter 3

The rain finally stopped. Jessica dismounted and stretched while she waited. The dog, whom she dubbed Bandit, came over and sat near the horse. His head was lowered and he sneezed twice - he looked every bit as miserable as she felt. A slight breeze sprang up and Jessica shivered in her wet clothes, wishing Howard would hurry up. Finally, a soft glow suffused the moonstone amulet.

"There's some kind of traveler's hut nearby," Howard told her. "I can't guarantee what shape it's in, but it's the best I can do. Just kept the river on your right for about an hour, then north for about ten minutes and you can't miss it. Just leave your moonstone out - it'll glow green to let you know you're on the right track."

"Thanks Howard." Jessica mounted up again.

"Jessica? Are you all right?"

"I'm fine Howard, I just need to dry off."

The traveler's hut was an unimpressive long, low building, but the roof was solid and the weathered grey plank walls would give them protection from the wind and rain. Other than a large supply of wood stacked just outside the door, it appeared to have been stripped of anything useful long ago.

There was a fireplace in the middle of the wall opposite the door, with a wooden chest beside it. The floor was strewn with dirt and decayed refuse, and it had a musty smell to it. The interior was dark enough that the ends of the room were lost to shadow, but a pile of straw could just be made out in the one side. Jessica lead the mare right inside, spreading the straw out for her to stand on.

After unsaddling the horse and depositing the pack and saddlebags on the hearth, she eyed the fireplace for a moment. Going back outside she returned with as much wood as she could carry. On her second trip outside it began to rain again.

There was a short, sharp, quizzical bark from the dog.

"I know it's wet," Jessica replied, as though he asked a question. "But so are we. And I'm not only wet, I'm cold. And I'm tired of being wet and cold and miserable."

She stacked several logs in the fireplace and stood back, contemplating the arrangement. The dog moved between her and the fireplace and barked a question.

"What are you doing?" she asked, irritation in her voice. "Oh, you think I'm going to mess this up like I did the fireball. Or the other time I tried to make a fire. This is totally different. Now get out of the way."

Reluctantly, the dog moved to one side, then retreated all the way back to the door. Jessica centered herself, the way Howard had instructed her the first time she'd used magic, reaching deep inside for that magical spark that had been hers since she first landed in this world. Focusing on the pile of wood in the fireplace she drew up the magical energy, not too much, pointed at the wood and released it.

A red glow shot from her fingertip to the pile of wood. The wet wood steamed, then with a "whoosh" began to burn. Jessica grinned, feeling pretty pleased with herself. She wished Howard had been around to see it.

"See?" she told the dog, "Piece of cake." She sighed, her elation fading. "I wish I hadn't said the word cake. I could really go for a piece of cake right now. A giant slab of Ellen's Oreo double chocolate fudge cake."

Ellen was her best friend, and roommate, in the mundane realm, as she'd taken to calling Earth. She topped the list of things Jessica missed about her home world. She missed her even more than indoor plumbing and pizza.

The mare stamped her foot restlessly and Jessica suddenly heard Gareth's voice in her head. One of his duties as a squire had been to teach her how to deal with horses and one of the first things he'd taught her was to always make sure her animal was well cared for.

"Your life will sometimes depend on your horse," he'd told her. "No matter how tired you are, remember that your horse has carried you whatever distance you travelled and it deserves to be looked after before you look after yourself."

Picking up a handful of straw, she rubbed as much of the water out of the mare's coat as she could manage. "It could be worse," she told her. "At least we have a roof over our heads tonight. And if it's any consolation, I'll be going hungry too."

The mare flicked an ear towards her and snorted. The dog

gave a sharp bark to get her attention and Jessica looked over to where he sat beside the wooden chest. "What's up with you?" The dog pawed at the box and woofed at her.

"If there's a mouse inside there, you're welcome to it," she said, giving the mare a final pat before going over to the dog.

"Yowsa!" she exclaimed, lifting the lid. "We've hit the jackpot Bandit."

The chest was filled with supplies. There were a couple of thick, warm blankets, a bucket that held a bag of grain for the horse, bread, cheese, apples, and what appeared to be strips of dried meat. Under the blankets were a couple of towels, a wineskin, and a tin cup.

"Bless you, Howard!" Jessica said aloud. There were places in heaven for thoughtful friends like him.

Since she'd let the mare drink from the river while they were waiting for Howard to get back to them, Jessica didn't worry about watering her. She dumped some feed into the bucket instead and set it down for her to feast on.

The fire was starting to take the edge off the cold and damp of the cabin. Reaching for one of the saddle bags, she pulled out a change of clothing, grateful beyond belief that Wendel, the hedge wizard she befriended in Ghren, insisted on magicking her horse's gear, saddlebags, and pack so they were waterproof.

She pulled off her leather jerkin and had just started unlacing her shirt when she remembered the dog. He was sitting in the shadows, tongue lolling out of his mouth. If she didn't know better, she'd swear he was smirking at her.

"All right you, out." She went over to the door and held it open for him.

He made a whining noise but, ears drooping, obediently headed out the door. Jessica grinned in his wake. Shaking her head she pulled off her boots and the rest of her clothing, quickly drying off using one of the towels. After dressing in fresh, dry clothing she opened the door and called the dog back in.

"Oh, don't give me that look," she told him as he slunk over to the fireplace. He moved as close to the fire as possible and sat there shivering. Jessica heaved a sigh and picked up the other towel. "C'mere," she said.

Head held low he glanced her way. "Oh, come on. Stop being a martyr." She shook the towel at him. "Come here and I'll dry you off."

Feigning reluctance, he came within her reach and stood patiently while she rubbed the towel vigorously over him. By the time she was done the fire was heating up things nicely.

"Okay. I don't know about you, but I'm starving."

Jessica piled a few more damp logs on the fire and using one of Bandit's knives, sliced off generous portions of bread and cheese. She sniffed the strips of jerky, shrugged and added a few to the pile. Bandit had his head tilted as he watched her curiously.

After spreading a blanket in front of the fire, Jessica divided the bread and cheese equally, but placed extra meat strips in one of the piles and an apple in the other. Sitting cross-legged near the pile with the apple, she gestured to the other.

"Well, don't just stand there, help yourself."

Bandit stepped gingerly onto the blanket and then lay down to eat. He wolfed down the bread and cheese and then settled in to start gnawing on one of the strips of meat. When Jessica picked up the wineskin his head popped up and he made a noise that was a cross between a whine and a whimper.

"You've got to be kidding!" she said.

He made the noise again and wagged just the tip of his tail hopefully.

Muttering under her breath she reached into the chest and pulled out the tin cup. Filling it half full, she set it in front of him. "That's all you're getting so don't spill any."

He wagged his tail and lapped carefully until it was all gone.

Jessica stared meditatively into the fire as she ate, alternating bites of the cheese with sips of the wine and chasing it down with bites of bread. Sending Reece and his family on their way, and the rest of the people who had been instrumental in helping her escape from Castle Ghren, seemed like the noble thing to do, but now . . .

She yawned, the day catching up with her.

"Jessica . . ."

The dog yelped and sprang to his feet at the sound of Howard's voice.

Jessica reached for the amulet. "What is it Howard?"

"I thought you'd like to know, the rain should let up tonight and the river will be back to normal by mid-morning. There's a place to ford it just a few miles downstream from the bridge and there's an inn just a few miles beyond that."

"Thanks Howard. And thanks for all the stuff."

"Stuff?" he repeated, confused.

"You know, the supplies. In the wooden trunk. You even remembered food for the horse. I really appreciate you taking care of me."

"Oh, that," he said, realizing that Paranithel must have magicked up the supplies for her. "It was nothing."

"No, it was something, and I just want to thank you."

"You're welcome Jess." There was a hesitation, then he asked, "Are you going to be all right?"

"I'll be fine after a couple of nights in a proper inn. I'll contact you then."

Howard's presence vanished. Jessica finished eating and then pulled the second blanket from the chest. Wrapping herself up in it, she lay down in front of the fire. Bandit settled down on the other side of the blanket still spread out on the floor and went back to worrying at the meat strips, glancing from time to time at the figure sleeping beside him. At last he, too, curled up and went to sleep.

Chapter 4

Howard sighed as there was a knock on the door to his apartment. There was only one person who would be bothering him at this time of night.

"Come in, Ellen."

The petite young Asian woman darkening his doorstep was Jessica's other best friend, and held Howard responsible for Jessica's disappearance. Howard could sort of understand it, but it wasn't as though he'd been trying make Jessica vanish. He really hadn't believed his teleportation spell would work. If anything, it was the fault of the two wizards from the other dimension who'd enhanced his spell. They'd failed to take into account the amount of power he'd been able to raise, which threw Jessica's landing in their universe way off.

"How's Jessica doing?" Ellen asked, by way of greeting, pushing him aside as though she had every right to be in his apartment. For such a small woman she could be a real force of nature.

"Still in the Darkwood Forest, but at least she's getting the hang of camping. She's not liking it much, but she's getting the hang of it."

"Poor Jess, she's never liked camping." Ellen went over to his coffee maker and helped herself to a cup of his favorite, and most expensive, blend.

"At least she's got some company now."

"How's that?"

"She accidentally turned some guy into a dog."

"What?" Ellen choked on a mouthful of coffee. "What did you say?"

Howard grinned. "Someone disturbed her sleep last night and without even thinking about it she changed him into a dog."

"Howard! That's not even remotely funny!"

"Oh, chill Ellen. It won't be hard to change him back, she just has to wait for a month."

"That's not what I'm talking about, you idiot!" Ellen paced, short angry strides. "First of all, this just proves she's not safe on her own! He could have just as easily slit her throat while she slept. And then there's the whole 'accidentally' thing. You need to teach her how to use her magic."

"Me? But I don't—"

"Yes, you. You've been studying magic since you were a little kid. Jessica told me so. All you've lacked is the power."

"But Thackery said—"

"Screw Thackery! You need to teach her at least the basics, a modicum of control, or who knows what she might unleash!"

Howard opened his mouth, then shut it again. "It's just . . . she has so *much* power."

"All the more reason that she learns to control it. And maybe you could add a couple of lessons in using magic for defense. She's been really lucky so far, but one of these days her luck is going to run out."

"I guess you have a point," he said slowly.

"Of course I do," she said. "Now, have you got any biscotti to go with this coffee?"

Jessica's sleep was plagued by nightmares, strange nebulous things that left her with a sense of foreboding when she awoke in the morning. There was nothing specific she could put her finger on, but she couldn't shake the feeling something bad was on its way. Maybe not today, or even this week, but there was definitely something in the offing.

She fed the horse first, then herself and Bandit. When he barked a question at the amount she put in front of him, she shrugged.

"No sense in it going to waste, and I, for one, intend to keep going today until we find that inn to sleep in."

They ate in companionable silence. Glancing at the fireplace, Jessica snorted when she saw the glowing embers. Figured. The one morning she didn't need a fire was the one morning it was still burning. She was never going to get the hang of roughing it.

There was an unshuttered window at the end of the building furthest away from the horse, and something glinted in a beam of morning sunlight. Finishing her bread and cheese, Jessica got up to investigate. The shiny object was almost on top of a pile of rags and refuse. She reached out with a hand, then jumped back suddenly as she realized what the pile really was.

"Ew!" She'd been about to desecrate a corpse.

She jumped again as a cold, wet nose pressed into her hand. "Holy Saint Christopher! Give me a heart attack why don't you?" She glared at the dog.

Bandit stepped closer to the pile and sniffed at the corpse. Jessica got a hold of herself and took a closer look. There were two bodies, not one, and they'd been there long enough that what little flesh remained was dried onto the bones. The shine came from a sword protruding from the body on top.

"Now what are you doing?"

The dog was pawing at the pile.

"Seriously, if you're going to start gnawing on one of those bones . . . well, that's just gross and you can forget it right now. What is that?"

He'd pulled what looked to be a leather pouch away from one of the corpses. Looking at her expectantly, he barked. Jessica looked from the dog to the pouch and gave a slight shudder. Bandit barked again.

"All right, all right. I just need a minute to psyche myself up."

Flexing her hand first, she reached out and gingerly picked up the pouch, surprised at the weight to it. Turning away, she was just about to head back towards the fireplace where the light was better when Bandit barked again.

"Now what?"

He pawed at the pile again, sending bones and rags tumbling. The sword sticking up from the first corpse fell over with a clang as it hit some other metal object.

"Oh, I get it. Where there's one pouch there's probably two." She sighed. "You realize this borders on grave robbing, don't you?"

The dog barked twice and turned his head to look pointedly at the pile.

The sword had fallen to the near side and Jessica picked it up to poke gingerly at the pile. The narrow blade wasn't the best tool for moving the bones around, but there was no way she was going to use her hands. Her patience was rewarded as she finally uncovered a second pouch.

Returning to the blanket in front of the fireplace, she tossed the pouches onto the blanket and threw a couple of logs onto the almost dead fire. The new fuel caught, giving her enough light to see by. Bandit came over to sit beside her.

"Okay then, let's see what else we've got."

She pulled the smaller of the two pouches towards her and upended it over the blanket. A veritable fortune in gemstones spilled onto the blanket. "Holy Saint Christopher! These can't be real, can they?" Jessica held one up to the firelight, just to see it sparkle.

She glanced over at the sad pile of human remains and then at Bandit. "What do you think, they were thieves who had a falling out maybe?"

He yipped and ducked his head.

Jessica upended the second pouch and more gems, as well as pile of coins of various sizes, shapes, and metals, joined the rest. "Wow. Looks like we hit the jackpot. But . . ." She stared uneasily at the bodies. "Why hasn't anyone discovered them before us? Did we just get lucky, or is all this booty cursed?"

Sitting back on her heels, she thought about it for a moment. This place was so out of the way that it was just possible that no one else had stumbled across them before. They weren't exactly on a proper trail any more. Plus, she had no idea how long they'd been lying there. And wouldn't her magic allow her to sense if there was a curse on the loot?

"Looks like we'll be sleeping in a real bed, provided we find that inn. And maybe even a hot meal. I think this calls for a drink."

Bandit woofed and wagged his tail.

She fetched the wineskin and filled the cup for Bandit. Taking a drink herself, she stared at the gems sparkling in the firelight. When the wine was gone she separated the gems from the coins and put all the gems into the larger pouch, stuffing it in the bottom of the pack. She'd deal with them later.

Turning her attention to the coins, she divided them into piles - gold, silver, and copper. "It would really help if I knew how much these were worth," she said.

Bandit cocked his head and woofed at her as she stirred the larger pile of copper coins with her finger. "Oh, I know, you could help." She sat up straight suddenly. "You probably know the exchange rate on these, don't you?"

He bobbed his head.

"Okay then, one bark for yes, two barks for no. Got that?" she asked with a grin.

He barked once.

"Great! Now, it looks like these silver coins come in two sizes, is that right?"

Lowering his head to take a better look, he barked once.

"Okay, let's separate these too," she muttered. When she was done she sat back again. "Now, I'm going count these copper coins out. When I get to the number that one small silver coin is worth, stop me." She grabbed up a handful of copper coins and let them drop slowly, one by one, to the blanket. When she got to fifteen, Bandit barked at her.

"Okay, so fifteen copper coins equal one small silver coin. Would it be safe to assume that two of the small silver coins equals one of the larger silver coins?"

Again Bandit barked once.

"All right, now we're getting somewhere. Let's do the same thing with the silver to gold." She snatched up a handful of silver coins and began dropping them one by one. When she got to ten, Bandit barked.

"Great. Fifteen coppers to a half silver, two half silvers to a full silver, and ten silvers to a gold." She sat back with a sigh. "Now if I only knew how much a copper was worth. I'm thinking a penny here will buy a lot more than a penny where I come from."

Bandit woofed at her, a distinctly different sound than the sharp barks he was using for yes and no.

"See, where I come from a penny, which is about a third of the size of one of these copper coins, isn't worth very much at all. It takes a hundred pennies to make a dollar. It takes five dollars to buy a cup of coffee from a specialty shop, and a decent meal will run you about twenty dollars and up. So it's really a matter of perspective. I have no idea whether I'm rich or I'm just looking at chump change here."

Having followed her monologue with his head tilted slightly to the side, Bandit got up and went to the open chest where he dipped his head in and came out with an apple in his mouth. Carrying it over to the blanket, he dropped it on the pile of copper coins. Then he went over and picked up the knife she used slice the bread and dropped it on the pile of silver. Sitting back on his haunches, he looked expectantly at Jessica.

"What are you doing?"

Giving a huff, he went over and picked up the strip of dried meat he hadn't finished and dropped it beside the apple.

Understanding dawned. "I get it, copper coins are used for buying small stuff like food and silver is used for bigger stuff, like weapons. So . . . how many gold coins would it take for us to get a decent room at an inn?"

Jessica picked up a handful of gold coins. "Okay, stop me when we reach the right price." She dropped one coin and Bandit barked at her. "Are you kidding me? Wow."

This windfall couldn't have come at a better time. As much as she'd been primed to stay in a proper inn, she knew it wouldn't have been for free. She had no idea if Howard would have been able to conjure up some local currency, the best case scenario had been being able to work for her room and board. But now she wouldn't have to.

Rooting around in her pack she came up with the small pouch Wendel had made her for when she wanted to hide her amulet. She scooped up a handful of the copper coins, a few of the silver ones, and after a slight debate three of the gold ones and dropped them inside. This one had a tie as well as a leather cord so she could hang it around her neck. It was a little heavy, but at least it was safe from pick pockets. The rest of the coins were deposited in the smaller of the two pouches and it too went into the bottom of her pack.

"I kind of feel bad that we're just leaving them there," she said, glancing at what was left of the two men, or who knew, maybe one was a woman.

Bandit barked, softer this time.

"Yeah, I know. The circle of life and all that. I'm just not faced with stuff like this where I come from."

Resolutely, she packed up the remainder of the food, save for one of the apples, and their gear. There was just enough room in the saddlebags for the extra blankets and towels. Offering the apple to the horse, she stroked the soft velvet nose as the mare crunched away.

"You've been very patient with me and I really appreciate it. With any luck tonight you'll get to sleep in a real stable and have someone who knows what they're doing groom you."

The mare flicked an ear in her direction. With a sigh Jessica threw the saddle blanket on the mare's back and then hefted the saddle on top of that. In no time at all, which would have surprised her two weeks ago, she had the mare saddled and all the gear loaded up. Silently she led her outside, the dog following at her heels.

Mounting up, she headed back they way she'd come without a backward glance.

Chapter 5

Jessica stayed quiet until they reached the river bank. The river had gone down considerably during the night but it was still too rough for crossing.

"I don't suppose you know some other place where we could cross?" she asked the dog. "Howard said something about there being a ford nearby."

He looked up and down the river, barked, and trotted along the bank. Jessica turned the horse to follow. About mid-morning he stopped and sat down. Jessica looked dubiously at the river and sighed. While it did look much less threatening, it still wasn't as shallow as she'd like it to be.

"I had enough of getting wet last night. Are you positive this is the best place to cross?"

He barked at her.

She looked at the churning water and sighed again. "And I suppose you're going to want a lift across that?"

He wagged his tail hopefully. Jessica looked at the river. The water was still muddy from the previous day's rain; there was no telling how deep it was. She knew dogs could swim, but she didn't know if even a normal dog could swim across that.

"All right," she said finally. "Do you think you can jump up on your own?"

He leaped for the saddle and Jessica pulled him across in front of her. Head and tail dangled on either side of the mare's neck, a most undignified position to be sure. He looked utterly miserable.

"What I wouldn't give for my digital camera," Jessica said with a smile.

The mare balked at the riverbank. Jessica sympathized with the animal's discomfort, but urged her on into the cold, swirling waters. It was not as deep as it appeared, though the mare's footing was unsure and the water came up almost to her belly. The river was not terribly wide and in a few moments they were climbing up the bank on the other side.

"Good girl." Jessica leaned over the dog to pat the mare on the neck. "With luck you'll have a nice, dry stable to sleep in tonight."

The mare snorted at her.

Squirming, the dog barked to get her attention. Jessica pushed him unceremoniously to the ground. He woofed as he hit and gave himself a shake.

"Okay, you're leading this parade. Which way now?"

The dog took a couple of steps into the forest, then turned and doubled back along the bank. When they were almost to where the bridge had washed out, he found the trail again and angled off into the woods.

They travelled for the better part of the day. Jessica let Bandit set the pace. Depression settled around her like a shroud; she didn't really pay attention to where they were going, trusting that the dog didn't want to spend the night outside any more than she did. The trail turned into a dirt road and a few miles later a short side road led them to the courtyard of an inn.

It was a shabby inn, but Jessica thought nothing had ever looked so beautiful. A ragged urchin met her in the courtyard as she dismounted, pulling her gear down with her.

"Rub her down good and give her an extra measure of grain. I'll be in later to see the job's done right. There's a copper in it for you if I'm happy with your work."

"Yes'm!" The young boy bobbed his head and led the mare away.

Jessica grinned at his sudden enthusiasm. Carrying the saddle-bags she entered the inn, the dog at her heels.

The tap room was empty. Jessica called out but there was no answer. It looked as though there had been a brawl here recently. Tables and chairs were overturned, a sword was stuck into the ceiling, a pile of wood near the fireplace gave the impression of once being furniture and, if she was not mistaken, that dark pool beside it was blood.

"Looks like a real fun place," Jessica commented. "Hello? Anyone here?"

"Keep yer shirt on, I'm comin'." The surly voice seemed to come from a back room.

Jessica leaned against the counter, the dog sat close to her feet. After a few minutes a woman came out. Jessica couldn't help staring at her. She had to be well over six feet tall, and at least two hundred and fifty pounds. Her long greasy hair was held back by a leather cord and she was holding a meat cleaver.

"What'd ya want?"

"A room, if there's one habitable." Jessica eyed the meat cleaver.

"There be a common room, if yer travellin' alone."

"A private one," she said firmly. "And a tub filled with hot water, and whatever you've got to eat that's hot." She waved a gold piece under the woman's nose.

The sight of money transformed the woman. "O course, our very best. Right away," She turned. "Ginny! Git out here!"

A thinner, younger version of the woman came scurrying out. She moved with sharp, jerky motions that reminded Jessica of a cockroach, and her face was flushed.

"You get Thomas 'n move the brass tub to the first room. Clean it and fill it with water. Mind it's hot now. Move girl!"

"Yes'm," Ginny replied. Without looking at Jessica she scurried away.

"This way milady." The older woman set the meat cleaver on the bar and led the way to the stairs off to the side of the room.

The room was small and smelled of dust and old sweat. Still, the bed looked soft and inviting. Jessica hoped it wasn't too badly infested with bugs. The woman bustled through the room, brushing imaginary wrinkles from the coverlet, giving the top of the wash stand a quick dusting off and opening the small window to let in a fresh, albeit cool, breeze.

"Will ye be wantin' the critter taken to the stable?"

"What?" Jessica had forgotten the dog. "No, you can leave him here for now."

"I'll see to yer meal then. And if there's anything ye be

needin', ye've only to ask for Hannah," she indicated herself with a jerk of her thumb.

"What do you think?" Jessica asked, after Hannah left.

The dog looked at the door and shook his head.

"That's what I think. But there's a good bolt on the door and one on the window."

"Just make sure you use them," said a disembodied voice.

Bandit started, then growled. Jessica pulled moonstone amulet free of her blouse.

"What's up, Howard?"

"I found a Well. Not a big one, but big enough for our purposes," Howard told her.

"And what purpose would that be?" Jessica asked. "You've already said it would take more than the power of a Well to get me home again. Isn't that why I'm travelling south in the first place?"

"Oh. I—oh." There was a pause as though she'd caught him by surprise and he had to search for the right words. "I was talking to Ellen last night—"

Jessica brightened immediately. "How is Ellen? I hope you're giving her a break in the rent. It *is* your fault I'm here."

"Of course I am. But she and I were talking and we thought . . . maybe . . . maybe I should try teaching you a few rudiments of magic. You know, more than just the basic control we were talking about."

The dog pricked up his ears.

"Are you sure about this?" As much as she'd been eager to learn magic a day ago, she also didn't want to blow anything else up. "Have you forgotten what happened last time?"

"Well, due to recent events . . ."

"This isn't just about preventing any more accidents," she said, glancing at the dog. "Ellen's worried about me being by myself and thinks I could use magic to protect myself, doesn't she?"

"Well . . ."

Jessica sighed. "I don't suppose I could have a couple of nights here first?"

"Actually, Jess, there's no rush. Take three or four nights if you like."

"You're so generous," she muttered.

"What'd you say, Jess?"

"I said, I think I hear my bath coming. Talk to you later, Howard."

There was a rap on her door. Thomas, who also looked like Hannah, brought the brass tub in, followed closely by Ginny, who was staggering under the weight of two steaming buckets suspended from a shoulder yolk. Thomas was flushed and sweating from exertion.

It took four trips in all for the pair of them to fill the tub. Jessica's chestnut hair was pinned up on her head, her boots off and she was just starting on the buttons to her blouse when she remembered the dog.

Too big to fit under the bed he was sitting as unobtrusively as possible in a corner by the door.

"Out, right now," she told him. "And don't get into any trouble or you're on your own." The dog sulked his way out of the room. Jessica waited until the door was closed behind him then grinned. He was, after all, only human.

By the time Jessica was done her bath and wrapped in a silk robe, a gift from the rat fink Prince Ewan that had somehow ended up in her pack, the shadows in the courtyard were getting long. Bandit pushed his way back into the room when Hannah delivered Jessica's supper. The innkeeper looked tired and overworked.

"Hannah, is everything all right with Thomas and Ginny?" Jessica asked. "I don't mean to pry, but they didn't seem well."

An alarmed expression filled Hannah's eyes. Jessica waited patiently while the woman wrestled with the truth.

"I've been hopin' 'twould pass," she said reluctantly. "Fact is, few weeks back one 'o the guests took sick. Ginny, she been keepin' company with 'im, if ye catch me meaning. I don't know as I can keep this place goin' if they both take sick."

"It might not come to that," Jessica said soothingly.

"Got word a few days back, that guest up and died. I just get by, cain't pay no healer."

"I might have something to help," Jessica said.

She rummaged around in one of the saddle bags and pulled out a cloth wrapped packet. Inside were several individually wrapped packets of healing herbs. They were a gift from Meren, wife to the tanner who who'd helped her escape from Ghren. They'd found common ground in their love of herbal remedies and exchanged a great deal of knowledge in the short time they were together.

She found an empty square of cloth and shook several different herbs in its center and then handed it to Hannah who was watching her, somewhat surprised.

"Boil a spoonful of this into a tea, you might want to add

honey, it'll be very bitter. Make sure Ginny and Thomas both have a cup of it before every meal until it's gone."

"Milady," Hannah stuttered. "How can I ever repay ye?"

"Don't worry about it," Jessica told her. "We women have to stick together."

After Hannah left, Bandit came over and woofed a soft question.

"Don't get sentimental on me," Jessica said. "It's a tough life for a woman alone, especially in this world. She deserved a break for a change."

Jessica shared her supper with the dog then, too tired to deal with her wet hair or get under the covers, she fell asleep across the bed.

Bandit watched her as the light from the fireplace cast flickering shadows across the curves of her body. At last he gave a very un-doglike sigh and he, too, slept.

Chapter 6

It was closer to midday than breakfast when Jessica awoke the next morning. She helped herself to some bread and cheese on her way through the kitchen and Bandit, following her example, snatched up a shank of meat left on a sideboard from the night before. Jessica checked on the mare and, finding everything to her satisfaction, wandered out into the woods.

Bandit barked at her.

"I know, you think I'm crazy going back into the woods. But it's a nice day and giving Hannah those herbs reminded me I have a way to earn an honest dollar after our stash of loot runs out. Back in my old life I made a study of plants and herbal cures. Plus I have this," she waved a leather-bound notebook at him. "It's sort of like a diary of indigenous plants and what they can be used for."

She and Meren, the tanner's wife, had spent a great deal of their time together pouring over the information held in the small book. Meren was studying to be an herb wife before she married Reece and never quite gave it up after. The book was hers and contained sketches of various plants, plus information about their uses as well as recipes. It contained all the information Meren had collected over the years and she insisted Jessica take it with her. "You never know when such a thing might come in handy," she'd said. "And who knows, perhaps one day you'll be ready to settle down and become a proper herbwife."

Jessica didn't see that happening, and had argued, "But won't you be needing this yourself? What if Reece gets sick? Or one of the children?"

"I have everything I need up here," Meren replied, tapping her head. "And something tells me you'll have a far better use for it than me."

There was nothing Jessica could do but thank her and accept the book.

Bandit followed at her heels at first, then wandered off to do some exploring of his own. It was a beautiful day, made all the more so because she knew there was no rush and she wouldn't have to spend the night out here. Jessica filled the bag she brought with her with wild herbs she was familiar with and since it was still early, followed a stream to see if there were some of the rare water herbs Meren had described.

Luck was with her. In a secluded glade she found a deep, clear pool. Along its edge she found several of the plants she was after and if she was not mistaken, the rocks supporting the waterfall were covered with the rare purple moss that could be used in small amounts in a recipe for an antibiotic, as well as a recipe for a brilliant dye. For medicinal purposes it needed to be dried thoroughly, but for the dye it needed to be kept damp. Meren assured her if she kept it wrapped in a wet cloth and then wrapped it in a second cloth treated to keep the water from evaporating she could sell it in any town for a huge profit.

She looked at the water and shivered. It wasn't as though she needed the money right now, but how long would her stash last? Quickly, before she could change her mind, she stripped off her clothes and stepped into the pool, totally unaware that Bandit was watching from the underbrush.

It was as cold as she feared and deceptively deep. She had to swim to the rocks. Her fingers were numb and the rest of her chilled to the bone by the time she'd prized off all the moss that could be of use. She came out of the water with a gasp.

Having nothing to dry herself with, she dressed as quickly as possible. Calling for Bandit, she hurried back to the inn. Bandit prudently stayed hidden a few more seconds before following.

Ginny was in the kitchen of the inn peeling potatoes with a knife of impressive size when Jessica poked her head in to ask if she had any spare rags or string. Unfortunately, she had neither so Jessica carried her bounty up to her room.

Bandit jumped up on the bed and lay there watching as she unpacked her bag and separated the herbs into piles.

"Now how am I going to dry these, and keep these from drying out?" she muttered. "What I wouldn't give for a roll of waxed paper and a ball of string."

She thought about it a moment longer and then went back down to the kitchen, returning with a jug of water and a couple of candles. Fishing around in her travel pack, she pulled out several articles of clothing and debated about which she could sacrifice for the greater good.

In the end it came down to a choice between a plain white shirt and pants made of a heavier material. The shirt won, mainly because she had more than one to spare. She only had two pairs of pants and she was wearing one of them.

Using the knife from Bandit's gear - why dull her own blade - she sliced the sleeves off the shirt and then tore one of them into small strips. These she used to tie the various herbs into bundles, which she hung from the mantel of the fireplace.

Next she pulled out the smaller of the two towels Howard had sent her and cut a wide strip off the bottom. This she soaked in the water from the jug and then spread most of the moss on it, folding the ends over to cover the moss completely.

Cutting a large square of cloth from the body of the shirt, she spread it on the stone hearth and then dug out her flint to light one of the candles. What she wouldn't give for a box of matches. The flint, as usual, gave her trouble and she was almost ready to risk using her magic when the candle caught the spark.

The candle actually gave off a scent of wildflowers. Jessica hoped it wouldn't interfere with the potency of the moss as she dripped wax over square of cloth. She was almost finished when a disembodied voice made her jump, dropping the candle.

"Hey, Jess. What're you doing?"

"Damn it Howard!" Jessica reached for the flint again. "Do you know how hard it is to light these damn things?"

"Why don't you use your magic?"

"And burn down the whole inn? I don't think so. I like having a bed to sleep in."

"That's why I'm here. I thought we could talk about a training schedule for you."

She sighed, almost blowing out the candle that she'd just managed to relight. "Fine. Whatever. But I'm not going to use magic inside the inn and it's too late to find someplace outside today."

The last few drops of wax went on the cloth and she placed the wet towel with the moss in it in the center of the waxy square. After folding up the edges of the cloth, she dripped wax along the seams.

"What are you doing?" Howard asked, watching through the scrying bowl.

"I'm preserving herbs," she said proudly. "And I'm telling you, it's not easy without an oven or waxed paper or even string. I don't know how people can stand living like this."

"It's all they've ever known," Howard said, with just a trace of guilt. And if Paran and Thackery had their way, it's all she'd know from here on in.

"Yeah, well it sucks. There's no electricity, no cars, and I'd kill for a pizza. I don't suppose you could manage to conjure me up a pizza, could you?"

"Sorry Jess."

"Why not?" she asked irritably. "You managed to conjure a whole trunk full of goodies back at that traveler's hut."

"That was different," he said, scrambling for an excuse. "The things in that trunk were already in your universe. I just had to move them to the trunk, not conjure them out of thin air."

The dog let out a woof suddenly. Howard couldn't shake the feeling the former man knew he was lying.

"If I had a recipe, and an electric stove, I could make one

myself," Jessica said with a sigh. "Of course they probably don't have pepperoni . . . or mozzarella cheese either."

"I'm sure we could find something similar . . ."

"Oh don't bother," she said, waving the candle in the air. "I'll just eat pizza for a week once I get back home."

The more she talked about getting back home, the more uncomfortable Howard became. "My treat," he told her. "Tomorrow morning I want you to look for a place you can start practicing your magic. A small clearing would be good. Someplace rocky would be even better and near water would be great."

"Okay, Howard," she said with a resigned sigh. "Say hi to Ellen for me."

"Will do, Jess."

His presence vanished.

Bandit watched her carefully as she started cutting up the rest of the shirt into squares, presumably to wrap the other herbs in after they were sufficiently dry. Once she was finished she set them aside and cleaned up the mess she'd made.

He sensed something was wrong but wasn't sure what it was. It was in his best interest to make sure nothing untoward happened to the witch, at least until she reversed her spell. But the very fact that she was willing to wait for the right time to change him back spoke volumes of her character, more so than his for sneaking into her camp. Most magic workers in the same situation would have just left him to fend for himself as a dog.

Once Jessica ran out of things to do around the room, she began to pace restlessly. Finally, she sat down on the bed with a sigh and then flopped backwards to lie down. Bandit shifted around and rested his chin on her stomach. Absently, she started to scratch behind his ears.

"You know, when Howard first sent me to this world, all I could think about was getting home - the thought of being stuck here scared the crap out of me. Now that I've gotten used to it I find myself almost enjoying it sometimes, and that scares me even worse."

Bandit tried to pay attention to what she was saying, but he was in a state of bliss from her touch. He'd never thought of ears as particularly erotic before - maybe it was just a dog thing. Whatever it was, he was thoroughly enjoying it.

"Howard claims I've got all this power inside me. What if he teaches me to use it and I start liking it too much? What if I like it so much I never want to go back?" She sighed again. "It's not fair, really. Howard's the one who's always been fascinated by magic. But where I come from magic isn't real. It's just a bunch of tricks used to entertain people. Howard would have a blast here."

Her voice trailed off and her hand stilled as she fell asleep. Bandit found himself drifting off as well and he couldn't help but wonder about the relationship between the witch and the disembodied Howard. Were they just friends? Or lovers as well? And why did it even matter?

Chapter 7

Jessica decided to eat in the tap room that night. It was a rough-looking crowd with few women about, but the sight of the shaggy, black dog at Jessica's feet seemed to discourage company. She had Ginny bring two bowls of her mother's stew - one for her and one for Bandit.

"Oh, my Lady Jessica. To see thee in such rough surroundings is like to break my heart."

Bandit growled low in his throat at the sound of the voice, but Jessica's face broke into a smile.

"Gareth? What are you doing here? Please, sit down and stop looking so woebegone. You've seen me in much worse surroundings. Bandit, cut that out. Gareth's a friend."

Giving the dog a nervous glance, the young squire slid into the chair opposite her. Jessica felt a pang of guilt as she looked at him. While she knew in this world children tended to grow up fast, he looked like he'd aged ten years since she last saw him. He'd been her first friend in this land, and her most loyal one. She hated that he'd become so entrenched in her problems.

"What on earth are you doing here? No, wait. Have you eaten yet?"

"Yes, my lady. Do not concern thyself—"

"Then a drink. You definitely look like you need a drink. Ginny, bring us some wine."

"My lady—"

"How did you know where to find me?"

"My lady, I—"

He broke off as Ginny hurried over with a bottle and two goblets. Bandit looked at Jessica and barked. She sighed.

"I'm sorry to trouble you Ginny, but could you also bring me a mug of the house ale and a bowl?"

"A bowl, milady?"

"Yes, please."

She suppressed a grin at the look on Gareth's face. He opened his mouth to speak, but snapped it shut again when Ginny returned to their table. Jessica put the bowl on the floor and filled it with the ale. Bandit woofed at her and began lapping thirstily.

"You're welcome," she said. "Just go easy on that stuff. Two's your limit."

"Thou givest thy dog ale?" Gareth asked, a bemused expression on his face.

"He's not your usual kind of dog," Jessica told him. "Now, what on earth are you doing here? I thought we were supposed to meet in Eglion. Were you looking for me specifically or did you just lose your way?"

"Nay, I came seeking thee—"

"What's happened? Is everyone all right?"

"Yes, my lady. As far as I know all is well with everyone," he said. "It is only . . . I will not be accompanying thee to the southern lands," he said, finishing in a rush.

Jessica blinked at him. "I'm sorry to hear that," she said at last, not sorry at all. In fact, she was somewhat relieved. One less person to feel guilty over. "What changed your mind?"

He ducked his head, flushing slightly.

She grinned suddenly. "What's her name?"

His head snapped up again. "I—how didst thou know?"

Chuckling, she just shook her head.

"Her name is Lynette. She is thy ladies maid Eleanor's younger sister."

"Former ladies maid, and I didn't realize she had any family, other than Reece."

"She joined us when we were but two days gone. She is most brave."

Jessica's lips twitched at the dreaminess in his tone of voice.

"I pray thee forgive my desertion of thee in thine hour of need."

"There's nothing to forgive, Gareth," she told him, reaching out and laying her hand over his. "As I recall, you were also travelling to the south with us in hopes of learning a trade."

"Aye, and now it's more important than ever I find the means to buy into a trade, so that I can ask for the fair Lynette's hand."

"What were you thinking of?" she asked. "And what do you mean by 'buying into' a trade?"

"I am too old to become an apprentice. My only hope is to find some menial labor and save up to buy a place in a trade. My skills lie in fine metalwork, such as is used for jewelry, but such a position would be costly indeed."

Jessica's eyes lit up, remembering the packet of jewels tucked safely away in the bottom of her pack. Bandit lifted his head and gave a slight whimper as she pushed away from the table. She ignored him as she patted the former squire on the back of his hand. The dog laid his head back down with a hefty sigh

"Stay right here for a minute, I have something for you."

Jessica rose from the table and hurried up to her room. When she returned she was carrying the small packet, which she pressed into Gareth's hand.

"Here," she said, "I want you to have this."

He hefted the weight of it and looked at her curiously. "What pray is this?"

"It's a custom where I come from to give a gift to friends who are getting married. This is my gift to you. But don't open it until you're back with Lynette."

"As you wish, my lady." Still puzzled, Gareth stowed the pouch away in his jerkin.

"So how have you been, Gareth? And how are Eleanor, and Meren and Reece, and the children?"

They went through an entire bottle of wine as they caught up on the news, and Bandit received an extra bowlful of ale as Jessica forgot to keep count.

"Master Reece bade me give thee a message," Gareth told her.

"Yes?" Jessica paused in the act of taking a drink.

"He bids you, do not fret over the necessity of his family leaving Ghren."

"But—"

"Nay," Gareth said forcefully. "None of what transpired was thy doing. The old king was harsh, but fair-minded. The new king however . . ." He shook his head and took a sip of wine. "Reece was fortunate he escaped with us. New taxes spring up like mushrooms after a rain and there is an edict forbidding tradesman from leaving without paying a hefty fine."

Jessica shook her head. "It's enough to make me wonder what I ever saw in him. I can't believe I thought I was falling in love with him."

At their feet, Bandit pricked up his ears. This conversation was starting to sound interesting. It was so frustrating not to be able to speak. Who was this "he" they spoke of that she thought she had been falling in love with? What king were they talking about?

Wait. They mentioned someone leaving Ghren. There was a new king there they said. What happened to the old one? Lifting his head, he took a closer look at Jessica.

There were so many things that puzzled him about his travelling companion. If she was as powerful a witch as he'd been led to believe, why did she know so little of magic? It appeared she was on the run from something, but he didn't know what. She definitely wasn't used to roughing it in the wild.

He'd recognized the packet she gave the young man, it was the one holding the jewels from their stash. Even one or two of those jewels would be enough for the man, Gareth, to buy his way into a trade, did she have to give him *all* of them?

"To be fair, thou wast not the only one deceived. And none knew of the amulet of Athelon, nor of its power."

Bandit knew about the amulet of Athelon. It was a charisma charm, used for everything from raising an army to recruiting followers for a religious order. Who else had the amulet been used on? He growled under his breath. Jessica must have heard him because she reached down and gave him a pat on his head, forgetting he was not a real dog.

"It was kind of sad, really. That he thought he needed something like that amulet to get people to like him."

"Trust me, my lady. Ewan was not a likeable man."

Bandit gave a start at the name. No, he thought, Ewan most certainly was not a likeable man. And he knew this from firsthand experience.

"Pretty is as pretty does," Jessica said with a sigh.

She had that much right. Ewan, at least the Ewan he'd known, had indeed been pretty to look at. And he could be quite charming when he wanted to be - he could only assume this skill had been honed as Ewan grew older.

"There lies another matter, my lady," Gareth said hesitantly.

"I'm not going to like this, am I?"

Bandit could practically feel her bracing for the worst.

"The king is offering a reward for thy return. As long as thou art on Ghren lands, thou art in grave danger."

If he'd been a true dog, he would have bitten the young man. In fact, he was tempted to do so anyway. You didn't just bandy about news like that. A quick check of the room caught the looks being exchanged by a group of men at a table by the fireplace. Had they heard Gareth?

Jessica sighed. "Like just trying to survive here isn't dangerous enough." Mustering a smile, she said, "Thank you for the warning, I'll be careful."

"Forgive me, my lady, but I must be off. My beloved Lynette awaits me in Old Bastion, and it is many leagues to the boat that will take me to her."

They rose together from the table and Jessica gave him a hug. "You've been a good friend," she told him. "I'm going to miss you."

"And I you, my lady."

She watched him leave and then picked up her goblet to finish up her wine. "Hey, Bandit. What do you say we take a walk before turning in?"

He got to his feet and woofed at her. She was a moody thing, this witch. And right now her mood seemed to have taken a downward turn. Maybe she was regretting giving all those gemstones to her young friend. He certainly was.

Trotting by her side, every inch the faithful dog, he kept on the alert. She tended to forget at times that he wasn't really a dog, which was fine by him. It made her say and do things in front of him that he was sure she wouldn't say and do in front of him if he were a man. He was beginning to get her measure and wished he'd met her under different circumstances.

It would have been easy to become bitter about his current condition, but the truth was he was getting off lucky and he knew it. He had, after all, been in her camp trying to rob her. She could have just blasted him, or decided to leave him a dog. Instead she was interrupting her own journey just to change him back. He couldn't help but wonder if she'd be this much at ease with him once he was a man again.

They reached a small clearing by a stream and Jessica sat down on a fallen log. Bandit sat near her feet and after a few minutes she reached out a hand to start scratching him behind the ears.

The other she used to pull the white amulet out so it was laying on top of her shirt.

"Hey, Howard, are you there?"

"Sorry, Jess. Howard had to step out for a while. You're stuck with me."

"Ellen? Holy Saint Christopher! Don't tell me you're starting to get magical powers too."

In the earthly realm Ellen snorted. "Hardly. Howard has your medallion hanging above his work table and has it voice activated or something. He had to step out and couldn't take it with him, so he asked me to sit in, just in case you needed something while he was gone."

"Where did he go that he couldn't take my pendant? Oh, never mind. I'm pretty sure he wouldn't want to be *anywhere* in public and have me start talking to him suddenly."

"So," Ellen said, changing the subject. "I hear you have a furry sidekick."

She'd always had a knack for knowing when Jessica needed cheering up . . . or at least when she needed distracting. Apparently it worked in either realm.

"Yeah, just what I needed," she said with a sigh.

"You know I'm a firm believer in things happening for a reason, Jess."

"Don't start with me," Jessica said, but she said it with a grin on her face. "What possible reason could fate have to compel me to turn someone into a dog?"

"Protection," Ellen said promptly. "You know I've never liked the idea of you being off on your own, this is fate's way of giving you some protection."

Jessica glanced down at Bandit. "There is that," she admitted. "Now tell me the reason for me ending up here in the first place."

"That was your own fault. Remember? You wished for some excitement in your life."

"As I recall, I asked for a *little* adventure. Emphasis on little."

Bandit lay down with a sigh as the two women fell to arguing.

Chapter 8

The next morning Jessica was in a much better frame of mind. Maybe it was her talk with Ellen the night before, maybe it was spending two nights in a row in a real bed. Whatever the reason, her spirits were high and she was ready to learn some magic.

"What about here?" she asked, stopping. She and Bandit had been following the meandering stream that ran near to the inn, trying to find a place that met Howard's requirements. Someplace with flat rocks, near the water, and preferably in the open.

This spot held a tumble of rocks, the ones closest to the stream flat enough to stand on comfortably. The stream itself was wider here, although the water cascaded quickly over the rocky bed. While trees overshadowed the stream on the far side, there were several huge boulders between the flat rocks and the tree line, giving a sense of space.

"It's perfect, Jess," Howard confirmed, checking the area with his scrying bowl. "Now, get comfortable. We're going to start by going over a few rules."

Bandit gave a huge yawn.

Jessica knew just how he felt. "You know," she told the dog. "You don't have to hang around. You can always go chase a rabbit or something."

He moved off a few paces, then turned and woofed at her.

"Don't worry, I'll be fine. Just don't wander off too far. I wouldn't want you to get lost."

Making a noise somewhere between a snort and a bark, he trotted off into the woods. Jessica made herself comfortable on the ground.

"Okay, Howard," she said. "I'm ready to start."

Several hours later, Bandit wandered back from his tour of the woods. Jessica's back hurt from sitting on the ground and her eyes felt like they'd glazed over. The most important lesson she'd learned was that Howard was the most boring teacher ever. In either universe.

"Look Howard," she said, interrupting him in mid-lecture. "My butt's numb and I'm starving. What say we pick this up tomorrow?"

"Oh. Well, it is important to make sure you refuel after working magic," he said.

She refrained from telling him she had yet to actually work any magic. Scrambling to her feet, she winced and dusted herself off.

"C'mon Bandit," she said before Howard could change his mind, "Let's go see what's for supper. Say hi to Ellen for me, Howard," she said, tucking the pendant back under her shirt. The dog at her heels, she hurried back to the inn.

Despite the fact it was busy, by virtue of the silver coin she dangled in front of Ginny's nose she was given a table for one in the corner by the fireplace.

Jessica felt a distinct prickle of unease as she ate. She glanced surreptitiously about the tap room but saw nothing out of the ordinary.

"I think we're being watched," she whispered, nudging Bandit. He finished his last piece of steak with a gulp and sat at attention again. To the casual observer he was every inch the faithful dog. He stiffened, growling low in his throat.

Edging around slightly in her seat, Jessica looked in the direction his nose was pointed. A few tables over there was a group of four rough looking men, talking low and glancing towards Bandit. One of them caught Jessica eyeing them. They conferred hastily, and he rose and made his way over to her.

"Good eve to you, mistress," he said politely, shifting his feet.

"Good evening," Jessica returned, warily.

"That's a fine looking beast, ye have. We was wonderin' if ye've a mind to sell him."

"I beg your pardon?"

"Yer dog. He's a powerful looking beast, too powerful for a lady like yourself to be handling, no offense intended. My mates and I be willing to take him off yer hands."

"I'm sorry," Jessica told him. "He's not for sale."

"We've a fair price to be offering."

"I said, he's not for sale. Not at any price."

Bandit curled his lip back in a snarl.

The man's face grew red. "Ye'll regret this, mark my words." He stomped back to his friends.

Jessica finished her meal without further incident and sat back to sip her wine. The men left soon after, and she caught them casting glowering looks back over their shoulders in her direction.

"I guess they're not used to people telling them no," she said to Bandit. He woofed in response.

After they finished, Jessica went out to the stable, as was her habit, to check on the mare. She fed her a couple of carrots she'd asked Ginny for and stroked the velvety nose.

"Well, well. Ain't that a picture."

Jessica whirled around, feeling for the rapier that she'd left in her room. There were three of the men from the tap room, looking even rougher in the dim light of the stable. They were fully armed, but they'd obviously continued their drinking after leaving the bar. The swords in their hands were held loosely.

There was a commotion behind her. Jessica heard growls and snarls and glanced back to see Bandit, at the other end of the stable, entangled in a net. The fourth man, obviously having come in from the other side, was attempting to drag the dog outside.

"Go get 'er, Will," the short, dark one urged.

Will swaggered forward, confident he could overpower a mere woman. Jessica flung out her hand towards him. No one was more surprised than she was when a fireball appeared and shot from her fingertips to his face. He howled and dropped his sword, beating at the flames in his beard.

The grins vanished from the faces of his companions. He fell back to give them their chance as Jessica snatched up his sword. She faced the largest, and least drunk, of the three.

"Now then, what're ye doin' with that there pig-sticker. Hand it over, afore someone gets hurt."

"Come and take it, you filthy sot." She held the sword firmly in a guard position.

His own sword wavered up. "If ye come quiet-like we can have a bit o' fun afore we turn ye over t' the king."

"We might have been willin' ta overlook the price on yer head if ye'd sold us the dog like we asked," said the one who'd approached her in the tap room.

Jessica lunged forward. The man was caught off guard and she nicked him in the upper arm. If anything, the pain only served to help him focus better on what he was doing.

The man was good. There was not enough room for Jessica's usual method of dancing around her opponent but she was able to dart in and out, nicking him hard enough to draw blood.

"Hold still, damn ye!"

Jessica made no reply. The sword was too heavy for her and she was beginning to tire. It was no longer a contest of skill, just a matter of who'd slip up first.

Her eyes widened at the thought, then quickly darted from side to side. She feinted a lunge and ducked as he took a swipe at her head. Quickly she turned on the offensive, forcing the man to back up. Almost there. His foot slipped in a pile of manure. The sword in his hand went flying and there was an audible crack as his head hit the stone floor.

The man she'd set fire to lay either unconscious or dead in the stable door. There was a thump behind her and Jessica suddenly remembered the third man. She turned just in time to see him slide slowly to the ground. Hannah stood over him, a mallet in her hands. She grinned.

"Us women gotta stick together. And the likes of them got no business attackin' payin' guests."

Jessica managed a thank you between gasps of air. Her breathing eased and she looked around. "Where's Bandit?"

"Bandit?"

"My dog," Jessica said, trying not to panic. "There was another man, he had my dog in a net."

"Didn't see no dog," Hannah told her. "But I seen a wagon out there earlier - it just left."

"Just left? Which way did it go?" Jessica was already saddling the mare.

"Most like to Pottswell if it be carryin' yer critter."

"Why Pottswell?"

"There be dog fights there, most every night."

"Dog fights?" Jessica blanched.

"He means more to ye than just a pet, I'm thinkin'," Hannah said shrewdly.

"I can't explain now," Jessica told her as she saddled the mare and mounted. "Just keep my stuff safe, I'll be back for it."

"Aye," said Hannah as she watched Jessica gallop off into the night. "Now that'll be a tale worth hearin'."

Jessica had the amulet in hand and was calling for Howard before she was even out of the inn's courtyard.

"Come on, Howard, we've got trouble. Big trouble."

"What is it Jess, running low on energy again?"

"Energy I've got. What I'm missing is one very large dog."

"What?"

"Bandit's missing."

"What do you mean, missing?"

She gave him a brief rundown on the men in the tavern and her encounter with them in the stables. The horse stumbled on the dark path and she was nearly thrown.

"This could be even worse than you realize," he told her.

"How could it be worse? My dog's been stolen!"

"Think about it, Jess. He's not a real dog."

"Hang on a second, Howard."

There was something wrong with the mare's gait. Jessica drew her to a halt and dismounted. Conjuring a small ball of light, she circled her horse. The mare was favoring her right foreleg.

"Damn! Damn, damn, damn!" Tears of frustration welled up in her eyes.

"What's the matter?"

"My horse is hurt," Jessica said. "My horse is hurt, I'm in the middle of nowhere, and someone stole my dog." One of the tears spilled over and she sniffled loudly. "I hate this place and I want to go home!"

"Take a deep breath, Jess," Howard said in his most soothing voice. "We'll get through this, I promise."

Jessica squatted down and hung her head, taking long, deep breaths. She concentrated on calming herself down. If she lost it now, she might never get it back. After a few minutes her breathing eased and her racing heart slowed. She raised her head.

"Okay, Howard. First things first, how do I help the mare?"

Howard's relief was almost palpable.

"Do you remember when you helped that kid?"

"Kieran? Yes, but I didn't really *do* anything. I was trying to put a splint on his leg and it just . . . happened."

"Your healing gift is intuitive; you should be able to just do it without thinking about it. Try running your hands down the mare's leg, the one that's hurt."

Jessica did as she was told, but she barely got below the knee when the mare shifted, pulling away.

"She won't let me."

"Try again. This time move your hands down her leg but don't actually touch her. You should be able to feel the heat from her injury."

This was actually harder, following the line of the mare's leg without actually touching yet staying close enough to feel the change in temperature. The first attempt she wasn't able to feel a thing, but on the second try . . .

"Okay, I feel it."

"Hold your hands steady and focus," he directed.

"Focus on what?"

"On healing. Remember how I had you looking deep inside yourself for the magic?"

"Vaguely.

"Do the same thing, only you'll need to focus harder until you can see different strands of color. You're looking for a cool, healing green. Remember? That was the color that appeared when you healed the boy's leg."

Filled with misgivings, Jessica did as she was told. Focus harder, he said. All she could seem to focus on was that every passing minute took Bandit further and further away from her.

Taking a deep breath, she tried again. She found the spark of magic in her and narrowed her focus. It was like a zoom effect.

Suddenly she was able to see the spark as a rope-like strand and the strand was made up of threads of many different colors.

It was beautiful. For a moment she was lost in the rainbow effect, then she focused on one of the green threads and gave a mental pull. The pale green color suffused her mind, spilling out of her hands and into the mare's leg. The color glowed for a moment longer before winking out. Jessica ran her hands down the mare's leg again and this time she didn't pull away.

"Your control is getting much better, Jess," Howard told her in admiration.

"Whoa." Jessica swayed in place. "I feel so dizzy."

"Healing used up your personal energy - it's going to take a few minutes for your batteries to recharge. I don't suppose you thought to grab some food or anything before you left?"

It never occurred to her. She'd been too intent on catching up with the men who'd stolen Bandit. "No, why?"

"Eating something might help. Even an apple or something."

"Sorry," she said. The air was suddenly starting to grow colder. She carefully stood up, leaning against the horse for warmth. "I think the dizziness is passing."

"Okay," Howard said. "Mount up. But maybe you should take it slow for awhile."

Jessica pointed the horse down the road, but kept her to a brisk walk.

Chapter 9

Dawn was just turning the sky through the trees pink when Jessica finally reached the town she assumed was Pottswell. There were no signs giving the town a name, and no trace of the wagon. There wasn't anything else along this road however, so Hannah had to be right - the men she was after must have brought Bandit here. But where to start looking?

She had to find them before the fights started. Bandit wasn't a real dog, there was no way he'd be able to defend himself in the ring. What kind of people were entertained by something as cruel as a dogfight anyway? It made her sick to think about it.

After watering the mare at the public fountain in the town square she stood off to the side, wondering what to do next. There were just enough people around that consulting Howard was out of the question, unless she could find some place out of sight. And even then it might be chancy. A lot would depend on the town's views on magic.

"There be a stable over yonder if ye be thinking to stay a bit," a young voice piped up. "I'd be happy to take care 'o yer mare for ye."

"Would you now," Jessica said with a flicker of amusement. She looked down at the raggedy urchin. He couldn't be more than ten - all skin and bone and shaggy hair. "And how much is this going cost me?"

The boy squinted up at her. "Three coppers."

"Tell you what." Jessica pulled the small pouch she had around her neck open and fished out five coppers. "Here's five. And if you take good care of my mare and gear there's another five when I get back."

The child's eyes opened wide. "I'll treat 'er like she's me own kin!"

"Hey!" Jessica called as the child led the mare away. "What's your name?"

"Sadie," the child said proudly, proving Jessica was wrong about her sex. "If'n ye be needin' anything else, just ask for Sadie."

She was so serious Jessica didn't dare crack a smile. "All right Sadie. I'll be back before dinner to fetch her."

"Yes'm." Sadie led the mare away, talking to her as though they were friends. Shaking her head in amusement, Jessica turned her attention back to the people in the square.

Having for the most part kept off the main routes, she had not seen many towns in her travels. It wasn't quite what she expected, but it wasn't as if she'd gone back in time; this was a whole new world. She had to keep reminding herself of that. With her ability to do magic simmering inside her, she shouldn't have such trouble remembering.

But maybe that was part of the problem. Although she could do magic, she hadn't really seen anyone else do it. Granted magic was frowned upon in Ghren, but the further from the castle she got, the more she expected things to be relaxed. Sure, Wendel was able to create charms that made it appear as though Eleanor and Meren had red hair, and give the illusion that Gareth was a red-haired woman, but she expected magic to be more in your face.

There were several permanent structures making a U-shape ringing three sides of the town square, some built of stone but most built of heavy timber, presumably from the Darkwood Forest. A market was just starting to set up. She wandered amongst the stalls for a little while, trying to get her bearings.

Anything her imagination could come up with was available in the market. Brightly colored cloth formed canopies under which business was transacted. The smell of the live produce competed with food both cooked and being cooked, from delicate pastries to full size pigs roasting on spits.

Jessica paused to admire the work being done by the goldsmith, who was carving an intricate design on a filigree necklace. Beside him a potter was calling out wares. Clothing of all descriptions and colors was offered for sale: embellished dresses that rivaled the ones she'd worn at court lay beside more practical skirts and trousers; shirts and vests and finely woven tunics along with complete sets of leather armor. Footwear ranged from jewel studded slippers to heavy leather boots.

Near the pens for livestock was a blacksmith and Jessica stopped to watch him work. Knifes and swords shared the space with cooking utensils and pots. She picked up a couple of the knives to test their weight, then put them down again.

Further down, where the live animals were kept, a man was

trying to sell puppies, citing them as coming from champion fighting stock. Jessica started paying more attention to what was going on around her.

She toured through the market again, this time making discrete inquiries about the dog fights and a man who might be having trouble with a large black dog. Late in the afternoon she gave up. Everyone she questioned seemed to shut right up as soon as she mentioned the word dog. She treated herself to lunch in a tavern, hoping to overhear something.

"Crops, weather and women," she muttered in disgust later. "And if even half their stories about women are true, then they don't have time to work their crops no matter what the weather."

The crowd thinned out late in the afternoon and Jessica began to lose hope. Howard had encouraged her to have faith in herself but it was hard when she'd spent all day getting nowhere.

"Milady, I found ye at last!"

Jessica turned to greet the breathless voice. It was Thomas, Hannah's son.

"Me ma sent me, thinkin' ye might have a bit 'o trouble. They don't take kindly to strangers here."

"So I've noticed," Jessica said dryly. "I haven't been able to find out anything."

"The fights ain't held in the town, they's held just beyond in a fighting barn."

"Thank you, Thomas. Do you know when the next fight night is?"

"Yes'm. T'night. It be an important one too, methinks."

"Bless you, Thomas. Can you take me there?"

"Aye, that's what I be here for."

Stopping only long enough to collect her horse and give Sadie her promised reward, she followed Thomas to the fighting barn.

Jessica drew a few curious glances; there were not many women present and what few there were bore the hardened look of the handlers. Though there was a picket line for those who arrived mounted, Jessica took the precaution of leaving the mare hidden in the woods.

As Thomas promised, it was an important fight night, judging by the size of the crowd. Though the fights took place inside a large, barn-like structure, the dogs and their handlers were spread throughout the trees surrounding it.

"This is going to take forever," Jessica said. "Maybe it would be better if we split up. We could cover more ground. What time did you say the fights started?"

"When the sun goes down, milady."

"Then we'd better hurry," she said. There couldn't be more than an hour until dark. "You see what you can find out in the barn while I keep looking around here."

With a nod in agreement, Thomas hurried away.

Jessica wound her way through the maze of tents and pens. The tents held the owners and their gear, the dogs not even having that much shelter. She didn't get far before she started feeling sick to her stomach.

Most of the dogs were kept in cages, several of them very small cages considering the size of the dogs within. Many of the animals looked half-starved. Some were terribly scarred and others were being tormented through the bars, the ones getting ready for on-coming fights she presumed.

Several times Jessica paused, half-minded to stop some petty cruelty, but fear of what might be happening to Bandit sent her on again. Though her heart cried out for her to do something the more sensible part of her knew she could, in fact, do very little.

If Bandit was indeed stolen with the dog fights in mind, the thieves were being very careful. No one she asked seemed to know anything about a big black dog, though several expressed a desire to see him if she found him.

Thomas finally caught up to her. "There be a rumor that a huge black dog be fightin' t'night."

"We've got to find him before they put him in that pit."

"I seen yer dog; I reckon he stands a good chance of winnin'."

"You don't understand," Jessica told him. "Bandit is different, he doesn't know the first thing about fighting."

Thomas looked at her oddly but didn't comment. Jessica pushed her way through the crowd and into the barn. The noise and the heat were stifling. She scanned the people around her, looking for the ones taking bets. There were several clusters centered around single individuals and she sought out the man at the center of the largest group. Elbowing her way in to him, she pulled a gold piece out of a pocket.

"I want to make a bet," she said.

"That's what I be here for. What dog and what fight?"

"I heard there's a big black beast, new to the pit. I want the whole thing on him."

"Aye, lot 'o action on that one. Black Devil they call 'im. Sixth fight, comin' up soon."

"Thanks," Jessica elbowed her way back out of the crowd.

"Thomas," she called when she reached him. She handed him several coins. "See if you can rent a wagon for the night."

He ogled the money. "With such I's can buy one."

"I don't care, just so long as you get it."

He left and Jessica tried to get near the dogs for the next fight but they were too well guarded.

"Sixth fight," someone called at last. "Fight number six, ready to go."

Jessica wished she was wearing her rapier so she could cut her way through the crowd. They stood elbow to elbow, six deep around the pit.

She managed to shove and bully her way close enough for a glimpse, and a glimpse was all she needed. Bandit was already in the pit, looking as out of place as was possible for a dog. They were having trouble bringing in his opponent, a huge mastiff who was trying to bite everything in sight, especially his handlers. One had only to see the rivulets of blood running down his sides to see why.

Jessica eased herself back out of the crowd. She had only a few minutes before it was all over for Bandit. She needed a distraction and fast. Hoping for the best she hurried back out of the barn.

There were only a few people about, none of them paying any attention to her. Quickly, she pulled out the amulet.

"Howard, you've got to help me."

Having been keeping a eye on her from the other realm, he was there instantly. "What do you need, Jess?"

"I need some kind of distraction in the barn in front of me, and I need it yesterday."

"It's going to take time, Jess."

"We don't have time!"

Fortunately he'd already worked out a couple of different scenarios. "I'll have to work through you, then, I can't just—"

"I don't care how you do it, just do it! Bandit's fight is about to start and he's going to be a chew toy for a mastiff any second now."

"Okay, here goes. Face the barn, and whatever you do, don't move."

Jessica held herself rigid as she felt power flow through her. It was an eerie feeling, like ants crawling on her skin. She shivered but forced herself to keep still. From her finger-tips a white glow snaked towards the barn.

Suddenly, there was screaming and people began streaking out of the barn. All at once the power left her and Jessica forced herself against the human tide. Whatever Howard had done was effective, people were trampling each other to get out. Even the mastiff was more interested in leaving the barn than in finishing off Bandit, who was unable to get out of the pit.

Jessica jumped down beside him. "Oh, Bandit."

He looked up at her, head drooping, sides heaving. His left shoulder was a bloody mess and he had a gash across his muzzle. As he moved to meet her he limped, favoring one of his hind legs.

"We've got to get you out of here before they come back," Jessica said. "Do you think you can make it out of here if I give you a boost?"

He woofed at her, a gruff sound. Though she tried to be careful a few whimpers escaped him as she helped him out of the pit. By this time the barn was empty. Both sets of doors were wide open, they left by the set that had fewest people lingering nearby.

She was a little surprised, but grateful, no one tried to stop them. Of course it might have been different had Bandit not been taking such a beating in the ring. He'd only been seconds away from being torn apart.

Thomas was waiting for them. He helped Jessica lift the injured dog into the wagon and they started back to the inn.

Chapter 10

It was still dark as they reached the courtyard to the inn and Thomas pulled the wagon around to the back so they could use the kitchen staircase, which was shorter and closer to Jessica's room. Even so, it seemed to take forever to get Bandit up the stairs and when they reached the room Jessica helped him up onto the bed. He closed his eyes, exhausted.

"Is there anything else ye be needing?" Thomas asked.

"A bowl of water, and some clean cloths if you've any to spare," Jessica said, unable to take her eyes off the dog on her bed.

Thomas slipped away and was back in a matter of minutes. She didn't seem to notice and he set the bowl and cloths on the small table near the bed before leaving again.

Jessica bit her lip and moved closer to the bed. Bandit's eyes were still closed. He was a real mess. She dipped one of the cloths into the water and began to wash the blood off of him, as gently as possible. Tears filled her eyes and she sniffled as she worked. In no time at all the water in the bowl was bright red.

Laying her hands on the gash on his muzzle, she tried to summon the healing energy. It was a struggle to separate the green strand, but she pulled, sending the healing magic into Bandit. She managed to create a faint green glow but it faded quickly.

Moving to the more serious gash in his shoulder she attempted to heal it as well but the energy wouldn't come. Making a noise of frustration in the back of her throat, she closed her eyes and tried again. The strand of green stayed just beyond her reach.

"Howard! I need your help!"

As though he'd been waiting for her summons, he was right there. "What do you need, Jess?"

"I'm here too," Ellen said.

"My healing power, it's gone. How do I get it back?"

"I'm sorry Jess, but like I've told you before it uses your personal energy. You haven't slept in two days and you healed the mare not that long ago. Without a Well it's going to take time to re-charge your healing batteries."

"What about the herbs and stuff you got from Meren?" Ellen put in. "You were always pretty good with the herbal cures."

"Herbs. Right. Thanks Ellen."

She upended the saddle bag onto the rug in front of the fireplace and sorted through the packages, laying aside what she thought she might need. Glancing up at the herbs still tied for drying, she plucked several from her make-shift line.

The next few hours were spent washing, bandaging and making poultices for the dog. Twice she consulted with Howard on procedure and once she sent Ellen down to their apartment for her book of herbal medicines, giving her specific remedies to look up.

By the time the sun was fully up, Jessica had done as much as she could for him. The worst of it was his shoulder, but without the healing magic the best she could do was stitch him back together and slap a homemade antiseptic poultice, made from the purple moss, on it.

"You've taken care of Bandit, now you need to take care of yourself," Howard told her gently.

"I just need some sleep," Jessica said vaguely.

"You need to eat," Ellen said firmly.

"That's one of the reasons you weren't able to heal Bandit with your magic. You've got low blood sugar, which means low energy."

"All right, all right!" Jessica threw up her hands in defeat. "You guys win. I'll go down to the kitchen and find something to eat." She glanced down at her blood-spattered shirt. "But first I'd better change my clothes so I don't scare anyone."

Rummaging around in her pack she pulled out a plain white shirt and changed it for the one she was wearing.

"Thanks guys," she said solemnly. "I couldn't have done it without you."

"Yes, you could," Ellen said. "But it was nice to feel useful for a change."

"He'll be much better after a good sleep. You both will," Howard told her. "And if he's still feeling bad after a few days, you should have enough energy to be able to use the healing magic on him."

"That's great," she said wearily. "Thanks again, guys."

Jessica used the back stairs to make her way to the kitchen. There was no one around so she helped herself to a tray and loaded it up with cheese, fruit, bread, and after a slight hesitation, a bottle of wine she found sitting on the work table.

By the time she carried her loot back up the stairs she was running on empty. She barely had a few mouthfuls before she was asleep in the chair.

When Jessica awoke, Bandit, too, was awake, and watching her curiously.

"How are you feeling?" she asked. "Howard said you'd be fine in a few days. Your shoulder took the worst of it. I needed to do some stitching, but nothing's broken."

She got up and paced around the room, then crouched by the bed to look him in the eye. "I'm sorry I took so long to find you. I did try, but . . . "

Bandit woofed softly, then suddenly swiped her face with his tongue.

Jessica sprang to her feet. "Ewww! You miserable—"

She looked down at the mischievous look in the dog's eyes. "I'm glad you think this is so funny, because there's something else Howard and I discussed."

She went over to the wash stand. "Just in case we ever get separated again, Howard came up with a way to trace you."

Bandit made a noise in his throat as she picked something up and came back over to him.

"I know it looks like a dog collar, but it's a link, like my amulet."

He tried to pull back but she was too fast for him. The collar snapped closed around his neck. It was black leather, made from one of her belts, with a glittering sapphire set in the center.

"It's the jewel, really, that's the link." She looked at him with a grin. "I wasn't crazy enough to give all of our loot to Gareth. And don't get any bright ideas - it won't come off until you're human again."

He shook his head and glared balefully at her.

"Look at it this way, at least people won't mistake you for a stray." She got up and stretched. "I don't know about you, but I'm ready for breakfast. Steak okay by you?"

Bandit was still glaring at her as she left the room. He laid his head down and sighed heavily as the door swung shut behind her. He supposed the collar was a small price to pay for his past misdeeds.

He hurt, but not as much as he should have. She must have taken care of his injuries. Even his shoulder didn't hurt as much as it should. At least it didn't until he shifted on the bed. Then pain spiked through him, eliciting an unintentional whimper.

It was hard to believe anyone would risk so much for a dog, let alone a dog that was once a man. Did she not remember he'd been searching her camp when she caught him? He deserved to get turned into a dog, because that's what he felt like. A real dog, for ever having tried to make a victim out of her.

He knew well enough from experience what it was like to be a victim. Being stuck in this form had given him plenty of time for reflection, and he didn't like what he'd become. Had he lost so much of himself that he would really have harmed her? For all her tough facade, she was very much the innocent in the ways of the world. In fact, she bordered on naive. What were her friends thinking, letting her travel alone?

He wasn't normally a thief, but he hadn't eaten in two days and the money he'd been offered for the amulet had been too much to resist. The wizard who hired him had assured him the amulet was his, and she was the true thief. But he should have known better. For one thing, the amount of money he'd been offered was too good to be true. And for another, the witch, Jessica, was nothing like he'd been told. She was a woman out of place and out of time and it appeared her luck was even worse than his. He couldn't help but admire her courage and perseverance.

He shifted on the bed again and realized that although he had an overall ache, only his shoulder really pained him. Even his sensitive muzzle didn't feel all that bad. It suddenly occurred to him to wonder what kind of scars he was going to end up with, and how they were going to translate to his human form once the month was over and he was changed back. Sighing heavily he decided it was no worse than he deserved.

Chapter 11

Paranithel eased the door of his room open, congratulating himself that he'd thought to oil the hinges earlier in the day to keep them from squeaking. He crept along the corridor, avoiding the squeaky floorboards, and made his way to the scrying tower.

Once he started up the stairs he relaxed slightly, secure in the knowledge that he'd made it this far undetected. He could have just magicked himself up to the scrying room, but it was a waste of power, and the ripple of his passing might have awoken Thackery and that was the last thing he needed. Besides, he could use the exercise.

It only took him a few minutes to set the wards to prevent anyone from discovering what he was up to, then a few more to set up the scrying bowl. Taking several deep breaths, he cleared his mind of outside influences.

Together he and Thackery had watched Jessica taking care of the injured dog. Thackery muttering about it being a waste of her time and energy, that the beast had no life-threatening injuries and could easily recover on its own. But Paranithel was filled with pride.

More than ever he could see her mother, Farenalyssia, in her - her strength, her courage, and especially her compassion. Once again he was filled with misgivings that they were doing the right thing, keeping the truth of who she was from her. It was an argument he and Thackery had been having since they brought her across the void.

He believed they should tell her the truth, that she'd been sent to her world as a baby to protect her from their enemy and that her journey now was not just to meet a potential teacher, but to be reunited with her family. Thackery, on the other hand, believed that she wasn't ready for the truth and such knowledge would be too dangerous.

Farenalyssia would not have wanted the truth kept from her daughter, of that much he was certain. And had it been her in Jessica's place, she would have been outraged that such knowledge was kept from her. Even now learning the truth could create a rift between Jessica and her father, and the longer the knowledge was kept from her, the larger the rift could grow.

Unfortunately, he'd given his word he'd abide by Thackery's decision. But there was another promise he'd made, to someone even closer to him than his son-in-law. He had thought he'd never have a chance to fulfill that promise but Jessica being in the Darkwood Forest put him in the position to do so.

Paran cast a summoning spell over the scrying bowl once, twice, three times, and then sat back to wait. He was starting to nod off before he finally got an answer.

"Who is it that summons me, and at such an hour?" The bell-like voice resonated within the room and a face appeared in the scrying bowl.

Silver hair was swept off her face, threaded with chains of amber and gold and wound about her head. Her ears swept upwards into high, delicate points and her cat-like eyes were a brilliant blue. The stern look on her face softened as she saw him.

"Paranithel! It has been a long time, my friend. To what do I owe this honor?"

"The honor is mine, Aracelia." Paran bowed towards the bowl. "I have news of Jesseminathus."

"Such an unwieldy name," she shook her head in amusement. "I have never understood the custom of the people of Mythago to favor such names. Now what news have you of our granddaughter?"

"She has returned. And even now she takes her ease on the borders of your realm."

"Truly? I am well pleased, for the sake of all involved. You know I was never in favor of sending her away. But what does she here in the Darkwood Forest?"

Without further encouragement, Paran launched into the story of how they reconnected with Jessica just as Howard was on the verge of experimenting with teleportation using her as the subject, and how they hadn't factored in the energy from the magic circle he raised, so instead of bringing her directly to them in the south, she ended up in Ghren. Then he explained the events that went on in Ghren and how she came to be in the Darkwood Forest with a price on her head.

"Extraordinary," Aracelia said, shaking her head. "And you say she knows nothing of her origins?"

"Nothing," he confirmed. "She does not even question where her sudden magical abilities come from."

"She may not take the news well when it is delivered. I hope

Kiranthus knows what he is about."

"Thackery. He goes by Thackery now."

She shook her head. "Whatever name he goes by, he is courting trouble. But that is his choice. Let us talk more of the magical strength of Jesseminathus."

Paran brightened immediately. "Her power is incredible. She crossed the lines of a Well and suffered no more than a slight backlash. Already she has performed Alchemy, Elemental, and Healing magicks, and her first attempt at healing was intuitive."

"Indeed." For most, healing magic was the most difficult to perform. "Do you believe she could be of Grand Master ability?"

He gave a deceptively casual shrug. "There is no way of telling without testing her first."

"Ah! The true reason you have reached out to me after all these years," she said with a knowing smile.

"I promised Farenalyssia, when Jessica was born, that I would have her tested. I believe she had a premonition that she would not be able to bring her to you herself."

"Jessica?" Aracelia asked.

"It is the name she was raised with and the name she goes by."

"Very well," she said, coming to a decision. "I will do as you ask. I will test our granddaughter. But I will do it in my own fashion, with no interference from you or Kiranthus. And she will receive no help from her would-be wizard friend in the other realm."

"But they are connected through the talisman you gifted Farenalyssia."

"Leave everything to me."

It took Jessica two more days to recover enough that she could finish the healing on Bandit. She placed her hands above his shoulder and reached for the healing green, smiling when it came easily to her this time.

"There, that should feel better," she said.

He woofed softly.

"You're welcome. Now let me see your leg."

Dutifully, he shifted until she could get at the injury on his leg.

"It looks like it's pretty much healed, but let's see if we can fix it so you don't scar. Hold still."

She already looked tired from healing his shoulder. The last thing he wanted was for her to expend energy on him for vanity's sake. He tried to pull away but she held him fast and worked her magic.

"Okay, try getting up and walking."

With a sigh he got up from the bed and walked around the room.

"How does that feel? Are you all right?"

He wagged his tail to show that he was feeling fine again.

"Great! What do you say we go for a walk in the woods?"

Bandit barked in agreement.

"This room is starting to feel a little claustrophobic. And I should probably search for some more herbs to replenish my supply."

Jessica picked up her empty pack, and slung it over her shoulder, leading the way out of the room and down the back stairs. On their way through the kitchen she pilfered some bread and cheese, just in case they got hungry.

It was a beautiful day. They followed the stream and when they came to the place Jessica had found to learn magic, they stopped. Bandit stretched out on a raised, flat rock to enjoy the sun. Jessica thought about contacting Howard to get a little magic practice in, but decided it was too nice a day for work. Instead she stretched out beside Bandit and in minutes they were both fast asleep.

A few hours later, Jessica woke with a start. Something was wrong but she couldn't quite put her finger on it. She sat up and looked around them, but other than the shadows being much longer, there didn't seem to be anything amiss. Her hand went automatically to the amulet to call Howard to check things out, but the amulet wasn't there.

"Oh my god!" She patted herself down frantically, but the amulet was gone. She got to her feet and gave her clothing a shake, hoping it was just a matter of the chain breaking and the pendant slipping down inside her clothing. But nothing fell out.

"Bandit, wake up!"

He lifted his head and looked at her blearily.

"It's gone! My amulet is gone!"

Her frantic voice got through to him and he quickly got to his feet.

"Ohmygodohmygodohmygod! What am I going to do? That was my only link to Howard. I am so screwed without him!"

She sank to the ground, eyes wide with panic. "I can't believe I lost it."

Bandit was sniffing the ground around them. Despite the fact he'd started out as a man, he'd acquired some of the characteristics of a dog, and a heightened sense of smell was one of them. He criss-crossed the rock, stopping suddenly to bark.

"What is it? Did you find it?" She turned a hopeful look in his direction.

He shook his head no, then pawed the ground and growled.

Jessica tried to see what he was looking at. "I don't -" There, in the loose dirt in a depression of the rock. "Is that a footprint?" Her voice rose. "Are you trying to tell me I didn't lose my amulet, someone stole it?"

Bandit dipped his head in a nod.

"Holy Saint Christopher! I can't believe I slept so heavily that someone was able to actually take my medallion off of me without waking."

Lifting his head, Bandit sniffed a couple of times with his nose in the air, then sneezed. He looked at Jessica expectantly.

"What?"

He repeated his actions and her brow furrowed in concentration. "Something in the air?"

His head went up and down in a nod yes.

"Something in the air . . . like magic? Someone used magic to spell us to sleep heavier?"

This time he barked and nodded.

Jessica's panic was burning away with anger. "God damn them to hell! Do you think you'd be able to track their scent?"

He stared at the footprint and then sniffed the ground around it. Catching the scent a little further on, he began to follow the trail.

"All right Bandit! Let's get the bastard, whoever he is!"

Chapter 12

Jessica had no idea how much of a head start the thief had, nor how long it would take to catch him. But catch him she would. Though she chaffed at the delay, she decided it would be prudent to go back to the inn for her horse and some supplies.

"Would you mind waiting here?" she asked Bandit. "I don't know how long we'll be, but I have a feeling we'll need more than just the snacks I snagged from the kitchen."

He barked at her and she took that as agreement. She practically ran back to the inn and up the stairs to her room. Grabbing up her saddlebags, she stuffed her blankets and spare clothing inside, and added the freshly dried herbs from the fireplace. Snatching up her empty wineskin and water bottle, she hurried back down to the kitchen where she sought out Hannah.

Handing her a gold piece, she said, "I'm sorry, I'm going to have to go and I don't know if I'll be back. Could I get some supplies from you? At least a couple of days' worth."

Hannah had been in business long enough to know when not to ask questions. She quickly put together a sack of apples, cheese, biscuits, and smoked meat and had Ginny fill the wineskin and the water bottle.

"Thank you," Jessica said, putting everything in the saddlebags.

"Good luck to ye," Hannah called after her. "In whatever ye be doin'."

Minutes later Jessica was back at the stream. "Okay, Bandit. Let's catch us a thief."

Nose to the ground he led the way, happy he was finally of some use to her. The trail led deeper and deeper into the Darkwood Forest. The thief seemed well versed in wood-craft, if it hadn't been for the scent Bandit would have been hard pressed to follow, and as a man he'd been an excellent tracker.

It was almost fully dark before they stopped. Silently Jessica made camp and built a fire.

"What am I going to do?" she wondered out loud, sitting huddled near the fire. "Without that amulet I'm helpless."

Up until now she hadn't realized just how much she depended on her link with Howard. It wasn't just his advice and magical assistance either, it was the connection to her other life, her real life. Although right now she could definitely use his assistance. How was she ever going to get home without him?

Now that her link was gone, Jessica had no idea what to do next. It was like going on a tour of a foreign country and missing the tour bus. This fear was why she didn't travel to foreign countries. Well, that and she couldn't afford it. She started to sniffle.

Bandit barked sharply at her. Jessica looked up. "You don't

get it, do you? I can still light a fire and do minor magic, but that's not going to get me back home, or change you back into a man for that matter."

Jessica rested her head on her knees. "Just go away and leave me alone."

It was so frustrating not to be able to speak with her. She had so much magic, burning just under her skin. If only she had faith in herself and her ability to use it. If he had even a fraction of her power he wouldn't be in this mess in the first place.

She didn't need her amulet, or Howard for that matter. They were just a crutch for her to lean on. Didn't she realize how far she'd already come on her own? Being able to talk to her friends was just a matter of casting a scrying spell. Simple really.

He had to remind himself that she wasn't from this world. From what he could gather, she was from a world where magic didn't exist. He remembered his teacher, long ago, talking about worlds without magic. They had something called technology instead.

Glancing over at her he could see she was well into a bout of feeling sorry for herself and decided to give her some privacy. He slipped into the woods to do some scouting ahead.

He was back, sitting by the dying fire watching her, when Jessica woke the next morning. Bandit barked once, sharply, and went over to the saddlebags. Jessica looked up as he started to tug at one of them.

"That's the wrong one if you're looking for something to eat."

He ignored her and continued to drag the saddlebag over to

her. Nosing it open he managed to get his teeth into what he was searching for and dropped the cloth wrapped packet in her lap.

"Sorry, that's healing herbs, not breakfast." Jessica picked the packet up. "Oh, I get it. I can use my herbal skills to pay my way. I already figured that one out, remember? And money's not the problem. I need to work magic."

Bandit gave an impatient bark, then upended the saddlebag.

"Now what are you doing, besides making a mess?"

The dog grasped a heavy book in his jaws and dropped it in her lap.

With a resigned sigh, Jessica looked at it.

"It's a spell book! But where . . . oh, I remember. It was in the wizard's tower at Ghren. Sebastian must have packed it for me." Her voice trailed off as she started to leaf through it. A sudden thought struck her. "How did you even know this book was in there?"

Bandit contrived to look innocent. He knew a lot of things she didn't.

"You better hope I don't find a mind reading spell," she muttered.

The book kept her attention for the remainder of the morning as Bandit pretended to search for the thief's trail. Sometimes she would absently gesture with her hand, or sound out a particularly long word, but for the most part she studied quietly.

Bandit wanted to give her enough time to get used to the idea of using a spellbook, so he disappeared into the forest, though he didn't go far. When he returned Jessica was staring intently into the pool of water they'd camped beside. He sat down behind her and barked.

Jessica nearly dropped the spellbook into the water. "Damn it! Did you have to do that? I almost had this scrying spell working."

She sat back with a sigh. "This is hard stuff, Bandit, real hard. I don't know if I'm up to it."

Bandit nudged his cold nose under her arm and she automatically started to scratch him behind the ear. Suddenly, she stopped and glared at him.

"Will you stop that! Were you able to pick up the thief's trail?"

He dipped his head and she got to her feet and started packing up. "Okay. Let's go then."

Whereas before the path the thief took was fairly straightforward, now it twisted and wound through the enormous trees. Jessica may not have known much about woodcraft, but she could tell this was definitely old growth forest. She hoped Bandit would be able to get them out again because she was definitely lost.

The trees were so dense it was hard to judge the time of day, but Jessica figured it was late in the afternoon when Bandit stopped and looked around uneasily. There was a faint shimmer in the air in front of them, as though there was a barrier of some kind. Jessica urged the mare forward but for once the steadfast beast refused to obey her.

"What is it?"

Bandit took a few steps forward and then stopped, whining in the back of his throat. Jessica swore to herself that the next time she turned someone into an animal she'd make sure they retained the ability to talk. He wasn't growling, so she didn't think whatever it the shimmer represented was dangerous, but he obviously didn't know what it was either.

She dismounted and, there being nothing small enough to tether the horse to, handed the reins to Bandit. "Here, make yourself useful," she said.

The shimmer was actually quite beautiful, a rainbow of colors in an intricate net-like pattern. Stepping slowly forward, she reached out and touched it. It tingled, like the pins and needles you get when a hand or foot has fallen asleep and is waking up again.

Emboldened, she kept moving forward. As she passed through the barrier it was like the world held its breath. She felt the shimmer over her skin, almost like absorbing a mild electric shock. Once she was through to the other side she turned.

"You're sure the trail goes this way?" she asked Bandit.

He woofed around the reins in his mouth.

"Okay. Well I don't know what this is, but I don't think it's anything bad." She crossed back to the other side and took the horse's reins from him.

"All right, sweetie," she said, stroking the mare's nose. "I know you don't like this thing, whatever it is, but I promise it won't hurt you." The horse flicked her ears and took a step forward. Jessica continued coaxing and cajoling and led the mare through the barrier. The horse snorted and tossed her head, but a few more soothing words and she was through.

Jessica turned back to look at Bandit. "Well don't just sit there," she said. "C'mon, you're next."

He approached the barrier slowly and reached out to touch it with his nose, pulling back with a yelp as though receiving a static shock.

"Oh don't be such a big baby, just do it."

Pulling back just a little, he drew his hind quarters underneath him and leaped forward. When he landed on the other side he shook himself vigorously, as though shaking water from his fur.

Jessica grinned at him. "Okay, braveheart, let's get back on the trail. But keep your eye out for some place to stop for the night."

He woofed at her and picked up the thief's trail again.

Chapter 13

"Paranithel!"

His name reverberated throughout the castle, causing three of his students to cringe and one to lose control of the wind imp he'd summoned. The imp shot around the classroom blowing papers all over the place before it could be banished. Paran sighed.

"Class is dismissed. And you may spread the word that the afternoon classes are cancelled for today."

He waited until all the students had left the classroom, then teleported himself to the scrying tower.

"You bellowed for me?"

"What have you done, old man?"

"I have done nothing," Paran said mildly.

"I am being blocked from my daughter. If not you, then who? Howard has neither the skill nor the knowledge to do so."

Paranithel sighed. "I would have thought you could figure it out yourself. Within the Darkwood Forest lies the third of the Elven Realms."

"But what have the elves - the third, you say?" Thackery's eyes narrowed. "And you thought not to warn me, to warn Howard to keep her away?"

"I made a promise to my daughter," Paranithel told him. "That I would see to it that when the time came I would make sure her daughter was tested."

"And think you I am not capable of testing my own daughter?" Thackery said angrily. "What right has she—"

"She is Jessica's grandmother. She has every right. And it was Farenalyssia's request that it be Aracelia herself that tests her child."

"I do not want—"

"It is no longer up to you," Paran said firmly.

"What was she thinking? You know what Elven testing entails. Nothing in Jessica's life has prepared her for this."

"Nothing in her life has prepared her for being in this world either, yet here she is," he countered. "I think you greatly underestimate your daughter."

But Thackery wasn't listening. "It's too dangerous. She must be warned." He waved his hands over the scrying bowl in preparation to summoning Howard's presence. When nothing happened he turned to glare at Paran once more.

"For the duration of the testing, you will not be permitted to contact Howard. Nor will he be permitted to contact us."

"This is utterly ridiculous!"

"At least you know she will be safe. Not even Anakaron can penetrate the shielding around an Elven Realm."

Thackery was far from being reassured.

"Hey, Howard. How's Jessica doing?"

Howard frowned into the phone. "I'm not sure," he said slowly. "You know we agreed to stop keeping such close tabs on her, to let her call us. She hasn't called in the last couple of days."

"I'll be right up."

Ellen took the stairs two at a time and didn't even bother to knock before bursting into Howard's apartment.

"What do you mean, she hasn't called in a couple of days. How many is a couple?"

"Two, maybe three. I can only assume things are going well for her. Or at least nothing bad's happened." At least that's what he hoped. Maybe she was just resting up from healing Bandit.

"I don't like this. What if something happened and she can't contact you?"

"I'm sure Paran and—"

"You haven't heard from them either?"

"No, but—"

"Damn it Howard, something's going on. I can feel it in my bones!"

She went to his work room, leaving him to follow in her wake. Going directly over to the pendent hanging above the work table, she said, "Do whatever it is you need to do to activate this thing."

With an exasperated sigh he spoke the words that opened the conduit between their world and Jessica's. "Jessica? Are you there?"

There was no response. "Jessica? Sorry to wake you if you're sleeping, but Ellen here is freaking out. I'd really appreciate it if you could get her off my back."

"Why isn't she answering?" Ellen said after a few minutes.

"She might not be in a place where she can hear me. After I contacted her in front of Sebastian without meaning to, I had Thackery help me set up a security system where she wouldn't be able to hear me if it wasn't safe, like if she was around other people."

"Then let's see where she is." Ellen pulled a bottle of oil off the storage shelf and poured it into the scrying bowl, then turned and looked at him expectantly. "Fire this thing up, Howard."

"Fine," he huffed. "But when we see she's all right will you go away and let me have some peace?"

"Of course," she said, not meaning a word of it.

Howard waved his hands over the oil and muttered an incantation. The surface of the oil rippled, then cleared. He peered into the bowl expecting to see Jessica either in the tap room of the inn or sleeping, but there was nothing.

Frowning, he repeated the incantation and tried again. Again there was nothing.

"What's the matter?"

"I don't know. This has never happened before."

"Are you sure you're using the right incantation?"

"I only know two for this. One for Jessica and one to contact the wizard school where Paran and Thackery are."

"Well try again!"

Howard closed his eyes and took a deep breath to relax. Opening his eyes again he shook out his hands and then waved them over the bowl as he recited the incantation. Once more the oil in the bowl rippled, but there was no image. He started to catch Ellen's bad feeling.

"I don't know what's going on," he said. "Maybe Paran or Thackery do." Once more he waved his hands, though with a slightly different motion. The incantation he muttered this time was a tad longer, and slightly different.

"Nothing's happening Howard."

"I know nothing's happening. What I don't know is why nothing's happening!"

Howard closed his eyes again and took another deep breath, trying to center himself. It didn't work. He was too freaked out to work the incantation.

"Deep breaths," Ellen told him, understanding the pressure he was under. "In and out, in and out."

He tried again and this time was able to muster a semblance of calm. He worked the scrying spell again, and again there was no response. Now he was really starting to panic.

"I don't understand. Even when Paran or Thackery aren't available they always leave one of their students watching in case of emergency."

"You don't think . . ." Ellen's voice trailed off, not wanting to believe the worst.

"I don't know what to think! This is bad. This is very very bad."

"Is it possible that they cut us off?" she asked slowly.

"What do you mean, cut us off?"

"I mean," she said, voice a little stronger, "is it possible they don't want us contacting them anymore and that's why we can't get through?"

"I suppose anything is possible." The very thought of it gave him a sick feeling inside. "But it doesn't explain why we can't get through to Jessica. I came up with the spell for the moonstone myself, it had nothing to do with the others."

"But these safeguards you came up with . . ."

"Again, it was my own work. Mostly. There was no reason for it not to work. Unless . . ."

"Unless what?"

"Unless she's hurt and can't answer, or unconscious, or . . ."

"Don't even go there!" Ellen glared at him.

"You have to face that it's a possibility."

"No I don't! I—"

"Oh enough!" a third voice said. A woman's face shimmered into view in the scrying bowl. Though she had silver hair that was done up in an elaborate style, she seemed ageless. There was a faint expression of irritation in her brilliant blue eyes.

Howard and Ellen faced her, identical expressions of astonishment on their faces. "Who the hell are you?" Ellen demanded.

"My, such language. And from such a lovely young woman."

Ellen flushed, unaccountably ashamed.

"Forgive us," Howard said. "We're just very worried about our friend."

"So I gather. That's why I'm here. I would like to assure you that your friend is fine but until she has completed the task before her she can have contact with neither yourselves nor her father and grandfather."

"What task?" Ellen demanded. At the woman's raised eyebrow she added, "If you don't mind me asking, ma'am."

"Are you an elf?" Howard asked, eyes trained on the slender, pointed ears.

"You are familiar with my kind?"

"Only myths and legends, and fairy tales."

"Ah. Of course. Yes, I am of the elvish race. And your friend's quest has taken her into the Elven lands, which are warded against magical intrusion."

"Magical—"

"She means the scrying bowl and the amulet," Howard told Ellen.

"Okay, so what kind of quest is taking Jess through the Elven lands?" Ellen asked with dogged persistence. "And why can't we reach Paran and Thackery?"

"Did Paranithel not warn you?"

"Warn us about what?"

She let out a huff of exasperation. "Of course he did not. How foolish of me to think otherwise." Shaking her head, her features seemed to soften. "Forgive me. Your friend has been set upon a quest to test her magical abilities. It is necessary that she receives no outside assistance for the duration of this test, which is why it is being given in the Elven Realm."

"Let me get this straight," Ellen said, still spoiling for a fight. "You've taken away Jess's only means of support and sent her off on a quest to test her for magic that up until a couple of months ago she never even knew she had and even now has only a vague notion of how to use?"

"That sums it up quite nicely," the woman said.

Chapter 14

"You know," Jessica said, "I really have to remember to thank Sebastian for stashing this in my pack. It's truly opened my eyes. According to this book, the more magic you use, the more powerful your reserves become. Theoretically, one could advance beyond needing a Well simply by using Wells for a series of powerful spells."

Bandit gave a bark to show he was listening. In truth, he knew this from his own magical studies.

"I'm not sure I understand it either," she said, misinterpreting his bark.

They'd spent the last two days tracking the thief and whenever they stopped to rest Jessica studied the magic book. Sometimes, trusting the horse to follow the dog, she even read while in the saddle.

Jessica sighed and closed the book. "Even the simple spells are hard. There's one for causing rain that calls for sixteen different hand signals - and even that won't work if there are no clouds to start with."

The dog woofed softly at her. She fidgeted under his scrutiny. "I know what you're wondering," she admitted. "No, I haven't found a transformation or reversal spell. But I'm sure I'm getting close, they're getting harder."

Another day's ride made Jessica more confident in her ability. Some of the spells relied solely on power, but others required little power, relying on incantations and hand movements. One love spell required nothing but dance movements.

"Howard always told me that wizards guard their spell books jealously," she said, "and it's no wonder. With enough power and physical dexterity you can do virtually anything."

Bandit gave another bark and nosed at the saddle bag.

"All right, all right. I can take a hint." She pulled the saddle bag closer and searched inside with her hand. Frowning, she opened it up fully and peered inside. "I don't know how to tell you this, but we're out of food."

His head drooped and he whined softly. Jessica opened the spell book again.

"You know, this is the perfect opportunity to test one of these spells. I'm sure I saw a spell for conjuring up a chicken dinner. If I can just—here it is! Chicken Flambé."

Bandit barked a question.

"Well it's chicken something or other, and it looks close enough to flambé for me to give it a try."

He prudently backed off a few paces to watch, rather dubiously, as Jessica prepared the spell. She sat cross-legged in front of the fire, spell book spread across her lap. After reading the spell over several times she finally nodded to herself and straightened her back.

Hands waving madly, she started. "Ip reel fela, shidd yib jev—jev—jev—" The fire snapped and flared as she paused and looked at the book. "Crelna, isit sin gallow!" With a flourish she gestured in the air.

The blast from the fire knocked her over backwards. She could hear Bandit's high pitched yelp over the roar of the flames. An indistinct but enormous creature towered over them.

Jessica levered herself up on her elbows, gaping in shock. Bandit circled round to stand beside her. The creature was gaining solidity and let loose an awful scream.

"It looks . . ." Jessica sat up properly and gulped. "Holy Saint Christopher! It looks like a giant, flaming chicken!"

Bandit barked urgently and nudged her arm.

"What?" He pawed the book in her lap. "Right, a banishing spell. Good idea."

The chicken let out another scream. Jessica scooted backwards away from it as she leafed rapidly through the book.

"Banishing, banishing . . ." She looked up quickly and felt the first stirrings of desperation. She had the feeling that if she didn't find the banishing spell before the creature finished taking corporeal form they'd be in a world of trouble.

It was a rooster, not a chicken, that was forming in all its flaming glory. It flapped transparent wings sending waves of heat in Jessica's direction. She coughed and backed away again.

"Here it is!" she exclaimed.

The rooster crowed, gaining substance. It swept its head downwards. Bandit started to bark, distracting it away from Jessica. A shower of sparks sprayed upwards as it spread its wings and swept around, following the dog.

Jessica raised her hands and started to gesture again. The words she spoke were lost in the roar as the rooster crowed again. Jessica finished the spell. With a whuff of displaced air the bird, along with their fire, disappeared.

"Well," Jessica said, dusting her hands off with a nonchalance she was far from feeling, "That wasn't so bad for a first try, was it?"

Bandit bared his teeth at her in a snarl.

"I'd watch my language if I were you. It wouldn't do to antagonize someone of my awesome powers," she said, teasingly. Then she sighed and her smile faded. "Who am I kidding? You saw what just happened, and that was a simple spell. If we don't get my amulet back so Howard can help me with the spell to change you back, I could end up making matters worse for you, a lot worse."

Bandit looked at her and woofed softly.

"Your faith in me is admirable," Jessica said soberly. "I just hope it isn't misplaced."

In the morning, after a cold and hungry night, Jessica pulled out Meren's book of herbs, hoping to find something edible amongst the abundance of plants growing around them. When she returned from foraging it was with an armful of fungus and mushrooms, which she emptied on the ground in front of the saddle bags.

Bandit looked from the pile to her, and back again.

"I could try stewing them up or something, if you like."

He shook his head.

"In that case, you go first."

Tilting his head, he gave her a look and then took a cautious sniff. Sneezing, he shook his head and backed away.

"There's gratitude for you," Jessica muttered.

She never cared much for mushrooms, and even then she preferred them sautéed in butter with onions and served with steak. With a sigh she broke off a piece from a spongy looking white fungus and took a taste. She froze as the taste hit her, then quickly spat it out again.

"That's totally gross!"

Bandit barked in agreement.

"Maybe we should keep our eye out for some berry bushes on our way today. And if we happen to run across a stream I could always try fishing."

He huffed a sigh as she saddled up the mare and packed up her gear. If her fishing abilities were anything like her magical abilities, they were doomed to starve.

Chapter 15

By mid-morning it was becoming apparent that Bandit was having trouble following the thief's trail. When he back tracked for the third time, Jessica called a halt.

"Do you hear that?" she asked, listening intently. She urged the mare forward. "It sounds like an animal in distress."

Bandit had no choice but to follow. It was either that or get left behind. Sometimes the witch could be like a dog with a bone.

As they neared the source of the noise the mare starting balking and side-stepping. Jessica was forced to tie her to a sapling and she continued on foot. Just a short distance away they found the source of the noise.

It was a wolf, at least she thought it was a wolf, having never seen one in real life before, and it was tangled in some kind of snare. The rope was wound around it like a net, and it was cutting into both one of its legs and its neck.

"Oh, you poor thing!"

The wolf snapped at her in reply. Bandit instinctively moved between Jessica and the frantic predator. Jessica pulled the knife out of her belt and pushed the dog aside. He wouldn't budge and she looked at him sternly.

"Look, I know this probably isn't the brightest thing I've ever done, but we can't just leave her to suffer. Who knows how long she's been here. And there's no way she's going to be able to get free on her own. We *have* to help her."

The wolf seemed to be listening as well, and had stopped struggling. But as Jessica pushed past the dog, the wolf snarled at her.

"It's all right," Jessica said in her most soothing voice, trying to project calm. "I know you're scared and you're hurt, but we only want to help." She continued with her quiet encouragement and slowly continued forward, approaching with her hands held so the wolf could see them both.

"That's right, I promise you'll be free in just a few minutes."

Jessica was within striking distance of the wolf, but the animal didn't attack. She didn't dare touch her, so she studied the arrangement of ropes, trying to figure out which would be the most advantageous to cut first. Deciding the rope wrapped around the animal's leg was causing the most distress, she followed it to the anchor in the ground.

Still making soothing sounds at the wolf, she sawed through the rope with as little movement as possible. To her relief, and great surprise, the wolf did little more than watch. As soon as the rope was cut the pressure eased on the wolf's leg and it was able to kick it free. But it yelped as it did so and Jessica could see the damage done to the leg itself.

"I think it might be broken," she said to Bandit. "I'm going to see if she'll let me heal it before I get rid of the rest of these ropes."

She made more calming noises and this time the wolf seemed to be listening. It trembled where it stood, favoring the injured leg, but didn't pull away as Jessica moved her hand close enough to the injury to summon her healing energy. Fortunately, the energy came easily this time, the green glow transferring easily from her hand onto the wolf's leg.

When she was finished she cut more of the ropes, leaving the one that was tight around the wolf's neck for last.

"Now I know you have no reason to trust me," she said, "but you have to know by now that I mean you no harm. And I did heal your leg. I'm going to have to cut this rope off of your neck, and to do so I'll have to put my blade between your neck and the rope. But if you let me do this, I promise I'll be as quick as possible."

The wolf trembled as Jessica lowered her knife, but allowed her to cut the rope and pull it away. As she did so, Jessica sent as much healing energy into the wolf's neck as she could, knowing that the animal was going to be gone as soon as she got the rope off her. She sawed through the strands as gently as possible and the moment she was through the wolf bounded away without a backward glance.

"Truly, you must be a most powerful Animagnus," a voice said behind her.

Jessica and Bandit both gave a yelp and whirled around in shock. They hadn't even heard the woman approach.

"Holy St. Christopher! Give a person some warning, would you?" Jessica said, hand pressed against her chest where her heart was pounding.

Standing behind them, a little off to the side, was a tall and slender woman, dressed in a green tunic with brown trousers. Her silver hair was confined in a thick braid that hung all the way to her waist, and sticking up through her hair were two slender, pointed ears.

"Are you a Vulcan?" Jessica asked. If magic was real, who's to say Star Trek wasn't?

The woman arched one perfectly shaped brow. "Pray forgive me. I did not mean to startle you. I know not what this "Vulcan" is. My name is Aracelia; I am an elf."

"Really? That's so cool! I have a friend named Howard who would just die to meet you. He's right into the whole elves and wizards thing," Jessica said, spirits suddenly high. "I'm Jessica, and this is my faithful dog, Bandit." Bandit gave a snort. "What's an Animagnus?"

The hint of a smile played around the elf woman's lips at Jessica's enthusiasm. "An Animagnus has a magical way with animals, including the ability to communicate and influence them."

"And you think I can do that?"

"I have just witnessed you doing this. Think you that just anyone could have freed the wolf?"

"But—" Jessica thought about the way the wolf seemed to calm down as she spoke to it, almost as though it knew she was trying to help.

"May I ask what you are doing so far from human trails? Be you lost?"

"Now that's a bit of a long story," Jessica said with a sigh.

"My camp is not far," Aracelia said, appearing to come to a decision. "Perhaps you and your four footed companion would care to share dinner with me while I hear your tale."

Both Jessica and Bandit seemed to brighten at the mention of dinner.

"If you're sure it's not too much trouble," Jessica said out of politeness.

"The hunting was good today and I was somewhat overzealous. You would be doing me a favor."

"In that case, it would be our pleasure."

Since the elf woman, Aracelia, was on foot, Jessica led the horse as she and Bandit followed her to her camp. True to her word, it wasn't far. It was set against a tumble of boulders that made a u-shape surrounding a flat space. The fire was neatly contained within a ring of stones and suspended above it were several mouth watering, small, animal corpses.

"You can secure your mare over there," Aracelia told Jessica, pointing off to the side where her own horse was tied. "Then please take your ease by the fire."

Aracelia's horse whickered a greeting to the mare, who perked up her ears. Jessica unsaddled her and spying Aracelia's saddle set neatly to one side, placed hers beside it. She hesitated over the saddle bags, then shrugged and left them beside the saddle, bringing only her travel pack with her to the fire.

"I'm sorry I don't have anything to contribute," she said. "We ran out of food yesterday."

"Then it is fortuitous we met," Aracelia told her. She handed her one of the spitted animals, having already given Bandit the biggest of the three.

Jessica tentatively bit into the succulent flesh and then took a much larger bite. It was the best thing she'd ever tasted. She was not the least bit curious as to what kind of animal it was - it looked to be either a large squirrel or a small rabbit and she really didn't want to know.

"This tastes amazing," she said, practically gnawing the bones themselves. "Is this how you make your living, hunting?"

"I have, at times. But tell me what brings you to the Elven Realm of the Darkwood Forest."

"The Elven Realm? Really?" Jessica's eyes widened. "That's what that shimmery curtain thing was, wasn't it? It marked the border of your realm. Oh, jeez. Are we trespassing? Because we didn't mean to."

"Be at ease, my young friend. Had the border sensed you meant ill, it would not have let you cross."

"If the border sensed? You mean it's alive?" Suddenly she felt slightly queasy.

"It has a certain sentience, enough to know the intent of those who wish to cross."

"Oh. Well, our intent was to find my medallion," Jessica said with a sigh.

"Indeed. Pray, if this medallion had such value to you, how did you come to lose it in the Darkwood Forest?"

"It was stolen," she said bitterly. "Someone cast a spell over us that put us to sleep and then like the coward they were, took the only thing I have left of my mother."

"I am sorry for your loss," Aracelia said quietly.

"If only you knew the half of it," Jessica muttered. "We've been tracking the thief for days. Well, Bandit's been tracking and I've just been following. But he seems to have lost the trail."

Bandit woofed softly.

"It's not your fault," she told him. "We'll just have to deal with its loss."

"Perhaps I can be of some assistance," Aracelia said slowly.

"Really? How?" Jessica didn't want to get her hopes up, but her gut had been telling her they weren't going to catch up with the thief on their own.

"As you have observed, I am somewhat skilled as a hunter. And I have a small gift for finding that which is lost. Perhaps I could assist you in tracking down the thief."

"That would be wonderful!" Jessica said.

"But alas, I too am in search for aid in a task."

"What kind of aid? And what kind of task?"

"The aid I seek is of the magical kind. And the task is a quest for a rare plant."

Jessica looked at Bandit and bit her lip. He dipped his head as though he knew what she was thinking and agreed with her.

"Perhaps we could help each other," Jessica said slowly. "Although I have to be honest with you, Aracelia. My magic . . . this is all pretty new to me. My magic isn't exactly dependable at the best of times."

"Though my own gift is quite small, I was well tutored. I could perhaps offer some instruction on what is needed. All elves are taught the seven thoughts of magic."

"Seven thoughts?"

"Alchemy, Animagic, Conjuring, Elemental, Healing, Mind, and Necromancy. They were named after the seven schools of white magic that once dwelt in Mythago."

It was suddenly driven home to Jessica how very little she knew of the world she was not living in. "You said once dwelt.

They're not there anymore?"

"Alas, Mythago itself is no more. It was destroyed many years ago by a blood sorcerer named Anakaron."

Jessica felt an inexplicable chill at the sound of the name.

Chapter 16

It was on the tip of Jessica's tongue to ask if Mythago was a city or a country, but she decided it didn't matter. She didn't want to think of magic so strong that it could level an entire city, let alone a country. She was still coming to grips with her own power.

"Why do they call them the seven thoughts of magic?" she asked instead.

Aracelia blinked, as though not expecting this question. "I know not," she said. "Perhaps it is because each of them requires a specific mindset of thoughts to master them."

Jessica nodded. "What exactly would you need me to do, I mean magically."

"I am not sure myself," Aracelia admitted. "It was prophesied at the beginning of my quest that one I would aid would aid me with what I seek."

Jessica brightened immediately. She was a firm believer in prophecies, signs, and fortunes, much to Howard's consternation. "A prophecy, really? How wonderfully cryptic!"

"Indeed. I have been on my quest for five days, drawing no closer to a resolution, and you are the first soul I have encountered."

"So you think if you help me, I'll be able to help you? It makes sense I guess."

"Please know that my offer of aid is sincere. Prophecy aside, I could not in good conscience allow you to wander the Elven Realm in search of a thief you may never find."

"Thank you," Jessica said. "At this point I could use all the help I could get."

"Then it's settled," said Aracelia, beaming. "Now, let us start at the beginning. What can you tell me about this medallion of yours?"

"Well . . . it's basically an oval disk made out of a moonstone. The setting and chain are silver."

"Are there any markings on it?"

"No. Yes!" she said, suddenly remembering. "Well, not on my half, but there's another half that has what I'm told is a magical symbol. It looks like this," she picked up a stick and drew what looked like a stylized letter 'F' with an arrow through it.

Aracelia nodded. "That is the Elvish symbol for protection. But you say there are two halves to this medallion?"

"Yes. I was wearing the one part of it and the other is in the keeping of my friend Howard."

"Then perhaps we should start by contacting your friend and—"

Jessica was already shaking her head. "The medallion was my only means of talking to him. He, uh, he's pretty far away. There really isn't any way to reach him other than through the medallion."

"I see. Then in that case we'll track the thief to retrieve the medallion. But I would suggest we begin in the morning. The hour grows late and your companion looks to be worn out."

Jessica glanced towards the fire where Bandit was stretched out, sound asleep.

It was the delicious smell of breakfast that woke Jessica in the morning. Bandit was already licking a shallow wooden bowl clean. When Aracelia saw that Jessica was awake, she scooped a serving of whatever was cooking over the fire into another wooden bowl.

"Your companion and I scouted about a bit while you slept," she said, handing the bowl to Jessica. "It was difficult, but we picked up the trail of the thief. He is headed east. When you are finished breaking your fast we can be on our way."

"That's wonderful!" Jessica said between mouthfuls. Breakfast was some kind of grain stewed together with fruit and nuts. "Could you tell how far ahead he is?"

"Two, maybe three days at most."

"So there's a chance we'll catch him?" Jessica said hopefully.

"There's always a chance," Aracelia told her. "Made even better by two of us tracking him now."

Jessica finished her breakfast quickly and they broke camp. They made good progress - the thief seemed to be following a game trail.

"He's slowing down," Aracelia said late in the afternoon. "I believe he thinks himself safe from pursuit. Either that or he's in familiar territory. He's getting careless."

"Do you think he could be one of your people, an elf?"

"All things are possible, but I highly doubt it. Elves are taught wood craft at an early age. Were he an elf even I would have an almost impossible time tracking him."

The second day of tracking, almost mid day, Aracelia declared, "We are very close now. I suggest we leave our gear and horses here and continue on foot. The horses make far too much noise - we would not want to alert him of our presence."

"Sounds like a plan to me," Jessica said. She couldn't wait to get her hands on the thief. She had a fist with his name on it.

Aracelia had them moving at a jog. Although Jessica tried to set her feet where the elf stepped, her passing was still the noisiest of the three of them. The trail twisted and then crossed a glade. Halfway across the glade Aracelia stumbled. Bandit and Jessica were hard on her heels and rather than bowl her right over they split to move to either side of her. They stumbled as well and all three of them were caught fast by the earth.

"Holy Saint Christopher! What's happening?"

"It is a sinking earth bog. This should not have happened. Warnings are posted to prevent anyone from becoming trapped in them."

"Never mind that, how do we get out of it?" Jessica was trying to pull her feet free but was not having any success. Her toes were growing numb.

"We cannot," Aracelia said, face pale. "Were there a vine or a tree branch within reach we could perhaps pull ourselves free, but there is nothing."

"We have something like this where I come from called quicksand. I read somewhere once that if you become trapped in quicksand you should lie flat and you won't sink. Then you can get to the edge with a swimming sort of motion."

"Nay, lying flat would only increase the paralyzing effect of the earth."

Jessica was about to ask about the paralyzing effect but figured it out for herself. Her feet were already numb and she could feel it working its way up her legs. Bandit whimpered, already up to his belly in the soft earth. Aracelia had her eyes closed and was reaching out with her hand.

"What are you doing?" Jessica asked.

"There is a growth of vines, right at the base of that tree." She opened her eyes and looked at Jessica sorrowfully. "I was attempting to use my magic to draw them to me but it is no use. My magic is not powerful enough."

By this time they were up to their knees in the earth, but the numbness was spreading up to their thighs. Bandit seemed to be faring somewhat better, at least he seemed to be sinking at a much slower rate, but there was no way of telling how badly the paralyzing effect was hitting him.

"Why don't I give it a try," Jessica suggested. At this point she was willing to try anything. "What do I need to do?"

"You must use your mind," Aracelia told her. "Focus on the vines and draw them towards you."

She made it sound so easy. Jessica looked over at the vines. She stared until all she could see were the vines - they filled her vision. It looked like some kind of ivy. Ivy was supposed to be strong right? They'd need that strength if they were going to be able to pull themselves out of this sinking earth.

The leaves rustled slightly. Bandit whimpered, breaking her concentration, but when she looked around to yell at him she couldn't. Only his back and head were showing above the earth.

Determined, she turned her focus back to the ivy. Just as Howard had taught her to submerge her awareness inside to find the magic, so now she focused that awareness on the ivy. She closed her eyes and concentrated on its strength, its suppleness, the roots growing deep into the soil. With a mental twist she started pulling it towards her.

Her eyes still closed she continued to pull. It was almost as though she *was* the ivy. She could feel the sap flowing through it, the leaves absorbing the sun and turning it into energy. If she focused harder she was sure she'd be able to submerge herself in the thoughts of the plant.

"Enough!" Aracelia called sharply.

Jessica's eyes snapped open.

"Forgive me," the elf said. "But you were in danger of losing yourself. And in any case, you have accomplished your task."

Jessica looked down and was astonished to see several life lines of ivy stretching from the base of the tree to where they were sinking. Aracelia was wrapping one vine around her waist and then another around Bandit.

"Forgive me," she said to the dog as she wound the ivy around his head and shoulders, "but I do not dare try and wrap this around your body."

She and Jessica began pulling themselves, hand over hand, out of the bog. It was slow work and their muscles were shaking, but as soon as they won free they turned to Bandit. By this time only his head and shoulders were showing. Together they began to pull on the ivy around him.

The ivy around his neck tightened and he began to thrash as

his air supply was cut off.

"Stop struggling," Aracelia called. "You might—"

But it was too late. The vine attached to him snapped and they fell into a backwards sprawl.

"No!" Jessica bounced back up again, watching in horror as Bandit slipped further into the earth. His eyes met hers in a soundless plea, the paralyzing effect having stolen his voice.

Without even giving it a thought, Jessica reached out her hand towards him and closed her eyes. Focusing the power of her mind she searched for and located Bandit in front of her and then drew his physical form towards her. It resisted, the earth had a strong hold on him. Reaching for the spark of magic within her, she channeled power into her mind and pulled steadily until she was meeting no resistance at all.

Opening her eyes, she looked down to see Bandit laying at her feet, eyes closed. Kneeling down beside him she ran her hands over his dusty fur.

"Bandit, are you still with us? Tell me I didn't take too long, that it's not too late."

With one hand on the side of his neck and the other on his back, she reached inside herself for her healing energy. Her hands glowed green and the green spread along his body. It flared brightly for a few seconds, and then was gone.

Bandit stirred as Jessica toppled over sideways, energy depleted.

Chapter 17

Paranithel jerked awake at the chiming sound of faerie bells. He and Thackery had suspended classes temporarily for the duration of Jessica's testing and were camped out in the scrying chamber. Thackery took a few moments longer to shake off the effects of sleep.

"You would be pleased at our granddaughter's progress," Aracelia reported to Paran. "She has passed every task I have set her. And she has proven herself to be both loyal and compassionate as well. These are, perhaps her greatest gifts, but the ones that will ultimately cause her the most difficulties, I believe."

"What good does loyalty and compassion do her if your tests kill her?" Thackery asked.

Aracelia arched an eyebrow at him. "She has never been in real danger, as well you know. Do you really believe I would seek the death of my own kin, however inadvertent?"

"What tests has she remaining?" Paranithel asked, forestalling yet another argument between these two.

"Prophecy and Necromancy," Aracelia answered.

"And just how to you propose to test her on these?" Thackery asked waspishly.

"I will take her to the Shrine of Mythania for the prophecy, and for the necromancy we will seek out the cold grave blossom." She braced herself for an explosion and was not disappointed.

"Mythania is chancy enough, but to expose my child to the dangers of the cold grave blossom . . . it is unconsciously stupid!"

"You will keep a civil tongue in your head while addressing me!"

"Civil tongues are for those deserving of them," Thackery countered.

They glared at each other through the scrying bowl.

"Once the tests are completed, will you lift the spell that prevents us seeking her out?" Paran asked, trying to defuse their rising anger.

Aracelia hesitated. "I will think on it."

"Think on it? Think on it? I am her father! It is my right to keep watch over her!" Thackery exploded.

"And what of Jessica's right to privacy?" she said angrily. "She does not even know of your existence, and yet you have been spying on her since her arrival."

"It isn't spying!" he sputtered. "It—"

"When she is being watched without her knowledge, it is spying!" The liquid in the scrying bowl vibrated with her anger. "Were she experienced in magic she would know the telltale signs and be able to prevent unwanted intrusion, but she knows nothing. I have misliked the notion since I first learned of it."

Thackery opened his mouth to argue, but Paran laid a hand

on his arm. "You are right," he said, surprising her. "It is not fair to watch her without her knowledge, but the scrying bowl is our only link with her. You have seen for yourself her naiveté, she cannot be allowed to hare off on her own with no safeguards. Perhaps a compromise can be reached."

"Perhaps," she agreed grudgingly. "Though the constant watch is unpalatable, perhaps I can come up with a different arrangement."

Paran inclined his head. "Thank you, that is most generous of you."

Thackery muttered something that sounded suspiciously like, "It's the least you can do," but Aracelia decided to let it pass. For all his faults, he *was* Jessica's father and it was only natural for him to worry about her. And he must have some redeeming qualities, for him to have won Farenalyssia's heart.

Her one regret in life was not taking her daughter's concerns regarding the rivalry between Kiranthus and Anakaron more seriously. Had she realized that Anakaron was a blood mage - had any of them realized - things might have turned out differently. Too late had she recalled that when Farenalyssia had been tested, though her overall results were somewhat disappointing, she'd tested strongly for prophecy.

By the time she'd reached Mythago, it had been too late. The city was in ruins and Farenalyssia was dead. But even having witnessed first hand the destruction of the city, she could not agree that sending Jessica away was the wisest course of action. She had offered to shelter all three of them in the Elven Realm but Paranithel believed it was best they separate.

"For what it's worth," she said to the two men pictured in the bowl, "Jessica has performed outstandingly in all aspects of her testing. I anticipate no difficulties with her remaining tests. I believe our girl is a Grand Master Sorcerer, with the potential to be the most powerful I've ever encountered."

Howard awoke, chagrined to find he'd fallen asleep with his head resting on work table again, not even sure what had awoken him. At the sound of a soft snore he turned his head to see that Ellen, too, had fallen asleep, head pillowed on the magic book she'd been reading.

The noise came again. A sound like crystal bells chiming. It seemed to be coming from the scrying bowl. Howard nudged Ellen awake and then peered into the bowl.

"Good evening," Aracelia said. "I did not wish you to worry needlessly about your friend. I am here to assure you she is fine and is showing great potential in her testing."

"I'm happy for her," Ellen said before Howard could form a reply. "It's just too bad that she doesn't know she's being tested."

"You're like a hound with a bone, aren't you?" Aracelia said mildly.

"You'll have to forgive her," Howard said quickly. "She hasn't had a lot of sleep recently and she's a little testy."

"Indeed. I am inclined to make allowances because you *are* Jessica's friends. So far she has excelled at every test she has been given. Her power . . ." she shook her head faintly. "Her power is incredible."

"How many tests are left?" Howard asked.

"She has but two tests to complete before she is done, that of Prophecy and Necromancy."

"How exactly can you test for prophecy?" Ellen asked. "Get her to predict something and then wait around to see if it comes true?"

"Not precisely. I intend on taking her to a shrine to see if the goddess speaks to her. She speaks only to those who have the gift of Prophecy."

"What happens if this goddess speaks to Jess and tells her what's really going on?"

Aracelia shrugged. "It is a possibility, but I think it to be unlikely. If such a thing comes to pass then perhaps I am also being tested."

Ellen and Howard looked at each other and Howard shrugged faintly.

"Okay, what about the Necromancy test? I would think that would be pretty difficult to arrange."

"Difficult," Aracelia admitted, "but not impossible. However, it is the most difficult of all the thoughts of magic to conquer."

"So what happens when the testing is over? Does Jessica get a diploma to hang on her wall or what?" Try as she might, Ellen just could not seem to curb her tongue around the elf. Aracelia just seemed to bring out the inner snark in her.

"When the testing is complete I shall give the results to her father and grandfather and then send Jessica on her way. "

"Will we be able to see her and talk to her again?"

Just as she had with Paran and Thackery, Aracelia hesitated. "Did Jessica know you were able to see her?"

Howard looked a little uncomfortable. "Well, no. That is, the subject never came up."

"And do you think she would appreciate such a thing?"

"I can answer that," Ellen said. "She'd hate the idea of being spied on. Even though we only look in on her occasionally, she'd still hate not knowing."

Aracelia nodded. "It is as I suspected. If Jessica was trained in the ways of magic, she would be able to sense when someone was watching . . ."

"But because she isn't, and she has no idea, it's not really fair, is it? No matter how much we want to see her."

"I have pointed out much the same to her father and grandfather," the elf said, looking somewhat relieved. "They were not as willing to see reason."

"Before we knew about Paranithel and Thackery," Howard said slowly, "I talked with Jessica through the moonstone pendant. We could go back to that sort of arrangement."

"But we'd be taking the chance of talking to her at the wrong time," Ellen pointed out. "What if she was in a public place, or someplace where magic's not tolerated?"

"I promised the wizards I would come up with a compromise," Aracelia admitted.

"It's too bad we can't just tell Jessica what's going on," Howard said. "And then teach her some kind of spell to protect against scrying. But something that would only be in place when we aren't talking."

"An excellent idea, my friend!" Aracelia said. "While it would be best to tell her the truth, there is no way to do so without revealing the presence of Paranithel and Thackery. But a charm . . . spelled to protect against scrying unless she's talking with you . . . I think it might be possible.

Ellen and Howard looked at each other.

"Thank you my friends. I will get right to work on it and let you know what I come up with."

And with that, the face in the scrying bowl vanished.

Chapter 18

When Jessica awoke it was night. Aracelia had made camp and was sitting on the opposite side of the fire. Bandit was sleeping between them. As soon as Aracelia saw she was awake she pulled a pot from the fire and poured the contents into a wooden mug, adding a generous dollop of honey before bringing it over. Jessica was sitting up by this time and took it automatically when it was passed to her.

"You depleted every last iota of your energy," Aracelia told her. "This is a restorative tea, it will help you feel better."

"Thank you," Jessica said. She took a cautious sip and was pleasantly surprised by the taste. Although there was the bitter under taste indicative of medicine, for the most part it was sweet and flowery.

Glancing over at Bandit, she said, "How is he?"

"He'll be fine, thanks to you. He is just resting now. The paralyzing effect had fully over taken him when you pulled him free of the sinking earth. Had you not used up your energy healing him . . ." Aracelia smiled faintly. "I would warn you against allowing yourself to become so depleted, but I suspect such a warning would fall on deaf ears."

Jessica smiled faintly in return, already feeling better from the potion in the mug. "I haven't had a great deal of training - I don't really know what I'm doing."

Aracelia nodded. "That is sometimes not a bad thing."

Before Jessica was able to question her on that somewhat cryptic comment, Bandit awoke. He struggled into to a more upright position and barked a question.

"She is fine, my friend," Aracelia told him.

Jessica grinned. "You two can communicate now?"

Aracelia grinned in return. "One does not need to understand the language to know the question." Her smile faded. "I owe you my life. There is a blood debt between us. Do not make little of this," she added as Jessica opened her mouth to refute her statement. "It is no small thing for an elf to owe a blood debt. And it is compounded by the fact I have failed you."

Her granddaughter wasn't the only one she failed, there was also the matter of the young elf whom she'd drafted into playing the part of the thief. Kiranthus would say it served her right for engineering such a complicated test, and perhaps he was right. But what was done was done.

"Failed me? Failed me how?"

Aracelia couldn't meet her eyes. "As you recall, we were following the thief's trail when we stumbled upon the sinking earth bog. I believe he preceded us into the bog."

"So in other words, my amulet is gone," Jessica said bleakly. Now her only hope for returning home was to continue her journey to the wizards in the south in hopes they could help her.

"I am sorry," Aracelia said quietly.

"It's not your fault," Jessica said automatically. "You couldn't have known."

Perhaps not, Aracelia thought, but she felt guilty all the same.

Contrary to the popular saying, things did not look better after a good night's sleep. At least they didn't as far as Jessica was concerned. She and Bandit were both rather subdued at breakfast the next morning.

"It seems the loss of your medallion is a far more grievous blow than I first realized," Aracelia observed.

"I feel so cut off without it. Sentimental value aside, it was my only way of talking with Howard."

"And does he perhaps have something to do with your other friend, the dog who is not a dog?"

"You know?" Jessica asked in surprise.

"That your companion is not a true dog? Of course. However, I did not wish to be impolite and ask about how he came to be so."

Jessica studied the elf woman. Her instincts told her she could trust her, and Howard had always told her to trust her instincts. She sighed heavily.

"You might as well hear the whole story," she said. "I don't come from this world."

"Indeed?" Aracelia exclaimed with faux surprise.

"My friend Howard was experimenting with magic and accidentally sent me here. And trust me, no one was more surprised than him when his spell worked. We don't have magic where I come from. At least there's never been any sign of it before."

"A world without magic - it must be a bleak place indeed."

Jessica shrugged. "It was home. Anyway, you can imagine my shock when I woke up here and suddenly I can work magic."

"Indeed."

"But despite the fact I'm getting used to being here, and I've made a few friends, my first priority is getting back home."

"Why can your friend not just retrieve you? Would he not just have to reverse the spell he first cast?"

"He would if he could, but he's not exactly sure what all he did to cast the spell in the first place. So, I was on my way south to this wizard everyone thinks can help me, when I accidentally turned Bandit into a dog."

"Perhaps this wizard could aid you with that as well," Aracelia suggested.

"Well, probably. But it's going to take months to get to him, and Howard said I only have until the quarter moon to change Bandit back before the spell is permanent. And that's in two weeks."

"I see." Aracelia was quiet for a moment, mulling over everything Jessica told her. "It would seem that other than the companionship of your friend, all that is truly missing is aid for your magic. Specifically, the means to change your companion back into his true form. Is this not so?"

"I guess that about sums it up," Jessica admitted. "Although it did have sentimental value as well. It was all I had of my birth mother."

"Birth mother?"

"I may or may not have been adopted," she said with a sigh. "We were just trying to figure that out when I got zapped here."

With every word that came out of her granddaughter's mouth, Aracelia grew more angry. What right did Paranithel and Kiranthus have withholding the truth from her? It was on the tip of her tongue to tell her the truth but something held her back. Was she not doing much the same thing? Deceiving the poor girl for her own ends?

"While there is nothing I can do regarding your amulet," she said, "I may be able to assist in creating a transmogrification spell."

"A what?"

"A spell to turn your companion back into his true form," she said with a smile at the dumbfounded look on her granddaughter's face.

Jessica brightened immediately. "That would be awesome!"

"Very well," Aracelia said briskly. "It will take me a few days to work out the spell, so in the meantime I would suggest locating a better site in which to camp. I mislike staying so close to the sinking earth bog."

"You said you were on a quest of your own," Jessica reminded her. "Why don't we continue on with that while you work on the spell?"

"You truly wish to do this?"

"It seems only fair."

"Very well. In that case our first destination is the Shrine of Mythania."

Because Bandit wasn't quite recovered from his ordeal in the sinking earth bog, Jessica offered to let him ride across her saddle. Aracelia fixed up a special pad of blankets for him to rest on and it wasn't too uncomfortable.

While they traveled, Aracelia asked Jessica many questions about the world she came from. Bandit listened to the conversation with interest, learning more of why Jessica seemed so out of place here and the marvels she took for granted on a daily basis.

"Like cooking on a stove, for instance," Jessica was saying. "You have complete control over the temperatures you cook with. And you don't have to kill and clean your own food. The only foraging you have to do is in the store where you buy it."

"It seems like a waste of good coin to buy what you could hunt for free."

"Well, some people still hunt, but they have to have a license to do so. And they can only hunt at certain times of the year. Most meat comes from animals that have been domesticated and raised for that purpose. The meat is packaged and sold in stores."

"I cannot imagine such a thing," Aracelia admitted. "Except perhaps in some of the large cities, and those we elves tend to avoid. We do not like to be closed in."

Jessica nodded. "You probably wouldn't like my world much. So much of it is closed in, and we all move so very fast."

"It must make it hard on the horses."

Jessica smiled. "This will probably shock you, but we don't use horses for transportation. We use machines to travel from place to place."

"You have no horses?" Aracelia seemed to be having trouble with this concept.

"There are horses, but they don't have the same importance as they do here. Mostly they're used for pleasure riding - equestrian events, racing, trail rides - that sort of thing."

"So very different is your world from ours," Aracelia said, shaking her head. "What of magic?"

"Magic has no place in my world," Jessica said sadly, "Save for tricks made to look like magic for entertainment."

Aracelia tried to imagine a life without magic and failed. "What do you miss the most of your world?" she asked finally.

"Indoor plumbing," Jessica said promptly.

"Indoor plumbing?"

"Yes. No more having to fill a tub in front of the fireplace with buckets for a bath, no more chamber pots or digging a hole in the woods. Instead, water is piped in to fill your tub at the turn of a tap, and every home has a permanent tub, or at the very least a shower, which is like an enclosed waterfall, only you can control the force of the water and the temperature."

"I think I would enjoy that," Aracelia admitted.

"There may be a lot wrong with my world, but there are a lot of good things as well. And a nice, long, hot bubble bath is one of them."

They rode in silence for a while, Aracelia with growing admiration for this granddaughter who'd been forced to leave so much behind, and Jessica waxing nostalgic for all the things in her life she'd taken for granted. Again Aracelia regretted the circumstances that prevented her from revealing her true relationship to Jessica, but the testing was not over yet.

The trail began to grow steeper, and the area rockier. The giant redwoods gave way to smaller evergreens until Jessica could almost convince herself that she was merely going for a trail ride. With an elf. And a dog she'd changed from a man using magic.

Chapter 19

The Shrine of Mythania was set in an alcove carved out of the dark grey rock. Inside was an altar with a statue of a woman with a bird's head, carved out of smoky white quartz. The altar itself was a piece of pale green marble with lines of gold threading through it.

Surrounding the altar were offerings of flowers, vegetables, jewelry, coins and gems. Melted wax coated the sides of the altar where people had burned candles as they said their prayers.

"This is beautiful," Jessica said in a hushed voice.

They'd left the horses tied a little ways away and followed the faint path up to the shrine. Bandit had opted to stay with the horses.

"I've never been to a shrine before," Jessica admitted. "What do we do?"

"First," Aracelia said, rummaging around in the pack she brought with her, "We light a candle." She pulled two candles out of the pack and handed one to Jessica. The other she placed on the mound of wax on one end of the altar. Pressing the wick between two fingers, she let go suddenly and it burst into flame.

It impressed Jessica enough that she wanted to try it too. After placing the candle securely on her end of the altar, she pinched the wick firmly between her thumb and her forefinger then let go quickly as it burst into flame.

"Awesome!" she said with a grin.

"Next we must stare into the candle's flame and empty our minds to allow the goddess to come and speak to us."

"Has she ever spoken to you before?"

"Never," Aracelia admitted. "But one can hope."

Jessica stared into the candle's flame but had a hard time emptying her mind. Extraneous thoughts kept intruding. Like the sound of the wind in the leaves of the trees, or whether she should ask Aracelia if the elves could help her learn how to use her magic.

Finally she was able to chase away the last stray thought and just focus on the candle's flame. It seemed to grow brighter and she began to speak.

"*The path that is without obstacles will have no satisfaction at the end. Even failures can bring triumph. Friends and family can be found where you least expect them. The dark one shall bring much happiness through the ill times ahead.*"

Jessica shivered and came back to herself, surprised to see that the candle had nearly burned itself out. "What just happened?" she asked.

"You have been blessed by the goddess," Aracelia said quietly. "Few who come to the shrine hear her voice and at most hear but a single sentence. To have her speak through you, and at such length . . ." She shook her head.

"Why don't I remember what I said?"

"That is the way of such things. Your prophecy was most interesting." Aracelia repeated the words of the goddess.

It was on the tip of Jessica's tongue to tell the elf that it just sounded like gibberish to her, but she didn't want to offend her. Instead she asked, "But what does it all mean?"

Aracelia shrugged. "The meanings can be as simple or as complicated as you wish to make them. You must take it one sentence at a time."

"Okay," Jessica agreed. "So . . . the path that is without obstacles - you could take that to mean that things that come too easily to you don't give you as much happiness as the things in life come through hard work. But what about failures bringing triumph?"

"Could that not refer to the loss of your amulet? Even though you failed to recover it you have still been triumphant in your use of magic. Had you the amulet when we were trapped in the sinking earth bog, would you not have called upon your friend for assistance? Instead you were able to act on your own."

"I guess that's true," Jessica admitted. "And I don't know about the family bit, but I've certainly been finding friends where I least expect it. But that last sentence . . . the one about the dark one bringing happiness through the ill times. What about it?"

"That one I could not say. It sounds as though it was a prophecy of the future."

"How about you," Jessica asked curiously. "You didn't say anything, but did the goddess speak to you?"

"Indeed she did, though she spoke to me, not through me. She advised me that the dead shall live again and the blossom that I seek can be found in the Field of Sorrows, beyond the Venom River in the grey lands."

"Sounds like a lovely place," Jessica said with a shiver.

"It was the site of the great civil war between elves," Aracelia told her. "Hundreds, maybe even thousands died there."

"I'm sorry," Jessica said.

"It was a senseless war, as are all wars. But it was a long time ago. Let us continue our journey. There is a camp site close to the Field of Sorrows that the pilgrims use. If we push ourselves we can reach it before night fall."

They made their way down the path to the horses. Jessica looked around with a frown. "Where's Bandit?"

"Perhaps he decided to do a little exploring on his own." Aracelia glanced around but couldn't spot which way he'd gone.

"Bandit! Where are you?" Jessica called. "We're ready to go. We don't have all day to wait for you. If you don't hurry up you'll just have to catch up."

"Wait!" Aracelia held up her hand. "Do you hear that?"

Jessica tilted her head and listened hard. Faintly she could hear what might be a dog barking. It didn't sound like he was in distress, but there might have been the slightest hint of panic in it.

"I think it's coming from over there," she said, pointing.

"It doesn't appear to getting any closer," Aracelia said after a few minutes.

"It figures that if there's any trouble out there he'd find it," Jessica grumbled. "You don't think he might be caught in a trap or something, do you?"

Aracelia frowned. "Trapping is not allowed in this section of the forest, but there is always the danger of poachers."

They followed the sound of the barking and found Bandit crouched down beside a bramble thicket, collar snagged on the lower branches. He wagged his tail hopefully as he saw them.

"How in the world did you—" Jessica's eyes narrowed. "You were trying to get rid of your collar, weren't you."

He managed to appear even more sad and pathetic.

"Save it," she said, reaching through the thorns to release him. "Now come on, you're going to have to ride up on the horse with me. We have a new destination and we want to make the next camp site before nightfall."

Aracelia stared at them thoughtfully as she followed behind. What was it the prophecy said? "*The dark one shall bring much happiness though the ill times ahead.*" Bandit was certainly dark, and she sensed a connection between the two. She wondered what kind of man he'd been, and whether he'd be changed by what he'd gone through. Would he harbor any animosity towards Jessica when he was a man again?

They rode in thoughtful silence towards the campsite and were startled to discover it was already occupied. Three elves arose at their approach.

"My lady Aracelia," said the oldest of the three, sketching a bow. "Forgive us. Had we known you intended—"

"Be at ease," Aracelia waved a hand. "There is plenty of room for us all."

Jessica was burning with curiosity. *Lady* Aracelia? But she was silent as they dismounted.

"Might we share your fire?" Aracelia asked politely

"Of course my lady," the elder elf said. "Please," he motioned for them to take a seat. "Kaelan will take care of your horses."

"It's my pleasure," said the youngest of the elves, hurrying forward. He took the reins from them and led the horses over to where their own horses were tethered.

"You will not remember me, my lady. I am Carwyn. This is my wife Sioned and our son Kaelan."

"How could I not remember the most talented silversmith in all the realm?" Aracelia said with a smile. "My companion is Jessica."

"A most beautiful and exotic name," Kaelan said, bringing their saddlebags over to them.

Jessica smiled back at him. "Thank you."

Hollywood would have loved Kaelan, Jessica thought. He was everything an elf should be. He was lean and beautiful, with brilliant blue eyes and long hair so blond it was almost white. His father was an older version of him, although a little broader in the shoulders. His mother was very similar to Aracelia, save that she had dark hair shot through with silver.

Jessica wondered if that was a genetic trait of the elves, the graceful way of moving, the tall and slender build, and the beautiful features. She felt positively dowdy in their company, although the admiring glances Kaelan kept shooting at her made her feel marginally better. Maybe he was just attracted to her because she was so different. In any case, a little harmless flirtation never hurt anyone.

Aracelia joined Sioned at the fire where they pooled their resources to make everyone something to eat. Kaelan loaded up two bowls and came over to where Jessica was sitting.

"Please, accept our poor fare," he said, passing her one of the bowls.

"Thank you," she said, taking the bowl from him. She indicated a spot beside her. "Please, won't you join me?"

He smiled and sat down with a grace she could only envy. "We do not see many humans within the Elven Realm," he said.

"Maybe it's your border that discourages them," Jessica replied with a smile to show she meant no criticism.

"I am glad it did not discourage you."

Bandit gave a sharp bark.

"It appears you have been forgotten, my friend," Aracelia said with a smile at Jessica's faint blush. She set a steaming bowl in front of him. "Never fear, I'll see that you do not go hungry."

"Sorry Bandit," Jessica called. "And anyway, I'm still peeved with you because you tried to get rid of your collar."

"You speak to him as though he understands you," Kaelan said with amusement.

"Oh, he understands more than you'd think," Jessica said. "He's pretty smart . . . for a dog."

Bandit didn't stop to analyze why the elf sitting so close to Jessica bothered him, he just knew that it did. The way he kept flirting with her was especially annoying - waiting on her hand and foot as though she was an invalid, smiling at her and leaning way too close as they talked. He needed to be taken down a peg or two. He didn't even realize he was growling low in his throat until he felt Aracelia's hand resting on his neck.

"Be at ease, my friend. 'Tis only a mild flirtation. It means nothing," she said quietly.

Her words did not mollify him, but he stopped growling.

"It is late in the season to be making the pilgrimage to the

Field of Sorrows," Aracelia commented.

"Yes, my lady," Carwyn said. "But my good wife was ill and could not make the journey sooner."

"I am sorry to hear that. Nothing serious I hope?"

"No my lady," Sioned said.

The talk segued into a discussion of minor illnesses and the most common cures, the current trade embargo on human weapons which had been found inferior to elven made weapons, and predictions for the oncoming winter.

When they finished eating and cleaning up, they spread their bedrolls near the fire. Kaelan casually placed his bedroll near Jessica's and Bandit came over and flopped down between them with a gusty sigh. Kaelan looked askance at the huge beast, while Jessica smothered a smile.

Chapter 20

In the morning, Carwyn and his family took their leave as soon as breakfast was finished.

"I hope that you will visit the elven city soon that I might take you to a proper dinner and we might learn more of each other," Kaelan told Jessica, holding her hand just a little longer than necessary. Bandit nosed his way in between them.

Jessica had to stifle a grin at his over-protectiveness. If she didn't know better, she'd think he was jealous. Not that she didn't find Kaelan attractive, but the last thing she needed was to get involved with the elf, no matter how sweet and hunky he was.

"We may as well leave the horses here," Aracelia told Jessica after they were alone again. "They will balk at the Field of Sorrows in any case."

The elf seemed pensive as they followed the trail towards the Field of Sorrows. Jessica had never visited a battlefield before. She tried to imagine what it would be like but it was hard to think of elves as anything but peaceful. Of course most of her knowledge of them came from fairy tales so it was hard to picture them doing battle - they were always the good guys in fairy tales. The ones she'd met so far, all four of them, did not seem particularly war-like.

Then she wondered how much of what she knew about elves was true. Like their aversion to iron, was that made up or was it true? Kaelan and his father both wore swords but she never got a close enough look to see what they were made of. They all had belt knives they used to eat with, but again she never paid close enough attention to know what they were made out of.

What else did she know about elves from the stories? The pointed ears, and being slender and beautiful was certainly true enough. Had whoever written fairy tales about elves actually met an elf before? What about the artists who did the illustrations for those stories?

The ones from Tolkien's books also had a much longer life span than humans. Was this true as well? Glancing at Aracelia, she wondered how old she was. While it was true she had silver hair, that was her only outward appearance of age. There was just something ageless about her.

The trees began to thin and the path they'd been following widened until they could walk side by side. When they got to the edge of the field, Jessica stopped. A vast plain stretched before them. There was no churned up earth, no monuments, just the slight rise and fall of the ground, bare patches of dirt, and slight mounds like moguls on a ski hill.

The plain stretched ahead of them, hazy in the distance. To either side she could see more of the Darkwood Forest, but there was no new growth. It was as though the forest itself held the field sacred and dared not encroach on the hallowed ground. That was when Jessica became aware of the silence, stark and total. She could almost hear her own heartbeat.

"Where do we start?" Jessica asked in a whisper. To speak any louder would have been sacrilegious somehow.

"The prophecy from the shrine mentioned the grey lands." Aracelia motioned to the misty distance. "I would presume that the blossom I seek lies in that direction."

"What was the name of that blossom again?" Jessica asked.

"It is the cold grave blossom. Until the goddess spoke to me, I was not even sure it existed."

"What exactly does it do?" Jessica asked as they started across the Field of Sorrows.

"It is said to be a cure-all. I—" Aracelia broke off what she'd been about to say as a whining noise registered.

They stopped and turned around. It was Bandit, standing at the edge of the field.

"Well don't just stand there," Jessica told him, "come on!"

He whined in response.

"I had assumed because his true nature is human he would have been able to cross. But it appears his dog essence is stronger than his human essence. Animals are not able to set foot on the Field of Sorrows."

"I guess you might as well go back and wait with the horses," Jessica told Bandit. "I have no idea how long we'll be."

He whined again, clearly unhappy with the situation. As the two women continued onward towards the mist, he began pacing back and forth along the field's border.

"There is an illness," Aracelia continued with her story. "So far it has resisted all of our efforts to eradicate it. One of the healers has the gift of prophecy, the same one who prophesied that I would find aid along the way, and she told me the answer lay within me. I remembered my mother telling me a tale of the cold grave blossom and its healing properties and decided I had nothing to lose by trying to find it. Legend has it that it can be found near to graves or cemeteries, so I have hope that it will be in these grey lands."

"I just hope after all this trouble it does what you hope it will," Jessica said.

"As do I, my friend. As do I."

They continued on for another twenty minutes, drawing ever closer to the grey mist. At last they came to the shore of a river, but a river unlike one Jessica had ever seen before. It only a few yards wide, but it was sluggish, filled with a thick, green-tinged fluid.

"The Venom River," Aracelia said.

"Good name for it."

"Yes it is. It is how the civil war was ended. Two Grand Master Sorcerers, one from each side of the conflict, drew the venomous feelings from the combatants and channeled it into this river. What you see before you is pure hate."

Jessica shivered.

"And look," Aracelia pointed to several rainbow hued flowers on the far side. "The cold grave blossom."

"I wonder how deep this thing is?" Jessica mused, staring down at the river. She didn't relish having to cross it.

"It matters not," Aracelia said bleakly. "This is the Venom River." She threw one of her gloves in and they watched it melt.

"We cannot cross."

"There has to be a way," Jessica said. "You can't have come all this way for nothing. What else do you remember about the stories your mother told you?"

Aracelia hesitated. "They were rather gruesome tales, but I rather liked that sort of thing when I was a child. One was of a living corpse who was trying to cure his beloved wife of the illness that killed him. And another had a necromancer reanimate a corpse to cross the river for a blossom to save his daughter."

"The dead shall live again," Jessica mused. "The goddess wasn't talking about the future dead you were saving with the blossom, she was talking about raising the dead to cross the river and collect the flowers."

"Alas, I know no spells that could aid us in such a task. Nor do I have the power." This was the tricky part. While it would be best if she had a spell prepared, there would be no way to explain it without acknowledging she'd known she would need it. She really should have worked on her cover story a little longer, but as usual she'd been in a rush. Still, she was sure that together she and Jessica could come up with something that would work. She had crafted similar spells in the past.

"Raising the dead . . ." Jessica said, a thoughtful look on her face. "I think I may have a spell for that, but it's in a book back at the camp.

"Truly?" Aracelia looked at her, eyes filled with feigned hope. Her granddaughter had a book of spells with her? How fortuitous. And how was it that she was armed with a book of spells and yet still despaired of the loss of the magical assistance of her friend? Did no one tell her how powerful, and valuable, such a book would be? A true thief would have been after the book, not the amulet.

"I stayed in a wizard's tower for a short while, and among the other things I was given was a spell book. I'm sure I saw a spell for raising the dead in it."

"I will be forever in your debt if you are able to do so," Aracelia told her. "Let us waste no more time."

They hurried back the way they'd come. Bandit met them at the edge of the field and followed them back to the camp. He sat down and watched as Jessica fished around in the saddle bags and finally withdrew the heavy volume of spells. Sitting down by the smoldering fire, she started flipping through the pages.

"Let's see, retying a tie that has become untied through magic . . . righting a wrong . . . here it is! Reanimating a corpse."

Bandit barked a question.

"I'm going to reanimate a corpse to send across the Venom River to pick some cold grave blossoms and bring them back to us." Jessica couldn't believe she just said that.

Placing his paw on the open book, he barked again. Rather sharply.

"I know what you're saying. You're telling me to remember what happened when I tried to conjure the chicken. I got rid of it again didn't I? And this will be totally different. Trust me."

"You tried to conjure a chicken?" Aracelia asked.

"It didn't go well. But this spell is much easier." She pulled the book out from under Bandit's paw. "The problem is I'll have to read it out loud. It's a little long and there's no way I'm going to be able to memorize it in such a short time."

"I have a quill and ink in my pack," Aracelia said. "And parchment."

"Great! Now I just need to write this down and go through it a couple of times and then we can go back to the river."

Chapter 21

"Be very precise as you copy down the spell," Aracelia advised Jessica. "One small mistake could spell disaster."

Jessica nodded in agreement. "Some of these words are unfamiliar - if you could pronounce them for me, I can write them out phonetically."

"Of course."

"Who comes up with these spells anyway?" the younger woman grumbled. She raised her head suddenly. "I wonder if the wizard down south will be teaching me how to come up with my own spells? That would be kind of cool." She bent back down to her task.

Aracelia had recognized the book the moment it came out of the saddle bag. It was one she had given Kiranthus, oh so many years ago. Many of the spells in it were of her own crafting. Was it just coincidence, or was there something larger at work here?

After the fall of Mythago she had offered shelter to Paranithel, Kiranthus, and Farenalyssia's child, but reluctantly agreed that it would only draw Anakaron's attention to the Elven Realm. She then argued that since Anakaron did not know of the child, the baby would be safe enough. But Paranithel said that Farenalyssia had had a vision before she died and had told him that her child would be raised among strangers. Fearing what this meant, she'd sworn him to secrecy.

After the baby had been sent to her new home, Paranithel journeyed to the south. Anakaron thought him old and broken by his daughter's death, more the fool he. His focus had been on finding Kiranthus, who became lost in the Shadow Mountains and emerged as Thackery. As Thackery he had visited the Elven Realm and Aracelia had given him a charm to mask his magical abilities as well as the spell book his daughter now held in her hands.

Anakaron, being so power hungry, would never believe a wizard could choose to suppress his abilities, and so Thackery had gone relatively unnoticed, turning up again in Ghren as a tutor to the king's young sons. Even Aracelia did not know why he had left so abruptly in the middle of the night, but she found it interesting that his daughter should end up in the self-same tower, and of all the things she could have brought with her, it was this particular spell book.

"Okay, I think I'm good to go on the whole zombie raising thing," Jessica said. "But what do I do once we're finished with him, or her?"

"To dismiss a spirit in your thrall you must tell them firmly three times to return from whence they came."

"Three times?"

Aracelia nodded. "Once risen, the dead are reluctant to

return. It takes the power of three to make them obey."

"I guess that makes sense," Jessica said. She tentatively touched the parchment to make sure the ink was dry. Howard would have loved this, writing with a quill and ink. She wondered how he was doing.

"What is it?" Aracelia asked, sensing her change in mood.

"I was just thinking about my friend Howard and how much he would have loved all this. He's really the magical one, not me. And he and Ellen must be freaking out, not being able to contact me."

"Have you tried getting in touch with them using a scrying spell?" Aracelia asked, knowing the answer. Had things gone as planned they would have recovered the moonstone and Jessica could have stayed in contact with her friends. But with the loss of her half of the moonstone another way of communicating needed to be found.

"A scrying spell?"

"It is the common method for magic-users to communicate with one another."

"Oh, I remember now. I tried to use one right after the medallion was stolen. I didn't have much luck."

"Perhaps you merely lacked the right materials. Or maybe you just need to practice."

"That would be really great, to talk to Howard and Ellen again," she said wistfully. "But first, let's go raise us some zombies."

"Zombies?" Aracelia repeated. "You've said that word before, but I am unfamiliar with it."

"Sorry, I guess you might call it a cultural reference. The

name's bandied about pretty freely where I come from, especially in games and horror movies." Jessica caught the look of confusion on Aracelia's face. "Which is also something that would take a lot of explaining. Why don't we walk while I talk?"

Bandit opted to stay in the camp with the horses. He hoped the elf knew what she was doing. Necromancy was the most difficult of all the thoughts of magic to master. In his travels he'd been to a land where it was practiced as a religion and he'd seen first hand what could happen if a Necromancer lost control of the soul he'd raised.

He knew, even if Jessica didn't, that she was being tested. But tested for what? And the elf, she was much more than she appeared. He could see the magic burning beneath her skin. She was far more powerful than she was letting on. And there was a distinct resemblance to Jessica - something around the eyes and in the facial features. They were related somehow, he'd bet his life on it.

Jessica and Aracelia were unhurried as they followed the path to the battlefield, giving Jessica a chance to finish her explanation.

"So, basically, where I come from, zombie is the name we give to animated corpses. Mostly you read about them in fiction - you know, things that are written to entertain?"

Aracelia nodded.

"Anyway, I think they had their origins in Africa or Haiti or someplace like that. It was some kind of religious thing, where the leader could curse people and turn them into zombies. Or raise the dead from their graves to do their bidding or something like that. But it also can just mean someone who's living who's just zoned right out - like, not really aware of anything that's going on around them or what they're doing."

"There is a chain of islands in the Mythric Ocean where the raising of the dead is religious in nature. But most Necromancers raise the dead for the gain of knowledge."

They reached the edge of the battlefield and began picking their way across.

"I can see where that would come in handy during a murder investigation," Jessica said. "I don't know much about Voodoo, the religion that's supposed to raise zombies, but I think it's just a combination of drugs that make it appear that someone has died so that the leader can make a show of bringing them back to life. And then more drugs that put them under the leader's control."

"It sounds utterly barbaric," Aracelia said. "Whether it be a drug or magic that is used, to take away one's will is the lowest form of crime there is. It does not just abuse the body, but the mind as well."

"Trust me," Jessica said. "Where I come from it isn't the lowest crime that's committed."

Aracelia looked at her, appalled. What kind of world was it that those stupid men sent an innocent babe to?

"Anyway," Jessica continued, "I guess it was just natural that the horror writers picked up on the whole zombie thing, so in horror fiction - that's fiction that's written deliberately to give you a good scare - zombies became animated, rotting corpses that go around wrecking havoc in search of brains to eat."

"Why would anyone seek literature written with the intent to frighten them? Is there not enough to frighten them in your world already? And why would an animated corpse need to eat anything, let alone brains?"

"It's not just literature, it's movies too. Movies are—" Jessica searched for the words to describe a movie. "Are you familiar with play acting?" she asked.

"Yes." The elf smiled at the memory. "I once attended the plays at the great amphitheatre in Mythago, and since then some of the smaller, enclosed theatres in many of the human cities."

"Okay, think of a movie as a play you can watch in a scrying bowl, only a scrying bowl as big as a pond."

"You truly have such things?"

Jessica nodded. "They're still called theatres, but instead of a stage there's a huge screen that the movie appears on."

"A most amazing magic, to be sure."

"Not magic, technology. People can go there to see all kinds of movies - adventure, romance, science fiction . . . even movies that are created specifically for the entertainment of children."

"And also horror."

"That too. People go to the movies to be entertained, to escape from reality if only for a little while. Personally I don't care for horror movies, but I have friends who like to go to them for the adrenalin rush of being scared or maybe it's just to reassure themselves that as bad as things are, they could always be worse."

"How sad," Aracelia said.

"I guess," Jessica said. "Maybe it's just a matter of perspective."

They reached the edge of the Venom River again and stood watching the faint greenish-grey mist rise up from it.

"Okay then," she said looking around her. "Any ideas where I should try my necromancy spell?"

"How about right there," Aracelia pointed to one of the mounds near the river.

"Are you telling me each of those mounds is where a body is?" Jessica felt slightly queasy. "Do you know how many of them I walked on? That is so gross!"

Aracelia looked at her with amusement. "You are about to raise the dead and yet you are repulsed by the idea of walking over a grave? I assure you, the spirits of the dead are long gone. There is none to care whether you walk over their remains."

"It's not the same thing," Jessica protested. "Okay, maybe it's close. But just—eww!"

She knelt down beside the mound. "Okay, here goes nothing."

Chapter 22

Jessica placed the parchment with the spell on it on the ground in front of her, anchoring the corners of it with four good sized rocks. That would be the last thing she needed, for the wind to come up suddenly and blow the parchment into the river. If anything went wrong she might be responsible for a zombie apocalypse. She couldn't help the faint smile that crossed her face.

"What is so amusing?" Aracelia wanted to know.

"It's just—" Jessica gave a short laugh and shook her head. "Everyone's always talking about the zombie apocalypse, where the zombies will rise up and humanity will be fighting for their lives. And here I am about to try raising the dead and if anything goes wrong I might actually be responsible for a zombie apocalypse."

Aracelica smiled. "If anything went wrong it would only be one or two of the dead who responded, not a whole army."

"So we're not in any real danger?"

"I did not say that. Our danger would be quite real. The dead do not take kindly to being disturbed and would seek to destroy us. And it takes a great deal of power to vanquish one who is newly risen from the grave if you lose control over him. There is no Well nearby from which to draw on, should such a thing happen."

"Jeez, no pressure or anything," Jessica muttered.

"My friend, you do not have to do this. I understand if—"

"No, it's all right, I *want* to do this. And it's not just that I promised, I truly want to help." She looked thoughtfully across the river. "If this flower is as powerful as you say it is, is there any way to transplant a few of them so you don't have to make this journey again if you need them in the future?"

Once again Aracelia was touched by Jessica's compassion. "I do not know," she admitted. "Until the goddess spoke to me, I did not truly believe in their existence."

"It probably wouldn't hurt to try," Jessica said. She realized she was just stalling for time. "Okay, here goes nothing."

The first part of the spell was written in a magical language that sounded to Jessica what she imagined Latin would sound like. These were the words that she had Aracelia sound out for her so she could write them down phonetically. It was intent, more than anything, that would make the spell succeed. Jessica did not intend to fail. Taking a deep breath, she began reciting the spell.

"Rhiamin dipthoriam evonicium mefamina tulaurini execianous reanium."

She repeated the phrase again, accenting the second syllable of each word. The third time she repeated the phrase accented the third syllable while at the same time kneeling down and placing her hands on the mound in front of her, sending energy downwards. Though she did not break her focus, she was slightly surprised when she felt something responding to her spell.

"Rise, o fallen one, taken before your time. Rise from the cold earth to walk again. Hear me guardians of the dead. Release these bones to do my biding for but a short span of time. "

This time she felt a definite stirring of the earth. Sitting back on her heels she raised her hands off of the grave.

"Rise, o fallen one, cut down unjustly in battle. Rise from the cold earth to walk again. Hear me keepers of the departed. Release what is left behind to work my will for but a short span of time."

The earth in front of her began to push upwards and she got to her feet, arms out in front of her at shoulder height.

"Rise, o fallen one, abandoned by thy spirit. Rise from the cold earth to walk again. Hear me worms of the earth. Release these mortal remains into my custody for but a short span of time."

The mound grew as something began to thrust upwards from below. The earth began to part and a skeletal hand appeared, searching for purchase. A second hand appeared and the skeleton slowly began to pull itself up out of the ground.

This was the most dangerous part. If she faltered here she'd lose control and then the skeleton (she couldn't really call it a zombie because somehow she'd always pictured zombies with flesh on them and this creature had none) would be loose to do whatever it wanted. The creature stood in front of her now and she could feel it testing the magical bond between them.

Jessica straightened her back and stood tall. "Your task is this:

162

you will cross the Venom River and gather the cold grave blossoms that are growing at the river's edge for five yards in each direction. Further, you will take care in gathering them so as to try and preserve the roots."

The skeleton remained immobile.

"You will do so now," Jessica said firmly, giving it a mental push.

Slowly, with the jerky motions reminiscent of a puppet, it began to stir. One step, two steps, it moved towards the river. At the river's edge it tried to resist, but Jessica was unyielding. Little by little it waded through the river and up onto the bank of the other side. Carefully it began pulling up the iridescent cold grave blossoms.

This is where most people lost control, when the re-animated creatures began to do their bidding. But Jessica stayed focused on the skeleton, willing it to do as she told it. She had forgotten to specify that it stay along the riverbank, so it gathered all of the plants within a five yard arc of where it had crossed.

It was rather more than Jessica had counted on. Hopefully Aracelia knew of a spell to preserve the flowers in case the plants couldn't be transplanted. She would really hate for them to go to waste. The skeleton paused in its task, as though sensing her mind had wandered. Jessica gave it another little mental shove and it finished its task, then leisurely turned and returned at a snail's pace.

She waited until it was standing in front of her again, and then said, "Set the plants on the ground before me."

It did as she told it and then stood upright, waiting for further instructions. Jessica did not need to consult her parchment to cast the spell of release.

"Rest now, o fallen one. Return to thy place of repose. Thy task here is done. Rest now, o fallen one. Return to thy inanimate state. For thy help I am grateful. Rest now, o fallen one. Return to the earth from whence you came. Know peace at last."

The skeleton quivered, changing from bone white to grey as it turned to dust and dissolved into a pile of fine powder beside the pile of flowers.

Jessica looked at Aracelia in astonishment. "I never meant for it to do that!"

Aracelia was beaming. She hugged Jessica tightly. "Congratulations, my dear. You have done it!"

"Holy Saint Christopher, I really did, didn't I?" Jessica grinned back at her. "I hope you're able to use all of these," she said, gesturing to the pile of flowers at their feet.

"Indeed. I have a preservation spell to keep them fresh."

Jessica was pleased to see there were at least dozen plants that had healthy looking root systems. Hopefully Aracelia would be able to find a gardener who could transplant them. If the cold grave blossom did even half of what Aracelia though it would, it needed to be preserved.

"I just had a thought," she said. "These are probably called the cold grave blossoms for a reason. When you get these ones," she indicated the ones with the good roots, "home you should try planting them in a cemetery. There's probably something in graveyard soil that they need to live."

"I will see to it personally," Aracelia said. "At the very least they will make a lovely decoration until they are needed."

Chapter 23

Bandit was sitting casually beside the horses but the tracks around the fire pit showed that he'd spent a considerable portion of his wait time circling the fire. He chaffed under the fact that he'd not been able to accompany them, not just because he wanted to witness Jessica raising the dead, but to be there to protect her in case something went wrong. And the fact that his desire to protect her had nothing to do with keeping her alive to cast the reversal spell on him didn't occur to him.

"It's too bad you couldn't have been there," Jessica told him. "It was totally awesome. It was like that old skeleton was just waiting for me to call him from the grave. And when it was over - poof! He was dusted. You would have thought I knew what I was doing even," she added with a giggle.

He woofed and looked at Aracelia. "She'll be fine after she's had some food," she told him. "She suffers a slight case of magical intoxication."

This was something his teacher warned him about. When there was no Well nearby it was possible for those with powerful gifts to pull magical energy from things around them - people, artifacts, even the land itself. But it was wild magic and somewhat unpredictable. And it tended to have a somewhat intoxicating affect on its users.

Jessica laid the flowers she was carrying down and then stumbled over her own feet when she turned around too quickly. She landed on her rump in the dirt and started giggling again.

"Maybe it's more than just a slight case," Aracelia said with a grin. "Why don't you just stay there," she told Jessica. "I'll fix us something to eat as soon as I attend to the flowers."

"Don't mind me," Jessica said, waving her hand. "I think I'll just stay right here."

Bandit wondered just how much energy she'd pulled from around her. They had been standing on hallowed ground, with a river of magic in front of them. And it hadn't just been a normal battlefield, it had been a field where elves had fought and died. And elves were magic themselves. His tongue lolled out of his mouth as he grinned. This could turn into something quite amusing.

Unfortunately, it didn't take Aracelia long to cast her spell over the flowers they'd brought back. She cut a chunk of bread and cheese for Jessica to nibble on while she put together another one of her stews. Bandit couldn't wait to get out of the Elven Realm. He was sick of stew. He craved a nice, thick, juicy steak.

Jessica was yawning before the stew was finished and could barely keep her eyes open while she ate. Neither elf nor dog were surprised when she curled up in her bedroll immediately after eating and went right to sleep.

Bandit was about to stretch out beside her when Aracelia stopped him.

"I would have words with you," she said.

He sat upright again and looked at her.

"Although Jessica may at times forget you were once a man, I have not. And I think perhaps you have seen and heard things that are best not spoken of in her presence."

She paced away from the fire and then came back to sit down near him.

"I can see that you care for her, as a man not a loyal dog." She said it more like a question than a statement and he dipped his head in agreement.

"There is much to be admired in her, but she has much to learn of the world she now lives in, which makes her vulnerable. I think she will need a friend such as you in the days to come."

She sighed. "I fear I make little sense, my thoughts are quite disordered where she is concerned. But I believe you can be trusted with the truth - for her sake. You are aware I have been testing her I am sure?"

He dipped his head.

"She is a Master Class Sorcerer. With training she will be a Grand Master one day. And although I am sure you have figured most of this out on your own, I will tell you what she does not know. She believes she was brought to this world by accident, but it was her father and grandfather who drew her back. They seek to bring her to them before revealing themselves and then to teach her how to use her power."

She shook her head slightly. "I do not agree with all this deception, but I must abide by their wishes, which is why I do not tell her who I truly am. Her father has a powerful enemy and I fear for my granddaughter's very soul, should she fall into his hands. The more spells she casts, the less recovery time she will need between them. I do not know whether this is good or bad. Not only is she a Master Class Sorcerer, but she is one of those rare individuals who is able to pull magic out of the air around her."

Bandit woofed softly at her.

"I ask that you protect her, and help guide her. I do not know why you were skulking about in her camp the night she transformed you, but I do know that you do not mean her any harm. The goddess spoke through her and said "*The dark one shall bring much happiness through the ill times ahead.*" I believe the goddess spoke of you."

Aracelia looked away from him and into the fire. "Perhaps I'm getting sentimental in my old age, but I also believe my granddaughter deserves any happiness that you may bring her. You humans tend not to believe in fate, but I am an elf and I cannot help but believe you were fated to be together."

She sighed and looked at him again. "You must see that she reaches the wizard school in the south. She will be safe there, and her father and grandfather wait to finish teaching her to use her magic. Magic is her birthright. But should she be unable to reconcile herself to the life she will lead there, bring her back to me and I will see that she returns safely to the world she was raised upon. To us it may be bleak and terrible, but to her it is familiar. It is her home."

He dipped his head and gave her another soft woof to show he understood.

"There is another matter... I know the loss of her moonstone pains her sorely, and I am sorry for it. It is not just the assistance with magic she misses, it was her only link to her friends. When the time comes, remind her she has magic, and then teach her to scry."

This time he felt the tell-tale tickle in his head that meant she'd placed the words in his mind. There was more to what she said, but he would not remember until the message was triggered by a key word or event.

Bandit lay staring into the fire long after the elf sought her bedroll. He thought back to the night he stole into Jessica's camp. When had he started thinking of her as Jessica instead of the witch? So much had changed. No, *he* had changed.

Never would he have guessed that the path he had taken would lead him to this time, this place. When his brother betrayed him, so many years ago, he thought his life was over. But he survived, just as he survived three years in the galley ships of Boctyn and two more in the streets of Aris Ny.

It took him five more years to work his way back to Ghren lands, where he was approached by a wizard named Braxton who promised to help him prove the truth of what happened to him if he first retrieved a magical amulet stolen from him by an evil woman who had been using it to prey on the weak and helpless.

His sense of outrage had been roused at the thought of innocent people being victimized by this criminal and he'd been so eager to prove that he was a champion of justice that he had not even considered checking out Braxton's story. More the fool he.

However . . . perhaps Aracelia was right, and the hand of fate *was* in this. Had he not been caught and turned into a dog, then he would never have had the chance to get to know Jessica better, and that would have been the biggest crime of all.

With a gusty sigh he laid his head down. He no longer desired to return to confront his brother, to prove to his father that he could be just as strong and ruthless as he was. He had a new desire, and it had nothing to do with revenge.

Aracelia was awake before either of her companions, and took a moment to contact Paranithel using her scrying mirror.

"What happened?" Thackery demanded, before Paran could even greet her.

"I have never seen the like," Aracelia told him. "Instinctively she contained the magic and raised only one skeleton to do her bidding. And when she was finished she even released the magic holding it intact and it returned to dust."

"Then the testing is over?" Thackery asked with relief.

"My testing is done, at any rate. Who's to say what tests she will face in the future?"

"Do not fence words with me! What of the results of your tests?"

"I begin to see some merit in her being raised elsewhere," she said slowly. "Her magic is pure, unsullied by greed or ambition. With training she will one day take her proper place amongst the Grand Master Sorcerers. When she comes into her full power she will make a most formidable weapon against your enemy."

Thackery looked appalled. "Never! How could you even think I would use my own child so! I would rather strip her power away myself than set her against Anakaron."

"I am gladdened to hear this," Aracelia said. "But the choice may not be yours."

"Have you *seen* something?" Paranithel asked quickly.

She looked troubled. "The visions of the future are murky, as though filled with a grey mist. But the goddess herself told Jessica there are dark times ahead."

"I fear there are dark times for us all," he said. "My cards, too, show a shadowy future."

"At any rate, the moon will be in position in three days hence for Jessica to return her companion to his original form, and then she will be free to continue her journey."

"A thief in the night," Thackery said. "I still say he should remain the dog that he is. Who's to say what mischief he will cause her once he becomes a man again?"

"Oh, a great deal of mischief, I am sure," Aracelia said, eyes twinkling with merriment. "I think you will be much surprised by his true form."

And with that she was gone.

Chapter 24

"I guess we'll be parting company," Jessica said after they'd had breakfast. "Bandit and I have a date with a Well in three days and we can't be late. And then I have a date in Eglion."

"At the very least allow me to escort you to the border. 'Tis but a day's ride and it's on my way. From there it's another day to the Well. Eglion is just beyond that."

"That'd be great," Jessica said, brightening immediately. She'd gotten used to the elf's company and was reluctant to say goodbye to her. It was more than just a comforting presence, there was something about her that felt very familiar.

She studied her surreptitiously as they rode side by side, Aracelia pointing out plants or land marks she thought might be of interest. It was late in the day when Jessica finally figured it out.

"I know where I've seen you before!" she exclaimed.

"Indeed?" Aracelia was startled, to say the least, and brought her horse to a halt.

"In the wizard's tower of Ghren, there's a portrait over the fireplace of a woman. She looks just like you. Well not exactly like you. Her hair is dark and she doesn't have pointed ears, but it's the same face, the same eyes." Jessica grew more excited as she recalled the portrait.

"It's what I imagine you would look like if you were human. Is she related to you in some way? Or maybe the wizard from the tower was fixated on you and commissioned the painting so he could have a part of you with him always."

Aracelia's bell like laughter rang out. "Such a romantic notion, as misplaced as it is. I assure you there was nothing romantic between Ghren's wizard and myself."

"But the portrait . . ." Jessica said stubbornly. "How do you explain that?"

"I cannot," Aracelia told her. "Not will not, but cannot. You must wait to have your curiosity satisfied by the wizards in the south." She removed a carved red stone from around her neck. "I would like you to have this, for protection. And if ever you wish to seek me out, know that you will be welcome in the Elven Realm. You need only cross the border and I will know you have returned."

"Thank you. I—thank you," Jessica said, throat tight. "I wish I had something to give you in return."

"You have already given me more than you can imagine," Aracelia told her. She disliked emotional scenes and urged her horse onward. Jessica, understanding, followed silently.

They made camp for the last time together, just inside the border. If there was still enough daylight that Jessica could have travelled a few more miles on the other side, neither of them mentioned it.

For their last meal together, Aracelia slipped into the forest and returned with a pair of fat rabbits which she deftly cleaned and then spitted. Jessica dug up some tubers she'd recognized and these were placed in the glowing coals. Bandit lay by the fire practically drooling as he watched the rabbits roast, much to the amusement of the two women.

When they were done, Aracelia and Jessica split one of the rabbits between them and gave the other to Bandit. They supplemented their meal with the tubers from the fire and some greens Aracelia had gathered on her way back from hunting.

"At least wait for me to pull the meat off the bones for you," Jessica told the dog. "It would be a shame to be so close only to have you choke to death on a bone before I change you back."

"I will miss your company," Aracelia said suddenly, then looked chagrined, as though she hadn't meant to say that.

"I'll miss you too," Jessica said sincerely. "Are you sure you don't want to come with us?"

The elf shook her head with regret. "Alas, I cannot. As you recall, I must deliver the cold grave blossoms to the healer."

Jessica gave her a guilty look. "I'm sorry, I'm taking you out of your way."

"Not at all. My way is much further along the border."

"It just occurred to me, we've been through so much in our short time together and yet I know very little about you," Jessica said.

Aracelia spread her hands wide. "What would you like to know?"

"Well . . . family for instance."

"I have two brothers, but they live in different Elven Realms so I seldom see them."

"Older or younger?" Jessica asked, genuinely interested.

"One of each. They both have mates, and several children between them."

"No mate for you?"

The elf smiled. "I am far too set in my ways. No sensible elf would have me, and I have not the tolerance for the non-sensible ones."

Jessica laughed.

"And what of you, my friend. Do you have a mate waiting for you on this other world?"

Bandit pricked up his ears, but only Aracelia noticed.

"No, just a few close friends."

"What of the wizard who sent you here?"

"Howard?" That brought a genuine smile to her face. "I may have harbored a few fantasies about Howard when we kids, but that was before he figured out he preferred men to women."

Aracelia reached into her pack and withdrew a wineskin, then two silver goblets and a bowl.

"I have been saving this for a special occasion," she said. "And I can think of none more special than tonight." She poured equal amounts in the goblets and bowl, passing one of the goblets to Jessica and placing the bowl in front of Bandit.

"I propose a toast. To friends, both new and old." She held her goblet up high.

"To friends," Jessica said. Bandit woofed in agreement and all three drank.

"This is amazing!" The wine seemed to evaporate on her tongue. Jessica sipped it slowly, the better to savor the flavor. It tasted of honey, and hot summer nights in a garden of exotic flowers, with a faint aftertaste of spice. "What is this?"

"It is faerie wine," Aracelia said.

Jessica's eyes widened at that. "You mean faeries are real too?" She clapped a hand over her mouth. "Sorry! I didn't mean to imply . . ."

"Yes, faeries are as real as we elves," Aracelia said with amusement.

"I really am sorry," Jessica said. "Where I come from elves and faeries are just in stories." She sat up straight suddenly. "Does this mean dragons and giants and ogres are real too?"

"Dragons generally prefer to live along the coast, although I have heard of the fire wyrm of the southern deserts. The giants seldom leave their mountains, but ogres can be found in many places."

Jessica closed her mouth with a snap. "I was just kidding," she said in a small voice.

"Do not fear, my friend. The giants and ogres tend to avoid contact with humans. And dragons are quite shy by nature."

"Of course," Jessica said faintly.

"But the hour grows late, and you have a much longer journey than I in the morning. I bid you good evening, my friends. And may the stars keep you and watch over you."

Somehow Jessica was not surprised that there was no sign of Aracelia when she and Bandit awoke the next morning. She understood all too well about hating to say good bye. There were a couple of sheets of parchment held down by a cloth-wrapped bundle where the elf's bedroll had been.

"Forgive me, my friend," Jessica read out loud, "But I dislike goodbyes. You have done a great service to my people in helping me to attain the cold grave blossoms, we are in your debt. If you are in need, and are able to do so, enter any of the Elven Realms and you will find friends. I have left a map showing the location of the Elven Realms, spelled so that only you will see the markings."

Jessica glanced down at the other papers and the top one was indeed a map.

"Remember that the wards I have shown you for protection must be set each night, as does the spell to repel vermin. Safe travels my friend. We will meet again."

Rifling through the other pages, Jessica gave a soft, "Oh!"

When she failed to share what had caught her attention, Bandit gave a bark to jar her out of her daze.

"It's the transmogrification spell," she said, looking over at him. "It's the spell I'll need to change you back into a man."

He woofed softly.

"Okay, let's not get maudlin," she said with a sniff. "Let's get going."

The border was so close that she led her horse to it, and then coaxed her through. As she was about to mount, she looked around with a puzzled look on her face. "Do you notice anything strange?" she asked Bandit. He looked around in confusion. "It's like everything is somehow . . . diminished."

The colors were not as bright, the landscape not as beautiful, as in the Elven Realm.

"Where I'm from there are stories about humans who've wandered into the faerie realms and end up staying there. Now I know why."

Bandit woofed in agreement.

"You're right. Enough lolly gagging. Do you want a lift?"

He shook his head no and she climbed into the saddle, pointing the mare in the direction of the Well.

Chapter 25

It was with genuine regret that Aracelia took leave of her granddaughter, her heart bidding her to stay. But she had not lied when she said there were healers waiting for the cold grave blossoms. The sickness she'd mentioned was real, and she'd already tarried too long.

Had she a choice she would have kept Jessica with her. But Jessica had a destiny to fulfill. It was not just wizardly machinations that brought her to the magical realm. There were higher powers at work here as well, powers Aracelia knew better than to meddle with.

The loss of the moonstone troubled her greatly. Sinking earth bogs did not just appear at random as this one appeared to have done. The moonstone was more than just a trinket - it was imbued with magical properties - elven magic. She could only surmise that someone was aware of this and wanted it disposed of. Had Jessica been the intended victim as well?

It was one of the reasons she'd gifted her with the blood tear. Not only for protection, it would ward against anyone scrying for her without her knowledge. This included her grandfather and father, and unfortunately her friends in the other realm as well. While the loss of communication with her friends was upsetting, it was not fair that the two wizards were scrutinizing her every move without her knowledge. Those two needed to be taken down a peg or two, and she was just the elf to do it.

Riding the Fae roads, it did not take her long to reach the city where the healers were waiting. She did not even wait to change out of her riding clothes, but went straight to the healing centre.

"Bless your swift return, my lady," Grania, the chief healer, said. She was tall and thin, her dark hair streaked liberally with silver.

Aracelia dismounted gracefully and handed the carefully wrapped cold grave blossoms over to the waiting apprentices. "There should be more than enough for your purposes, and I've preserved some of the roots as well."

Grania looked dubiously at the package she was handed and bit her lip.

"I know what you're thinking," Aracelia said. "We have thus far been unsuccessful in our attempts to cultivate these plants. But think on the name - cold grave blossom - and then think upon where they are to be found. We have tried many places and types of soil to grow them in, but never once did we think to grow them in the burial grounds."

The older elf's eyes widened in surprise. "In truth, it had not occurred to me." She wandered away, muttering under her breath at her own shortsightedness.

Aracelia smiled faintly. She took pride in the fact it was her very own granddaughter who had thought of planting the blossoms among the graves. Was it the human factor that gave her such insight? She hoped to one day find out.

Her horse had been led away to the healing center's stables and she knew her gear would be taken care of. Having served her purpose, and badly in need of a bath, Aracelia walked the short distance to her home.

Hot water filled the tub in the bathing chamber and a tray with fruit and cheese rested on a table beside it. Drops of condensation beaded up on the decanter sitting on the tray and she knew it would have one of her favorite wines in it. It was good to have servants who anticipated her needs.

She sighed as she slid into the tub after shedding her travel clothes. The scent from the fragrant oils wafted upwards. Reaching for the decanter, she poured herself a glassful of wine in a crystal goblet and sipped, the light, fruity taste echoing the scent of the oils, as she'd known it would. Coming home to this was what made journeying worth while. Perhaps one day she'd be able to share such luxuries with her granddaughter.

The thought of Jessica brought a smile to her lips. So much power in such a small human. But though her father and grandfather doubted her ability to control it, *she* had no doubts, or at least very few. Jessica was stronger than they realized - perhaps they had not been wrong to send her away to be raised after all.

The bath water had turned tepid and Aracelia sighed again, this time with resignation. As much as she'd like to keep putting it off, there was still something she had left to do.

Once properly dressed again, she went and stood before the large mirror she preferred for scrying. Might as well get the worst over with first. Taking a deep breath she chanted the incantation softly, then waved her hand in front of the mirror.

"It's about time!" Thackery's angry voice filled the room. "What have you done with my daughter?"

"I have done no—"

"Why can we still not see her image? I knew letting you test her was a dangerous idea. You have no idea . . ."

Aracelia merely raised an eyebrow as she waited for Thackery to wind down. Perhaps she should have contacted him sooner, he appeared to have a great deal of anger stored up.

"I gave her a blood tear," she said abruptly, when he showed no sign of stopping.

"You what?"

"Bad enough you sought to watch her like a feline with a rodent, but you thought to run her life through her friends. I will not have it. You do not wish her to know of you? Then she shall not. But neither shall you be able to spy on her unawares."

"I did not spy!"

"Then what would you call it? "

Thackery sputtered and blustered and glared at her. "I have every right to help my daughter stay safe."

"Ah, yes." Aracelia nodded in agreement. "And how exactly did you do that?"

"Well, I—"

"Did you assist her in scaling the cliff at Death's Head?"

"I—"

"No, that's right, you didn't know where your spell had sent her. Did you assist her in learning to control her magic, warn her that it would be best to keep it hidden?"

"No, I—"

"No, you decided to keep yourself hidden instead. Perhaps you saw to her safety when she was in the dungeon in Castle Ghren?"

"You know very well I—"

"Yes." She let the anger she'd been holding back leech into her voice. "I do know. You stood there watching from your tower in the south and worked your magicks through that poor boy in the other realm."

"That's not fair!"

"You're right, it's not fair. Neither is spying on Jessica when she doesn't even know of your existence. The creature she travels with smells of magic, and not just that which turned him into what he is. Once he is human again he can show her a simple scrying spell so she can contact her friends again."

"What about us?"

"You had your chance. Now you will just have to wait until she reaches you."

"And just how do you know this creature she's with can be trusted? That he will not lead her astray?"

"We will just have to have faith," she told him, and waved her hand in front of the mirror to break the spell.

"Well, that went rather how I expected," she murmured. "Now for the ones who are not so deserving of this."

The chant was slightly different this time, but the gestures were the same. The image that appeared in the glass was of the inside of Howard's work room. Before Aracelia could call out to him, she heard footsteps and Howard rushed into the room.

"Lady Aracelia!" he exclaimed. "I wasn't sure we'd see you

again, now that Jess has passed her tests and all."

"You were expecting someone else, were you not?" she asked shrewdly.

Howard took a half step back from the scrying bowl. "Oh, I . . . that is . . ."

"Be at ease," Aracelia said with a laugh. "It is Paranithel with whom you converse, is it not?"

"Well . . . yes."

She nodded. "It gladdens my heart to know he does not forget our granddaughter's friends. In truth, were he not already continuing your studies in magic I would have made the offer myself."

"Really?" Howard said in surprise.

"Most assuredly. He and I are alike in our desire to make sure potential such as yours is not wasted."

"Even the small magicks, like the ones I'm able to work in this realm, are amazing," he told her.

"Indeed. Just think what you could accomplish were you to visit us here."

"I hope some day I'll be able to do so."

"I hope so too," she said. "Howard, it is with regret I must tell you that you will no longer be able to converse with Jessica through scrying unless she contacts you first."

He was nodding his head as she spoke. "Yeah, I kind of got that feeling. I—what do you mean, unless she contacts me first? You think she might try?"

As much as she hated to squash the hope she saw on his face, she had to be honest. "I have given her a talisman to prevent her being watched from afar - I have misliked what her father has been doing from the beginning."

"Okay, I get that," Howard agreed. "I have to say I thought watching her without her knowing was kind of creepy too. But what's this about her contacting me?"

"The man who was once a dog who travels with her . . . he has some magical ability of his own. Should he teach her to scry, she will be able to find you through the moonstone, just as you found her."

"That's awesome!" Howard's whole face lit up. "I can't wait!"

Aracelia smiled in return. These humans, it took so little to please them.

Chapter 26

Jessica studied the transmogrification spell as she rode, sounding out a word here and there, trying out the odd hand gesture. She was only going to have one chance at it and she wanted to make sure she got it right.

She felt the pull of the Well long before she saw it. They'd left the Darkwood Forest behind and were crossing a series of long, low hills dotted with clumps of boulders and the occasional grove of trees.

"Doesn't look like much, does it?" she commented as they stared down at it the top of a hill. Bandit woofed in agreement.

Unlike the Well at Ghren, there was nothing special to mark this one's place. Like most Wells it was set on a slight rise, but the plain brown circle could easily be mistaken for an old camp site, the tall rocks on three sides offering shelter from the wind.

"Okay then. Now that we know where it is, why don't we spend our last night together in style? I think there's a dinner with our name on it waiting for us in Eglion."

Bandit woofed in agreement, a definite spring in his step as he followed in the horse's wake.

Eglion was a border town, rather than a market town like Pottswell. It was smaller, and though it did not have a huge market it did boast a sizeable village green centered on a crossroad.

The Blue Bull, the inn where Jessica was to meet up with Sebastian, was on the far edge of the town. She gave the stable boy a handful of coppers and carried her saddle bags and pack into the taproom of the inn, Bandit at her heels.

Going up to the bar she said, "I'm looking for Quillan."

The short, barrel-chested man wiping down the counter didn't even pause as he said, "I be Quillan."

"I have something for you, from a mutual friend." She handed him a token Sebastian had given her.

Reluctantly, he stopped what he was doing and glanced at the token. His whole demeanor changed. "Any friend of the bard . . . How may I be of service to ye?"

"A room, if you please. And dinner for two."

"Rooms is a half silver a day for a private room and meals is included. Yer dog'll have to stay in the stable."

Jessica produced a gold coin. "How about this," she countered, seeing the way Quillan's eyes lit up. "You take this and I get a private room for a week, meals included, and the dog stays with me."

"Done!" He plucked the coin from her fingers and it vanished into the pouch at his belt. "Dell!" He snapped his fingers.

A large, sandy haired youth shuffled out of the kitchen.

"Show the lady to room three." Turning back to Jessica he said, "Yer dinner will be waiting for ye when ye come back down."

"Great. And I'd like wine with mine, and ale in a bowl for my dog."

"Drinks be extra," Quillan told her quickly.

Suppressing a grin at his avarice, Jessica flipped him a full silver. "That should take care of it."

Dell grudgingly carried her saddlebags but she carried her pack as she followed him to her room. He dropped them just inside the door and handed her the key. She thought about tipping him a couple of coppers, but he disappeared back downstairs.

Sebastian hadn't exaggerated about the quality of the rooms here. Besides the bed, there was a washstand and a tall, narrow armoire. There was rough quality glass in the window and she couldn't help but wish it was cold enough to light a fire in the large, stone fireplace. There was a chair in one corner and a thread bare rug on the floor.

The bed was huge, almost as big as the one in the wizard's tower in Castle Ghren. It had four wooden posts holding up a canopy, and faded green velvet curtains that matched the spread. She couldn't wait to try it out.

She cast the spell Aracelia had taught her that would get rid of any and all bedbugs, fleas, and other vermin. With luck the room would be clear when they returned.

"I don't know about you, but I'm starving," she said to Bandit. "Let's see if the food is as top notch as the rooms."

He woofed in agreement and she paused only long enough to

set a protection spell around the room. Locking the door behind them, she led the way back down to the tap room.

Dell showed her to a corner table where there was a plate of beaten metal with what looked to be half a chicken and a variety of root vegetables waiting for her. There was a clay carafe with moisture beading it, along with a stubby goblet. On the floor there was a wooden bowl filled with chunks of medium rare beef, a bowl of ale beside it.

Jessica hadn't realized until that moment how hungry she really was. She dove into her meal with gusto, only dimly aware that Bandit was doing the same. It was sheer heaven to eat something she actually recognized.

The tap room had started out with only a handful of customers, but by the time they were finished it was about half full. Jessica wondered if it would fill up once Sebastian was here to entertain them.

In one corner a group of men were playing some kind of game of chance, while the table closest to them held two men arguing the merits of horses versus mules for a caravan headed north. A sudden shower of rainbow sparks drew everyone's attention to the table nearest the door.

"Here now - we'll have none of that in here. You know the rules. You want to be using magic, take it outside."

"Sorry Quillan, the lad just got excited, that's all," the elder of the two men sitting at the table said. "It won't happen again."

"Dammed magic workers," Dell muttered under his breath as he cleared away Jessica's plate and Bandit's bowl. "Will yer beast be needing more ale?"

"Just one more," Jessica told him. "What was that all about?"

She nodded towards the far table.

"Quillan don't allow magic in here - too easy for it to get out of control. I seen it cause more damage than a full out brawl."

Jessica merely nodded and looked a little closer at the two men. The elder looked rather angry while the younger looked downright sullen. She thought briefly of going over to introduce herself - maybe they could help - but dismissed it as a bad idea. Somehow she thought the fewer who knew about her magical abilities the better.

The ale was flowing heavily in the tap room, and by the time Jessica and Bandit finished their drinks the crowd was getting rather rowdy. She understood now why Dell had put her in the dark corner. There were only a few other women in the room and they were drawing a great deal of attention.

That seemed to be the idea, she decided as a few coins were exchanged and one of the women disappeared into a back room with a man who had the look of a farmer to him. Deciding that discretion was the better part of valor, Jessica decided to slip up to her room before she was noticed.

"I don't know about you," she said to Bandit as she locked the door behind them, "But I could sleep for a week."

After unlacing her leather jerkin, she sat down on the bed to take her boots off. Her eyes widened. "Holy Saint Christopher, this is a feather mattress!"

Quickly getting rid of her boots, she lay down on top of the covers for just a moment. That was her first mistake. Her second was closing her eyes. All at once her days of travel and fitful nights on the hard ground caught up to her and she was asleep.

Bandit gave a snort of amusement. How did she do that, fall asleep so quickly? He waited a few more minutes, just to be sure, and then jumped up on the bed beside her. If he'd been in his human form he would have groaned. The bed was every bit as soft as she'd said.

He contemplated the woman snoring softly beside him. With any luck this would be their last night together with him as a dog. He couldn't help wondering what she'd think of his true form and was vain enough to hope she liked what she saw. Of more concern was her reaction when she found out who he really was. As much as he'd like to hide the truth from her, she had enough people lying to her already and he wasn't about to do that.

In the short time they'd been together he'd come to know her pretty well. She was stronger than she realized but her tender heart and impulsiveness were going to get her in trouble. What she needed was a protector, and he was just the man for the job. Or he would be after moonrise tomorrow.

When Jessica inquired about a bath in the morning, a surly Dell informed her there was a public bathhouse beside the glassmaker, just down the street. But she'd better get there early because the water in the tubs was only changed once a day.

"I'll bet I'd get a different answer if Quillan was around," she grumbled to Bandit as she made do with a quick wash up using the pitcher and bowl provided on the wash stand in her room.

Breakfast consisted of freshly baked bread slathered with honey and stewed fruit for Jessica and a bowl of leftover stew for Bandit. Afterwards she went back up to their room where she studied the spell Aracelia had given her. It seemed straight forward enough, but it never hurt to be sure. And it was never far from her mind that if she screwed this up she was condemning a man to life as a dog.

More than ever she missed being able to talk to Howard. She could really use his advice. Aracelia told her she needed to have more faith in herself but it was easier said than done. She was still too much of a newbie when it came to magic.

"Aracelia said it didn't matter when the spell is cast, just so long as the moon is up, but I don't want to take any chances. What do you say to having our last supper at the Well?" she said to Bandit, who was alternating watching her and pacing in front of the fireplace.

He woofed in agreement. Jessica picked up her travel pack and an oddly shaped bundle, then renewed the protection spell on the door to the room before leading the way down to the kitchen. By slipping the cook a half silver, she came away with a loaf of bread, a half round of cheese, a roasted chicken leftover from lunch, and a skin of wine.

As they travelled back to the Well, Jessica wondered what kind of man Bandit had been. Obviously he'd been a thief, but was he a career criminal or driven to it by circumstance? As fond as she'd grown of him she had to be practical, so she ignored his confused bark when she continued on past the Well to a grove of trees a few miles away.

Dismounting, she took the bundle over to one of the trees and unwrapped it. He watched silently as she placed a small bundle of clothing into the crotch of the tree and leaned his sword up against the trunk. Finally, she turned her attention to him.

"Look, no offense, but I have no idea why you were stumbling around in my camp that night but I was too far from the trail for it to be by accident. We've been through a lot in the last month, but for all I know the spell is going to wipe that from your mind. Your stuff should be safe here. The Well will protect me from any ill intent and my horse and gear are already under a protection spell."

Turning away, she mounted up and led the way back the way they'd come. To be on the safe side, she built her fire on the other side of the boulders bracketing the Well. They didn't really need a fire, but she found comfort in the familiar task.

Pulling most of the meat off the chicken, she put it in a bowl for the dog, along with a couple of slices each of bread and cheese. Her own appetite deserted her, but remembering Howard's insistence that she replenish her energy, she nibbled at some bread and cheese while she stared into the fire.

"It's time," she said at last, getting to her feet.

It was a crisp and clear night and the quarter moon shone brightly. Bandit stayed hard on her heels as she climbed the rise to the Well. The power Jessica felt emanating from it gave her a heady feeling.

"I'll say goodbye now," she said, locking eyes with the dog. "Using the power from the Well, it shouldn't take long to re-energize myself so by the time you get your stuff and get back, I'll be gone."

She stepped into the circle. "Good bye Bandit," she said softly.

Jessica let the power of the Well flow into her, ignoring Bandit's barking. It was an amazing feeling. Blue flames of energy licked upwards, swirling around her as she chanted the words of the transmogrification spell, one hand pointed upwards at the moon, the other towards Bandit.

Something wasn't right. Jessica's eyes widened and she began to tremble. Pain, such as she never before imagined, lanced through her. It wasn't supposed to be like this! With a supreme effort of will she held her position and finished the spell. The last thing she was aware of was Bandit's frantic barking before the night shattered into a thousand splinters of light.

Chapter 27

Jessica was floating. She felt buoyant, detached from everything. She wanted nothing more than to just keep flying through the layers of softness, but a persistent voice nagged at her. If only she could make it stop.

"Damn it, Jess, don't you dare die on me."

Maybe she should make an effort. The voice sounded so concerned.

"You said she'd be better by now."

"I said," a second voice replied, "that I know very little about this kind of illness but in time she should recover."

Jessica made a supreme effort and half opened her eyes. A tall, dark haired man dressed in black was threatening an older, smaller man dressed in healer's grey. Her eyes wouldn't stay open any longer.

Much later she woke again. This time her head ached and the buoyant feeling had left. Too bad. She was lying in a very soft bed; vaguely she wondered what she was doing here. It seemed to be evening, there was a fire burning low in the fireplace. Beside her bed the dark haired man was sleeping in a chair.

She studied him curiously. He looked worried, even in his sleep. Black, wavy hair framed his face and curled down to the collar of his shirt. The sapphire he wore at his throat seemed vaguely familiar. He was still dressed in black, his clothes looked like he'd slept in them. She decided that without the worried look he'd be very handsome.

A sudden thought struck her. "Bandit?"

His eyes snapped open. The worry left his face - his smile was breathtaking. "I never thought I'd be glad to hear that name again."

"What happened? Where am I?"

"Just relax." His broad hand held her back as she tried to sit up. "You're back in your room at the Blue Bull. The Well was more powerful than it seemed. The backlash almost killed you. Didn't anyone ever tell you not to try casting a spell while standing on a Well?"

"Backlash," she repeated, leaning back against the pillows. "But how did you get me here, my protection spell . . . "

"Was only effective against those who intended harm."

"Oh." Jessica was suddenly at a loss for words.

"I know we have a lot of talking to do," he said, "but it can wait until you're fully recovered."

"How sick was I?"

"Are you," he corrected. "The healer said you'll have a few lucid moments, like this, but it'll be a long time before you're fully recovered."

"A long time . . ." her voice trailed off and then grew stronger again. "How long since I cast the spell?"

"Five days."

"Five days? So why are you still here?" The question may have seemed casual, but she couldn't quite meet his eyes. His answer was more important than she was willing to admit.

He was suddenly very interested in his hands. "After all we've been through, I owe you at least this much."

"Oh." She was suddenly very tired again.

"Go to sleep, Jessica. We have all the time in the world."

"Wait," she fought to keep her eyes open. "One more question. What is your name?"

"Dominic," he said with a smile.

Dominic, she thought as she drifted back to sleep. Somehow it sounded just right.

Dominic watched her fall back asleep and breathed a sigh of relief. She'd woken a few times, but not enough to do more than stir. The last couple of times she managed consciousness for longer periods, but both times she'd made no sense. The first time she'd spouted snatches of poetry and wanted to know where her teapot was. The second time she'd stared around the room but didn't appear to be aware of where she was. This time at least she'd made sense.

He sent a little prayer up to the powers that be, thanking them.

His heart had stopped, up there on the hill when he realized she was going to cast her spell from atop the Well. He tried to warn her, but of course all that came out of his mouth was barking. When the spell was complete and he was a man again he'd carried her down to the fire and wrapped her up as best he could to keep her warm while he rode to where she'd left his clothes and sword. Riding bareback, naked, was not something he'd care to try again anytime soon.

As he hurried to get dressed a small pouch fell out of the bundle she'd made of his clothing. It wasn't his. Curiosity getting the better of him, he opened it up to see what was inside. He went still for a moment at the glint of silver and gold in the moonlight. Even though she'd taken precautions for her safety because she didn't know if she could trust him, she made sure he was provided for.

The mare couldn't move fast enough to take him back to her. Jessica lay shivering beside the fire. He kicked dirt over the dying flames and gathered her carefully in his arms. Mounting the horse, he headed back towards Eglion.

The horse was slow with its double burden and the sun was just pinking the sky as they reached the town. Rather than stopping at the inn, he'd gone straight to the healer's, kicking the door with his boot because his arms were full.

The healer was a cantankerous old man and didn't take kindly to be awoken so early. However, one look at Dominic's face and he reluctantly invited him in.

"I am not set up to receive patients," he said peevishly. "Usually I'm summoned to them."

"There's no time," Dominic told him. "She's been unconscious for hours."

"Set her down here," he said, indicating what looked to be the kitchen table. "Now, what happened, she get out of line and you hit her a little too hard?"

"No!"

"I don't see any blood . . ."

"She wasn't wounded. She's a magic worker, and—"

"Magic worker!" the healer spat. "I might have known. She's probably just exhausted herself. She'll be fine in a day or so. Now take her out of here and let her sleep it off."

"You don't understand! She was standing on a Well when she cast a spell—"

"Then I can't say much for her master to let her do something so stupid. She's probably suffering from backlash. I don't know much about backlash illness but it's rarely fatal. Depending on how strong the Well was, it can take anywhere from days to weeks to recover and she won't be doing that here!"

"But—"

"She'll be far more comfortable in her own bed."

"If it's a question of money . . ."

"Trust me, if was a question of money I'd be the first to let you know," the healer said wryly. "The only thing she'd be doing here is cluttering up the place."

With no other recourse, Dominic gently picked Jessica up again. "Isn't there anything I can do for her?"

The healer sighed. "Keep her warm. She'll be awake off and on over the next few days. Try and get her to drink something when she's coherent - tea or wine, broth would be even better."

Filled with misgivings, Dominic gave the healer a silver for his trouble and brought Jessica back to her room in the Blue Bull. Once he had her settled in bed there was nothing left for him to do but keep a silent vigil.

Over the next few days Jessica was awake more often and gradually for longer periods of time. She dutifully drank the restorative teas Dominic persuaded the healer to part with, along with the occasional glass of wine and bowl of broth.

She chaffed at how long it was taking her to recover. The slightest exertion left her exhausted. Getting out of bed was a major achievement - managing the stairs to have a meal in the tap room was out of the question. But if she had to be ill, she couldn't ask for a better nurse than Dominic. He was every bit as faithful as a human as he had been as a canine.

No matter when she woke up, he was there, if not in the chair beside her bed, then at least somewhere in the room. He patiently fed her the broth he bribed Dell into bringing up from the kitchen. He placed cool cloths on her forehead when she felt like she was burning up with fever - this was after his initial alarm that she had a fever at all. He'd all but kidnapped the healer to come and look at her, only to discover it was a common side effect of backlash illness. He was also there for her when she had nightmares about what she'd suffered in the Ghren dungeons - never pressing her for details, just soothing her until she slept again.

If she wasn't careful, she could get used to being looked after like this.

Chapter 28

"Can I ask you something?" Jessica said after finishing a whole bowl of vegetable stew, making Dominic insanely happy.

"Ask away," he said easily.

"I couldn't help but notice that I'm not wearing the same clothes I was in when I did the spell casting . . ."

"That's right."

"But how—I mean, did you—"

He raised his right hand. "I swear I kept my eyes closed the whole time."

It was hard to feel embarrassed when he was sitting there with a cheeky grin on his face.

Jessica bit her lip. "I don't recall owning anything like this," she plucked at the nightshirt self-consciously. "Did you buy this for me?"

"I sent Dell's lady friend to the market for something for you to sleep in. If you don't like it, I—"

"No! It's fine, I—Dell has a girl friend?"

"Hard to believe, isn't it?" he said with a grin.

"No kidding. But what I wanted to ask is if there's another one. I'm feeling so much better right now and I'd love to get cleaned up, but I've been in this same nightshirt for close to a week."

His mouth pulled down into a frown. "The healer said—"

"Look, no offense but I met healers like him in Ghren and what they know about real healing could be carved on the head of a pin. Next thing you know he'll be wanting to stick leeches all over me."

Dominic's eyes flickered. If she hadn't been watching for his reaction she would have missed it completely.

"He did suggest leeches, didn't he?"

"You'll notice I didn't take him up on his offer," he pointed out.

"Lucky for your hide," she muttered. "What I want is a bath, and a fresh change of clothing."

He was already shaking his head. "A bath is out of the question."

"But—"

"You're still a long way away from having your strength back."

"I don't need a lot of strength to have a bath, I just need to sit in the tub."

He seemed to realize this was an argument he wasn't going to win. "I'll arrange for a bath to be brought up, but I'm not leaving you alone." He held up a hand when she opened her mouth to argue. "You could easily slip or have a sudden attack of weakness. If I'm outside the room you could be hurt or drowned and I'd never know it. Look, there's a privacy screen for dressing," he pointed towards a corner of the room by the fireplace.

Jessica dutifully looked and was surprised to see a sectioned screen propped up against the wall.

"We can have the tub set next to the fire and then the screen on the other side. That way you can have your privacy and I can be right here in case you run into trouble. What do you say?"

Jessica weighed her options and decided it was probably the best deal she was going to get. "All right," she said grudgingly.

A surly Dell brought the tin tub up and set it in front of the fireplace, carrying bucket after bucket of hot water. Jessica almost felt sorry for him but she remember how he'd lied to her before about there being a tub available.

As worried as Dominic was about Jessica attempting to have a bath, he couldn't help but find some amusement in the way she was all but salivating at the oversized tin bucket and its steaming contents. Once Dell was finished filling it, Dominic made her wait until he arranged a stool for her to sit on beside the tub with towels within easy reach. Instead of another nightshirt, he had a proper nightgown folded up for her. He just hoped she liked it.

Once everything was arranged to his satisfaction, he helped her from the bed to the stool, then arranged the privacy screen around the hearth.

"Okay," he said, moving over to sit on the end of the bed. "If you need anything, just give a shout. I'll be right over here."

"I'll be fine," she answered.

It was at that point Dominic realized that although the frame of the privacy screen was solid wood, the panels were made of something much thinner. With the fire blazing in the fireplace, he'd built it up himself so Jessica wouldn't take a chill when she got out of the tub, everything between the fire and the screen was silhouetted.

Hardly daring to breathe he watched as she pulled the nightshirt over her head, his imagination filling in the details of what the screen still hid. His mouth went dry. As she stepped into the tub, his sigh was an echo of hers. Dominic closed his eyes and tried not to picture her in the tub, a task made more difficult by the sound of the water sloshing.

"This soap is amazing," she called out after a few minutes. "Where on earth did you find it?"

"Eglion has quite a varied marketplace," he told her. It wasn't a lie, the town did have a decent market. The soap didn't come from there however. Somehow he didn't think she'd appreciate that he'd cadged it off one of the whores in the tap room.

The water sloshed again. His eyes opened enough to see her silhouette again as she stood up in the tub. Quickly shutting his eyes again he shifted uncomfortably on the bed. Maybe he *should* have waited outside the room for her.

She seemed to be taking a long time drying off. He could almost see the towel sliding over her skin, taking the drops of moisture with it. Again he shifted, trying to find a more comfortable position.

"Would you like some help?" he called out hopefully.

There was a small crash, followed by a muffled curse. "No!"

He was already on his feet. "What was that crash? Are you all right?"

"I accidentally kicked over the stool," she said, coming out from behind the screen. "Thank you."

"For what?" he asked, unable to take his eyes off her.

Her skin had a rosy hue from the hot bath and the heat of the fire. Her hair was confined in one of the towels and somehow wound around her head. The white night gown enveloped her like a cloud, making her look like an exotic princess.

"For the bath, the soap, this beautiful night gown," she said, waving her hand downwards. She took a step closer. "For taking care of me when you didn't have to."

"I—" His throat seemed to close up.

"Could I ask one more favor of you?"

"Anything," he croaked.

"Could you go down to the stable and check on my horse?"

Dominic blinked. "What?"

"She and I have been through a lot together and she's been alone in the stable for almost a week."

His eyes narrowed at the impish look in her eyes. "You want me to check on your horse?"

"Please? And maybe take her an apple."

With a heartfelt sigh he helped her back to bed. "I will check on your horse, but you will lie down and close your eyes until I get back."

"Deal." To prove her sincerity, she snuggled down in the bed.

"No cheating," he told her, knowing full well she'd be sitting up the moment he was out the door.

She turned a wide-eyed, innocent gaze on him. "Me? Would I cheat?"

Dominic snorted, but left to do her bidding.

Jessica waited until the door was closed before sitting up to deal with her hair. Just about the only thing Dominic hadn't thought of was a comb. She tried finger combing it but quickly gave it up as a lost cause.

She heard the rap on her door with relief. "You couldn't possibly have made it down to the stable and back already. But since you're back . . . how are you at braiding hair?"

"I must admit, I've never had the pleasure of braiding a lady's hair, however I've braided both a horse's mane and tail in my time."

The slightly amused masculine voice was most definitely not Dominic's. It was, however, familiar. Jessica turned her head, eyes widening in surprised pleasure.

"Sebastian!"

"One and the same," he said with a huge smile. A few steps brought him over to the bed where he pulled her into a hug.

"Sebastian, I can't believe you're here!" Jessica's voice was muffled by his shoulder.

"We were supposed to meet here, were we not?" he asked, releasing her and making himself at home on the bed beside her.

"Yes, but it's been so long . . ." her voice trailed off, emotions churning.

"I've missed you too," he said with understanding. "Now, my friend Quillan has been telling me tales about you. You have backlash illness? Again? What have you been up to, my friend? And who is this dark, mysterious man that has been taking care of you?"

"Quillan's got a big mouth," Jessica muttered. "Yes I have backlash illness. Again. I cast a major spell while standing on top of a Well. Apparently I'm lucky to be alive."

Sebastian shook his head solemnly. "It appears I've arrived

just in time. Now what about this man Quillan told me about? Where did you find him?"

"She didn't find me, I found her," said Dominic from the doorway.

"Oh! You're back," Jessica said weakly. "I know how this must look . . ." Sebastian had gone very still beside her.

"Do you now?"

Dominic had never sounded so menacing, even when he was threatening the healer. If he'd still been a dog, she suspected his hackles would be raised and there'd be a growl in his throat. How was she going to fix this?

Sebastian rose slowly to stand beside the bed, facing Dominic. "So . . . You're the mysterious stranger who's been taking care of my lady, Jessica."

Jessica looked from one man to the other.

"*Your* lady?" Dominic asked. He took a intimidating step closer.

"Wait a minute guys. Why don't we all just sit down and talk about this?"

"I think the time for talking has passed," Dominic growled.

"I agree," Sebastian spat out.

There was nothing Jessica could do but watch, heart in her throat, as the two men took another step closer to each other. In the next moment they'd met and were hugging each other.

"Dominic! Of all the men I'd ever thought to see here, you would be the last."

"Sebastian, my old friend! I would never have believed to find you so close to Ghren."

"You two know each other?" Jessica asked in disgust as they

continued to laugh and pound each other on the back.

"I told you about Dominic," Sebastian said, one arm slung around his friend's neck. "Remember? That's why I was in Ghren, I was looking for clues to figure out where he'd disappeared to."

"You went back to Ghren because of me?" Dominic asked. "I am truly touched, my friend."

"Wait a minute," Jessica was thoroughly confused. "First of all, you never told me your friend's name. And second, you said he was Ewan's older brother."

Dominic looked distinctly uncomfortable as she turned her searching gaze on him. "I was waiting until you were stronger to explain," he said quietly.

Oblivious to the undercurrents, Sebastian proudly announced, "My lady Jessica, I present to you his royal highness, Prince Dominic of Ghren."

Chapter 29

Jessica heaved a sigh. Her energy had run out shortly after hearing the revelation about Dominic's true identity and she'd fallen asleep. Though she'd stirred a couple of times to the sound of male voices talking quietly throughout the night, she didn't awaken enough to hear anything memorable.

Now she was wide awake and they were gone for who knew how long. After bullying her into eating a bowl of oatmeal for breakfast, the two men had taken themselves off to the market to buy her a change of clothing. From what she could gather, it was some kind of competition. As far as she was concerned, it was just another way for them to avoid answering her questions.

From what little she could piece together, Ewan had somehow been responsible for Dominic's disappearance, but she still had no idea why Dominic was back in Ghren nor why he'd been stumbling around in her camp. It was so frustrating!

Now that his father was dead he could be back to claim the throne. But if that was the case, why had he stayed to look after her? He could have just paid someone to do it.

There was a strange flutter in the region of her heart at the idea of him leaving. Every day, it seemed, they learned a little more about each other and somehow she'd envisioned him travelling south with her. But even if he did, she'd have to say goodbye eventually. Maybe it would be better to do it sooner rather than later.

Why did the thought of saying goodbye hurt so much?

Both Sebastian and Dominic were in a good mood as they perused the market in Eglion. Apparently old habits really did die hard - as teenagers they often turned even the simplest tasks into a competition, always trying to out do each other. The fact that this time the competition involved a woman they both cared about brought a smile to Dominic's face.

"What are you grinning about?" Sebastian asked.

"I just never thought to see the day where we'd be competing to impress the same woman."

"Yes, but for very different reasons," Sebastian pointed out. "You aren't seriously going to buy her a dress, are you?"

"What's wrong with a dress?" Dominic asked, bristling. "All women like dresses."

"Have you ever seen Jessica in a dress?"

"A dress wouldn't have been appropriate for the travelling we've done."

"I've seen her in full court regalia," Sebastian said smugly. He'd almost given up hope of ever setting eyes on his friend again. It felt amazing to be able to bait him again.

Dominic struggled with himself for a few moments, then finally broke down and asked, "What did she look like?"

"Absolutely beautiful." He went on to describe in glowing terms her dress, her hair, and even how much of her breasts were showing. Then he described how much she hated the whole thing.

Dominic still wasn't convinced. Every woman he'd ever known loved to dress in finery. But then he'd never met a woman like Jessica before. He had to find the perfect clothing for her.

"Why don't we split up," he suggested, "and meet back here in a candlemark. We'll take our booty to Jessica and let her have the final say."

"I agree," Sebastian said. They shook hands on it and parted company.

They met in the tap room of the Blue Bull, each with a bundle under his arm. Dominic eyed the package Sebastian was carrying. Was it bigger than his? It didn't matter. Jessica was going to love the dress he found for her. The fabric was as soft as down, and the dark blue would bring out the green of her eyes.

"Shall we?" Sebastian asked.

Dominic nodded and followed him up the stairs. He knocked on the door, then threw it open to announce, "Awake, my lady, your swains have returned with treasures untold!"

Stepping into the room, Dominic frowned. "Jessica?"

The bed was mussed, as though she had risen in a hurry. The small table beside it was knocked over and the bowl and pitcher from the wash stand were shattered on the hearth. There was a scorch mark on the wall beside the door.

"What happened here?" he asked.

Sebastian frowned as he took in the damage. "I'll ask Quillan what he knows about this."

He slipped out the door and down the stairs. Dominic took one more look around the room, as though Jessica would somehow magically appear, before following slowly. By the time he reached the tap room, Sebastian and Quillan had Dell backed into a corner.

"They said she was naught but a thief," he whined. "The likes 'o her got no reason ta be in a respectable place like this."

"Who said?" Sebastian demanded, his sword pricking the skin of Dell's throat.

"Them guards who was here."

"What color was their uniform?"

"Black!" Del yelped as the sword pressed a little harder. "They was black with no markings. And big."

Sebastian cursed and let him go. "C'mon," he said, grabbing Dominic by the arm. "We've no time to waste."

"You know who they are?"

"Yes," Sebastian said curtly. They reached the stable and began saddling their horses. "Ewan had special guards imported. They're resistant to magic."

"Ewan's behind this? They're taking her back to Ghren?"

"That's not the worst of it," Sebastian said, mounting his horse. "They'll have witch binding with them - they've used it on her before."

Dominic paled. Witch binding was insidious enough on its own. There was no telling what it would do to Jessica in her weakened state.

"Let's ride," he said grimly.

The witchguards must have shown up just after they left for the market. They'd spent far more time trying to outdo each other buying clothes for Jessica than they realized which meant the guards had a good head start on them. When it became too dark to track them they were forced to stop for the night.

"Have you any idea how many there are?" Sebastian asked. The Dominic he'd grown up with had been an exceptional tracker.

"There's six horses, but one's leaving much lighter impressions than the others so I figure that's the one Jessica's on. That leaves five guards."

"Heavily armed, impervious to magic, well trained guards."

Dominic shot him a look. "Your point?"

"No point," Sebastian said with a shrug. "Just an observation. I also observe that we're quite close to the river."

"And you have an idea?"

"These guards are from the east originally, which makes them unaware the river would be a swifter route to travel."

"So you're suggesting we take to the river . . ."

"We could get ahead of them and take them by surprise. I know this kind of guard, they'd never expect a rescue attempt to come from in front of them."

"It sounds good to me. But mark my words," Dominic said darkly. "This will be no attempt. This will be a rescue."

The night was still and the fire burning low, but Dominic found it hard to sleep. His mind was too full of Jessica and what she must be suffering. The stronger the magic worker, the worse the affect of witch binding on them, and he knew even better than Sebastian just how powerful Jessica was. But she was also still very weak from the back lash sickness, so maybe that lessened the effects. Or maybe it was weakening her to the point of death and if they didn't catch up to them quickly it would be too late.

And just when had he developed such strong feelings for her anyway? He sighed loudly.

"You realize that since we are no longer trying to follow in the footsteps of the witchguard, there is nothing impeding us from continuing on towards the river." Sebastian's voice came out of the dark. "I only mention this because I cannot sleep either."

Dominic sat up. "It will be slow going in the dark, but every step forward is a step closer to finding Jessica."

"My thoughts exactly."

They reached the river as day was breaking and came out close to the village of Falls Reach where they were able to secure passage on a caravel that was headed downriver.

Dominic eyed the small, square-sailed ship dubiously. "Are you sure this thing will get us there?"

"I know this ship, and its captain. It's the fastest on the river." Sebastian glanced over at him and frowned. "Is there a problem?"

"No." At least not one he was willing to share, even if it was with his best friend. Dominic had spent time as a galley slave and ships of any kind still made him uncomfortable. "I just wanted to be sure it's fast enough."

"With both the current and the wind with us, we'll be in Ghren before you know it."

"That's what I was afraid you'd say," Dominic muttered under his breath.

Chapter 30

Sebastian half sat, half leaned against a salt encrusted barrel on the deck of the ship, absently picking out a tune on his lute while keeping an eye on Dominic where he stood at the rail.

A grin slid across his face at the thought of Dominic as a dog. What he wouldn't give to have seen that! Dominic was more than just a friend, he was a brother. Brothers of the soul, that's what Thackery had told them. They'd taken a blood oath to that effect under the light of a full moon, standing within the circle of stones around the Well of Ghren. When he'd heard that Dominic had disappeared and was presumed dead, it was the blood bond that had Sebastian sure that he was still alive.

Now Jessica, she was the sister Sebastian had always wanted. From the first moment he laid eyes on her there was a connection, and not just because she'd seemed so utterly lost. She had a quick mind and a fiery spirit - he couldn't imagine a better pairing than Dominic and Jessica. She would have been totally wasted on someone like Ewan, even if he hadn't been evil incarnate.

There was a time when he thought Ewan had taken everything from him . . .

Some minor nobility Ewan had befriended when he fostered in the East paid a visit and a feast was held in their honor. Dominic had not been required to attend, but Sebastian, being one of the few musicians in the castle, was.

The hour was late and wine and mead had been flowing freely when the talk turned to the eastern custom of castrating young male singers to keep their voices pure. It was Ewan who suggested they do the same to Sebastian, and Randor was just drunk enough to listen to him.

Before Sebastian realized what was happening, he'd been stripped naked and held in place over one of the trestle tables, amid much drunken laughter. The eastern lord had tried to tell Randor that Sebastian was too old for it to make a difference, but Randor, goaded on by Ewan, was beyond listening to reason.

In the days that followed, Dominic had stayed by his side, blaming himself for his brother's actions. When Sebastian had been well enough to travel, his mother had taken him away from Ghren, where he learned to deal with his loss. Until Jessica gave him a greater gift than he could have ever hoped for.

Just before they parted ways at the edge of the Darkwood Forest, she'd asked for a moment to say goodbye. There was a whispered consultation with Howard, via the moonstone pendant, and then she had approached him with a determined glint in her eye.

"Sebastian, you are the only one besides me who knows just how truly evil Ewan is," she'd told him. "And I shudder to think what might have become of me if it hadn't been for you."

"My lady, I—"

She put a hand on his lips. "Not your lady. Your friend. Your friend with all this power seething inside her just begging to be used."

"I don't—"

"No, you don't," she said with a crooked grin. "But I think I might. All I ask is that you trust me and hold still."

One arm went around his neck so her hand could pull his head down for a kiss, the other hand rested on his groin. Before he could pull away he'd felt heat - searing heat where the scar tissue marred him. She swallowed his yell, not letting go of him until the heat began to fade.

What she'd done, regenerating the flesh that had been taken from him . . . He thought he'd come to terms with his loss, but realized at that moment that he'd only been living half a life. It went beyond owing her. They were joined together in spirit from that point on, just as he was joined in spirit to Dominic.

And now she was being taken from them both, back to that demon in human form, Ewan.

"You're thinking too hard my friend," Dominic said, turning from the rail. "I can hear your thoughts all the way over here."

"And what thoughts might those be?" Sebastian asked, glad of the distraction.

Dominic cocked his head to one side. "You're thinking of the past - I can see it in your eyes."

"Good guess."

"You must think me mad," Dominic said, turning to look out over the water again.

Sebastian set his lute aside and joined him at the rail. "Far madder would it be to not follow to rescue Jessica. In fact, to leave anyone in—"

"Not that, you idiot. My feelings for her. And after such a short acquaintance."

"Ah."

After a moment, Dominic turned to look at him. "That's all? Just 'Ah'?"

"What would you have me say? I can understand you thinking I'd think that, but I don't. I think your attraction to our lady makes perfect sense. I'm worried about her as well, and I am not the one in love with her."

"Love?" Dominic's eyes widened and he gave his friend an alarmed look. "Who said anything about love. I—"

Sebastian laughed at him. "If I was not sure of it before, I'm certain of it now. Tell me, did you fall in love with her while you were still in the guise of a dog, or did it happen during the short time you were together after you were human again?"

Dominic's shoulders sagged. "Sometimes it feels as though I have always loved her. You have no idea how frustrating it was for me - she would go careening from one mishap to another and there was nothing I could do to help, or stop her."

"She does seem to stumble across trouble quite easily."

"Stumble across it? She seeks it out and bids it come to her!"

"Clearly she needs looking after," Sebastian said with a sly glance at his friend.

Dominic was too fired up to notice. "Clearly! And she has no sense of self-preservation. A normal witch would have turned a thief into a dog and left him as such. But no, she turns him into a pet, even going so far as to rescue him from the dog fights and then using up her magical energy to heal his wounds."

Apparently he'd been saving up his angst for a while now. Sebastian let him rant.

"And money . . . Did no one think to school her on the value of a coin?"

"No, I—"

"She would have used the booty we found on a dead thief to buy a single meal, if I hadn't been there to set her straight. And what did she do with a king's ransom in jewels? She gave them to a lowly squire so he could buy into a trade. He could have bought a small village with the jewels she gave him."

"You found a dead thief?" Sebastian asked.

"At an abandoned way station," Dominic said grimly.

Sebastian smothered a grin at his indignant tone of voice.

Dominic rounded on him. "How could you have let her go off by herself so ill-equipped?"

Spreading his hands in protest, Sebastian said, "At the time it seem like a good idea. And she had Howard to advise her in magic."

"Howard." Dominic snorted. "The fool leading the foolish. And you know as well as I that most of his magic is borrowed." The irritation left him suddenly. "I cannot believe she is Thackery's daughter."

"It does seem impossible, doesn't it? I did not realize he had any family."

"I did. He mentioned it once, when he was in his cups, that he'd lost both his wife and his daughter, though he hoped one day to be reunited with his daughter."

"And the task falls to us to make it so," Sebastian said.

Jessica was dying. At least this is what she'd always imagined dying would feel like. It hurt everywhere. While she could tell she was lying on some kind of hard surface, she couldn't really tell what it was. And she was so cold she doubted that even the fires of hell could warm her up again.

The witchguard had taken her completely by surprise. She'd been napping, determined to stay awake later to ask some very pointed questions of Sebastian and Dominic when they got back from the market. Suddenly, the door to her room burst open and three burly men dressed in black forced their way in.

She managed to summon up a couple of fire balls to hurl at them, but a searing pain in her head made it hard to see whether she hit them or not. Her legs tangled in her nightgown and the bedding, and she couldn't reach her sword. Then one of them threw a net made of shiny silver cord around her and she'd passed out.

Using her tiny reserve of energy, Jessica cracked one eye open. Her vision was blurry so she tried the other one as well. It took several moments of blinking rapidly before her vision cleared and when it did she wished she could just close them again and slip back into the sweet oblivion of darkness.

The hard surface she was lying on was the ground. In front of her were the dying embers of a fire. In the light of the rising sun she could make out three black clad figures on the other side of the fire - two were drinking out of metal cups while the third appeared to be packing something up.

"She's awake," one of them said.

There was movement to one side and she felt the toe of a boot as she was turned over.

"Sit up," she was told.

It was all she could do to keep her eyes open, sitting up was out of the question. "I can't," she said, voice a mere whisper.

There was an impatient sounding noise and then she was jerked, none too gently, upright, back propped against a tree.

"Drink this."

A cup was thrust into her hands and her fingers curled around it reflexively. Able to see clearly now, Jessica counted two more, making five altogether, of the black clad guards Ewan claimed were impervious to magic.

Her hands were shaking so badly she spilled most of what was in the cup. It was almost disappointing to find that it was just water, not some drug to knock her out again. A dry throat had her drinking it all, but a few moments later she was wishing she hadn't as another problem presented itself.

She had to clear her throat twice before she had enough of a voice to speak. "I need to visit the privy."

The leader glared at her. For a moment she thought he was going to backhand her for speaking, but one of the other guards whispered to him. He glared some more, but then jerked his head at the guard closest to her. He and one of the others pulled her to her feet and half carried/half dragged her into the underbrush, several yards from the camp.

When she held up her hands in a mute appeal to have them unbound, the guard shook his head firmly. She blinked back tears of humiliation as they watched her relieve herself as best she could. When she was done, the other guard grabbed her roughly by the arm and dragged her back to the campsite where the leader threw a dark, homespun robe at her.

Jessica almost fell over as it hit her - only the guard's iron grip on her arm saved her from falling. She grabbed at the material reflexively.

"Put it on," she was told.

She stared dumbly up at the leader, who nodded at the guard holding her. He finally loosened the witch cord binding her wrists. Refusing to be humiliated further, she pulled the robe on over her nightgown. She was glad she had because although the robe was split for riding, the material was itchier than it looked. Ten minutes with that against her skin and she'd be in serious discomfort.

The robe hadn't even had a chance to settle around her when she was hauled towards one of the horses and lifted into the saddle. Her hands were re-tied and then secured to the pommel, while her feet were joined by a cord running under the horse. The hood of the robe was jerked up over her head.

The next few hours passed in a blur as she slipped in and out of consciousness. It was just as well she was tied to the saddle, she couldn't have kept her seat on her own. At one point she roused as they splashed across a body of water, though she couldn't tell if it was a river or a stream. Could it be the same river she and Bandit had crossed what seemed a lifetime ago?

No, it was too soon, unless she'd spent more time unconscious than she realized. Although . . . their side trip into the elven realm *had* taken them out of their way - they'd had to circle back to get to Eglion.

If it was the same river, and she could just loosen her bonds a bit . . . she could make her way to Hannah's inn. She'd bet her last dollar that Hannah could find a way to hide her.

Jessica shifted in her saddle again. Her bonds were just too well tied, and she was too weak. In fact, that was probably why she was tied in place, otherwise they'd be stopping every five minutes to pick her up off the ground.

Tears welled in her eyes. It wasn't fair. She never asked for this, not any of it. Not being zapped into another dimension, not the magic . . . she was sick and weak and she wanted to go home. Her only real crime was a little harmless flirting, and thinking Ewan was a better man than he turned out to be.

God only knew what he had in store for her. And what about Dominic and Sebastian? Did they know she was missing yet? Dominic . . . there was something there, between them. She didn't believe in love at first sight, but there was an undeniable attraction, in spite of the fact he was Ewan's brother.

A tear slipped down her cheek. Now she'd never see him or Sebastian again. There was no way they'd be able to save her this time. With no hope left in her, Jessica let the darkness take her away again.

Chapter 31

It was late in the day when the caravel put in to shore and Dominic and Sebastian disembarked.

"Where are we?" Dominic asked, looking around curiously.

"Tamblin," Sebastian said.

"Are you sure? I remember Tamblin quite well. We used to come here frequently for the entertainment. This place, it is as though all the joy was sucked out of it."

"There's little joy to be had anywhere, this close to Castle Ghren," one of the sailors, overhearing, told them. "That's why this is as close as the ship will go. Another season or two and it probably won't even come this far." He looked furtively around and lowered his voice. "'Tis like a sickness, it is, spreading from the Castle. The closer in you get, the worse it is."

He moved off and Sebastian and Dominic shared a look. Dominic opened his mouth to speak, but then shut it again when Sebastian gave a shake of his head. They gathered up their travel packs and left the docks, passing through the marketplace on their way to an inn.

Though the denizens of the market seemed to be doing brisk business, there was none of the laughing and joking one normally associated with such goings on. In fact, it was almost eerily quiet. People spoke only when necessary, vendors did not cry out with gusto extolling the virtues of their wares. There did not even appear to be any street urchins lurking about ready to scoop up a dropped bit of produce or lift a purse from the unwary.

They found a room in the Grey Swan, an inn of respectable size. Though the tap room was more than half full, there was little laughter and the conversations were subdued and they retired to their room as soon as they finished eating.

"We need a plan," Dominic said. "Have you any idea how we're going to rescue Jessica without an army to back us up?" Sebastian always was the better of the two of them for coming up with plans.

"First we need to figure out where exactly they are. How are your scrying spells these days?"

As a boy, Dominic had been forced to hide his magical aptitude from his father, but his tutor had not been fooled. He'd been delighted when Thackery included lessons in magic along with his regular studies. One of the first spells he was taught was to make fire, just like Jessica. But unlike her, he'd been taught a number of other, simple, spells as well. The one he had always been most proud of was how to scry with a bowl and water.

"Rusty, I'm afraid," he said regretfully.

Sebastian looked around the room and spotted the large bowl atop the wash stand in the corner. "Why don't you give it a try anyway. It doesn't need to be a clear image, just enough that we can make out where they are."

He brought the bowl over to the table and filled it from the jug of water.

"You always did have more faith in my magical prowess than was warranted," Dominic said with a sigh as he positioned himself in front of the bowl.

"And you always had too little," Sebastian said with a grin, standing so he could look over his friend's shoulder.

Dominic took a deep breath, then let it out again. He took another and this time began to chant softly, almost under his breath. His hands gestured above the bowl. The water seemed to shiver, but that was all that happened.

"See? I told you so. If the guards are impervious to magic, they are most likely protected from scrying as well."

"Try again," Sebastian urged. "I'll warrant their mounts are under no such protection - try scrying for them instead."

With a sigh, Dominic did as he was bade. This time he pulled out the gem that had been in his dog's collar. Jessica said it would help her track him, hopefully the reverse was true as well. If nothing else, it helped him focus on what he was trying to do.

This time the water in the bowl churned and boiled. When it cleared again there was an image in the bowl. He kept chanting to keep the image steady.

"They seem to be camped for the night," Sebastian said.

He knew from experience Dominic needed someone else to do the actual viewing. If he broke his concentration for anything the image would vanish, so Sebastian committed as much detail to memory as he could. "Is it possible to give a longer view? I am not quite sure where they are camped."

Sweat beading his brow, Dominic changed the chant slightly.

He'd only tried this once or twice before, and that had been when he was much younger.

The picture in the bowl began expanding, as though seeing through the eyes of a person who was moving away from above. Unfortunately, Dominic could not control it and the image popped like a soap bubble. He slumped in his chair.

"Good work!" Sebastian slapped him in the back, nearly knocking him over.

"Were you able to determine where they were?"

"Yes, and we made better time on the river than I hoped. They're just at the edge of the Darkwood Forest, which puts them two days from Helsenberg."

"And?"

"And they must cross the river at Helsenberg and it is there we can rescue Jessica."

Sebastian went over his plan again as they rode to Helsenberg. It seemed simple enough, and Dominic tried not to dwell on all the things that could go wrong. If things did not happen just so, or if the guards did not react as expected . . .

"There's a way-station a little over half a day's ride from here," Sebastian said. "If the witchguard are pushing it the way I suspect they are, they should reach it just after sunset."

"Then maybe we should go meet them instead," Dominic suggested. "A direct confrontation might be a better course of action. We could take them by surprise and—"

"And Jessica might be hurt or killed. And if we killed all the guards, as you know we'd have to, then Ewan would just send more. No, this is the only way."

Dominic heaved a sighed. "You're right, of course. I just hate all this prevaricating."

"You need to trust me," Sebastian said. "This'll work"

As they wandered the Helsenberg market in search of items that would help with the plan, Sebastian suddenly stopped in his tracks.

"What is it?" Dominic asked, hand on his sword as he looked around them.

"If I'm right, something that will ensure we get away safely," Sebastian told him. "Wait here."

Dominic watched curiously as Sebastian threaded his way through the crowd, stopping when he reached a shaggy haired young boy dressed in brightly colored clothing. The pair carried on an intense conversation involving much hand waving before the boy spit in his hand they shook on whatever agreement had been reached.

"What was that all about?" Dominic asked when Sebastian returned.

"That was about how we're going to get away unnoticed. The boy was a gypsy, from a caravan camped just outside of the town and he's agreed to take a message to their leader. If it's the group I hope it is, then once we have Jessica we can travel with them until we're safely away from here."

Waiting was the hardest part. There was no entertainment - Ewan had put a ban on music of any kind - the inn they found was even quieter than the last one. Fortunately they had an excellent selection of wine, so they retired early to their room to get drunk.

"A pox on Ewan," Sebastian said after they'd finished the first bottle. "And all who follow him."

"A curse upon him for everything he's put Jessica through."

They solemnly drank their toast. Sebastian hesitated a moment and then resolutely brought up another matter that had been plaguing him.

"You do realize her greatest desire is to return to her home?"

"I know," Dominic said, uncorking the second bottle of wine.

"And?"

"And what?" He refilled both their goblets.

Sebastian sighed. "You are both dear to me and I would see neither of you wounded when the time comes to part."

"Why do you believe we must part?"

"But—"

"It's a long journey to the southern lands, many things could change. Jessica could decide to stay, or we could find ourselves incompatible after all. But should our feelings be true and she still wishes to return to her home, I intend on accompanying her."

Sebastian opened his mouth and shut it again, not doubting him for a second. "Should that come to pass I will miss you both greatly," he said.

"What I don't understand is why Ewan is so obsessed with her," Dominic said.

Sebastian hesitated. As a bard he heard many things, people would tell things to a bard they'd tell to no one else - rumors, stories, legends . . . Not all of them were pleasant.

"You've thought of something. What? What is it?"

"A story . . . more a rumor of a belief really by the people in one of the eastern lands."

"Sebastian . . ."

"There are people who believe that the elves hold the secrets of all things magical. And that there is a ritual whereby elven blood can be used to grant magical abilities to a non-magical person."

Dominic looked at him, appalled. "He was always jealous of the fact I could work magic and he could not. Thackery once offered to test him for magical ability, even though he was positive he had none, but Ewan's mother would have none of it."

"It might explain why he's willing to go to such lengths to capture her."

"It would be much diluted elven blood . . . And how would he even have made the connection?"

"Her elven blood may have nothing to do with it. Perhaps he wishes to attempt the ritual because of her power. He said he knows a priest who is able to drain a witch's power. What if instead of just draining it, he wants to steal it?"

"Then we must hope this plan of yours works."

"Then let us away. I hear the church bell tolling midnight. Time to collect the last item we're in need of for our plan to work."

Dominic grimaced and got to his feet. "I think this is the part of your plan I like the least."

Two figures, anonymous in their dark cloaks, made their way swiftly from the inn to the church yard. Despite the curfew, they were not the only ones abroad this night, although they all took great pains to avoid each other.

Once in the church yard, the two figures were joined by a third and the click of coins being exchanged was heard. They were led to an open grave and then the third figure vanished again.

One of the figures hissed in displeasure. "You'd think for the amount we paid he could have cleaned her up."

"Keep your voice down!" the second figure demanded. "And what difference will it make once she's been in the river for a few hours?"

"Fine. Just jump on down and hand her up to me."

"This was your idea, you jump down there."

Muttering under his breath, the first figure did as he was bade. Taking hold of the body in the grave, he heaved it upwards to his companion. The second man grunted under the weight, but pulled the body upwards. Quickly he wrapped it in a dark blanket. When the first man joined him again he slung the bundle over his shoulder and they headed towards the river.

Sebastian was playing his flute, waiting on the bridge as the witchguard entered the town with their prisoner. They were forced to ride in pairs, the bridge being only as wide as a cart. There were five of them - one in the lead, then two in front and two behind Jessica. Either they were sloppy or confident she was too weak to attempt an escape because although her hands were bound she did not appear to be bound to the horse. Perfect!

Finishing his song, he smiled and nodded at the few coins that were tossed in his hat. Putting away the flute, he pulled out a pipe and put it to his lips instead. The first note was more a puff of displaced air, but before he could try again, chaos broke out.

Pedestrians screamed and scattered as the horse Jessica was on reared and plunged, careening into the side of the bridge and sending her toppling into the water. The witchguards had to fight to get their mounts under control before they could search for their prisoner, yelling and striking out at anyone in their way. One of them gave a shout, pointing to a body floating face down in the slow moving river. They fought their way through the remaining traffic on the bridge, as near to the bank as they were able.

One of them attempted to ride his horse into the water but the bank was too high. In any case, the body had already floated out of reach, spinning lazily in the current. The leader shouted and the group began following in its wake, trying to find a place they could enter the water.

After a few minutes there was a piercing whistle and anyone paying attention to such things would have seen a man helping a woman in a green cloak who had obviously slipped into the river during the commotion on the bridge.

Dominic had been waiting under the bridge and as soon as Jessica hit the water he'd been there to unwind the witch binding from her wrists and pull the nondescript brown robe from her, transferring both to the corpse he and Sebastian had obtained during the night.

Jessica had been too weak from the witch binding and dazed from her fall into the cold water to protest, though her eyes had widened when she saw what he was doing. By the time he released the corpse back into the current, she was shivering from the cold. The green cloak was a welcome weight around her shoulders, despite the fact it was mostly wet.

"Bandit?" she asked, voice a mere thread.

"We'll talk when you're safe," he promised

With the witch binding gone, some of her strength began to return. But she was not quite able to believe she was free as he half lead, half carried her away from the bridge. They didn't have far to go to where he had a horse waiting. Lifting her up into the saddle, he mounted behind her and kept the horse to an unhurried walk out of town.

Chapter 32

Jessica must have dozed off because when her eyes opened again they were in some kind of camp surrounded by brightly painted wagons. A group of laughing women, dressed in vivid colors, surrounded them.

"They're going to look after you for a bit," Dominic told her. "I'll be with you as soon as you're settled."

"But—" She was given no chance to protest. He dismounted, taking her with him, and then passed her over to the women who half dragged, half carried her over to a tent set up beside the wagons. Jessica was still too dazed to properly object. All she could do was trust that Bandit, Dominic, knew what he was doing.

The women chattered a mile a minute, as though this was some great adventure rather than life and death, and Jessica had a hard time understanding what they were saying. They sat her in a chair and a crone-like figure the others seemed to defer to gave her a wooden mug filled with a fragrant, steaming tea.

Whatever was in the cup had amazing curative properties to

it. Jessica vowed to make sure she didn't leave this place, whatever this place was, without the recipe. The women took her cloak from her, hanging it over the back of a chair off to the side, then leaned her back over a table to wash her hair. At least that's what she thought they were doing until she caught sight of the dark dye on the hands of the woman who gave her an incredible scalp massage.

When they were done with her hair they dressed her in the same kind of outfit they were wearing - a many-tiered skirt in red, orange and yellow, short sleeved blouse of bright red, and a brown leather vest that laced up tightly, keeping everything in place. When they were done, they led her, amid much laughter, to a wagon painted red and trimmed in yellow.

Inside it was rather homey, with chairs and a table on one side and a padded bench that was long enough for a person to recline on along the other. At the very back was a curtained alcove with a larger bed.

Jessica lay down, just for a moment to test its softness, and before she knew it, she was asleep.

A while later, when he was done talking with Nicolai, the gypsy leader, Dominic found her lying on the bed with her eyes closed. For a moment he just stood in the doorway looking at her, reassuring himself that she was really there. As though she could sense his presence, her eyelids fluttered, then opened.

He grinned. "Fetching as you look with a gypsy's black tresses, it's a bit unfair to those who don't know you."

"How so?" she asked, sitting up.

"The red hair gave fair warning of your temper."

As she stared at him open-mouthed, he sat down beside her. "How are you feeling?"

"All things considered, surprisingly good. They gave me some kind of tea that's even better than one of Sebastian's remedies. Speaking of Sebastian, am I safe in assuming he's around here somewhere too?"

"Of course. He'll be here soon. Now," he peered closely at her. "How are you really feeling?"

"I—" Tears welled up in her eyes. "I—" The tears spilled over and suddenly she was crying in his arms. "I thought I was going to die." Her voice was muffled against his chest. "And part of the time I wished I could."

Dominic held her tightly, unashamed of the tears pricking at the corners of his own eyes. He rocked her back and forth like he would a child, letting her cry herself out. Even after she was done he kept holding her, just because it felt so good to be able to offer her comfort.

When he'd been a dog he'd longed to be able to hold her, especially when she was sad. And when she was ill he'd fantasized about the day he could hold her in his arms. He knew it was insane to believe she felt the same way about him, but he was a patient man. He could wait until she came around to his way of thinking. And he had no doubt whatsoever she would. Eventually.

She sniffled and he reached into his pocket, pulling out a handkerchief. He glanced down as she gave a strangled laugh before taking it - the handkerchief was a bright purple with narrow green stripes - and he had to grin as well.

"Where are we?" Jessica asked, getting a hold on her emotions.

"We're in a camp of Valarian gypsies," he told her, finally loosening his grip. "We—"

Someone pounded on the door of the wagon. The door opened and Sebastian climbed in looking particularly pleased with himself. "I haven't had this much fun in ages," he announced. "Not since . . . not since we broke you out of the dungeon at the castle."

"Sebastian," she said as he came over and gave her a hug. She looked from one to the other. "How did you two find me? What's going on? Are we safe from the witchguard?"

"Yes, we're safe," he said, knowing which question she'd want answered first. "At least for now. The guard thinks you drowned."

"Drowned? But—"

"I think we'd better start from the beginning," Dominic said. "But first, Granny Warrick tasked me with making sure you took another dose of the medicine she made up." He pulled a vial out of his pocket.

"I'll fetch some tea to put it in," Sebastian announced, and was out the door again before either of them could say anything.

"What's in this?" Jessica asked, taking the vial and giving it a sniff. It didn't smell like much of anything.

Dominic shrugged. "Damned if I know. You're the expert in herb craft. All I know is you're to take half in a cup of tea once you were awake, and the other half in a cup in the morning."

"Hmm." She sniffed it again. "I wonder why I can't just drink it straight from the bottle?"

"Probably to make sure you take in enough fluids," Sebastian said, coming back in with a clay mug. At their surprise he was back so quickly he added, "There's always a kettle of tea brewing over the communal fire, it was just a matter of dipping up a cup."

He passed the mug to Jessica and then turned to one of the cupboards.

"What are you looking for?" Dominic asked, taking the vial back from Jessica and tipping half of the contents into the mug.

"Did you not hear me say the tea has been brewing over the communal fire? It'll be strong enough to blister paint. I'm looking for something sweet to put in it. Ah, here we are." He pulled out a small jar of honey and added a generous dollop to the mug.

Jessica smiled as Dominic found a spoon and gave a stir. He tried not to chuckle at the face she made as she took a sip of the tea. Even with the honey it would strong.

"Okay, enough is enough. Spill!" She looked from one to the other. "Tell me how you guys found me and got me away from the witchguard."

"It was Sebastian's plan," Dominic said, suddenly unsure of himself.

"I don't deserve all the credit," Sebastian said. "It was more of a joint effort. But it happened thusly . . ." And he launched into a recitation of everything that happened from the time they returned to the inn to find Jessica gone, to the day's events that led them here.

"So you counted on the witchguard having to cross the river in Helsenberg," Jessica said. "What if you'd been wrong?"

"Then we would have had to come up with a new plan," Sebastian said promptly.

"So . . . How did we end up in a gypsy camp?"

Sebastian grinned. "I was travelling through the eastern province of Chestley . . ." he began, and then launched into the tale of how he helped drive off a band of ruffians who were after a lone traveler, not caring that the man was a gypsy and not knowing he was a gypsy prince. "They're a roving people, the gypsies are, but I never expected to find them this far north. And for Nicolai himself to be here."

"So this is the same Nicolai you saved?"

"Actually, it's his son. But the life debt the original Nicolai owed me was passed down by the entire tribe, and this Nicolai was more than happy to have a part in settling it. An honorable people, these gypsies, and they dislike owing a debt."

"The hour is growing late," Dominic put in. For some reason he didn't care to examine too closely, he was suddenly feeling a little overwhelmed with emotion. He needed to get out of the wagon before he said something foolish. "Why don't I see if I can scare us up something to eat and then we can all get some rest?"

"He was almost beside himself with worry when we went back to the inn and you were gone," Sebastian said quietly, as the door shut behind him.

It had been on the tip of Jessica's tongue to call Dominic back and send Sebastian instead, but the bard's words caught her attention."Really?" There was a perverse part of her that couldn't help being pleased by this.

"I know you don't really know each other well, but after all the time you two spent together . . ." He shrugged. "Even if he was a dog for most of it there are still bound to be . . . ties."

"Oh." Jessica looked away from his probing stare. Ties indeed. But ties of a loyal dog to its master or those of a man towards a woman?. "What?" she asked irritably when she glanced back at him and caught sight of the grin on his face.

"Nothing," he said cheerfully. "Nothing at all."

Chapter 33

The next morning the Gypsies broke camp, and if there was an extra wagon at the end of the caravan, no one realized it but them.

"Are you mad?" Dominic demanded. "You do realize we're travelling further towards the heart of Ghren, don't you?"

"I do."

"Then I ask again, are you mad? We should be taking Jessica as far away from Ghren as we can, not deeper into it!"

"First of all," Sebastian said calmly. "The caravan was headed in this direction when we joined it. To change course now would raise suspicion. And second," his voice rose as Dominic began to protest. "Look at her. Would you suspect her of being the sword-wielding witch you first met?"

Dominic snapped his mouth shut and turned to look. They were stopped for the night and Jessica was with the other women near the central fire. She was dressed in a full skirt of dark red, her blouse a vivid yellow under the brown leather vest. On her head was a scarf of matching red that set off her black hair.

Bangles and chains adorned her wrists and gold coins winked and twinkled in the fringe of the white scarf around her hips. The gypsies were teaching her to dance.

He stared at her in admiration for several moments and then grudgingly admitted, "No, she does not look like herself."

"And where better to hide than right under Ewan's nose?" Sebastian pressed his advantage home.

He, too, was sporting a dye job, although his hair was a nondescript brown, and he had a large, heavy gold ring hanging from one ear. The clothes he wore had been given freely, all the men of the tribe wanting to contribute to the fulfillment of the debt. His lute had been traded for a fiddle, which he used to entertain them in the evening, much to the delight of everyone.

"It's just . . . I just . . . ."

"You want to keep her safe," Sebastian finished for him. "I understand that, my friend. And I applaud the sentiment, but until we get her to her father there is no place that's entirely safe for her."

"She needs to go back to her own world," Dominic said reluctantly.

"Do you really think so? Do you think she'd be any safer there? From what I hear her world is fraught with just as much danger, if not more."

Dominic turned to him in surprise. "And just who have you been talking to that you know of her world." To his surprise, Sebastian's face reddened as he answered.

"I may have had an opportunity or two to speak with her friend Howard," he admitted. "But that was before Jessica and I parted ways at the edge of the Darkwood Forest." There was a grin on his friend's face that had Sebastian scowling. "I hardly know the man. Plus he's in another world."

"Howard's an interesting person, isn't he?"

"That he is," Sebastian said with a sigh.

Jessica was having a blast, learning to dance like a gypsy. She was feeling rather gypsy-ish too with her dyed black hair and bright clothing. She'd always loved folk-dancing and had once tried to talk Ellen into take a class with her at the local high school. Ellen proved to be not as enthusiastic as she was about it and in the end she'd taken the class by herself. It was all coming back to her now though.

She'd been summoned for a chat with Granny Warrick, who apparently was really a granny although the title was also an honorific one, who cautioned her to allow herself time to recover physically before she tried to recover magically. Jessica could see the sense in that and agreed readily.

Then Granny eyed her sharply and said, "But do not think to suppress your magical nature. It cannot be done and great harm would befall if you try."

Jessica had given a guilty start. "I never asked for all this magic," she said. "All it seems to do is cause trouble wherever I go."

"There will come a day when you will embrace the magic within. And it will be a good day for all. I do not say this will be an easy thing, but it will be a necessary one."

"Is this a prediction?"

Granny shrugged. "It is more just common sense. Here," she passed her a heavy copper medallion. "Wear this."

"It looks old," she said, taking it from her. "What is it?"

"I could tell you it is merely a magical trinket, but that would be a lie. It is a powerful amulet, passed into the keeping of my family for one who would be of need of it."

"Oh, I couldn't." Jessica tried to hand it back but Granny refused to take it.

"We have only been safeguarding it, it was never meant for one of us. It was meant for the one who was to come, someone of great power."

"You mean like me?"

"No, I mean you specifically. I knew it the moment I saw you."

"I don't understand. What is it for?"

"It will hide your power. While you wear it the strength of your power will be masked."

Jessica looked at her in surprise. "You mean it'll be like I'm just an ordinary person?"

"It cannot hide your true nature, but you will seem no more than just a minor magic-worker."

She put the chain around her neck. The medallion hung just below the stone Aracelia had given her. "But what if I need to work some kind of a magic spell?"

Granny grinned a gap-toothed grin at her. "That is the beauty of this amulet. It will not impede your use of magic in the least."

"How can I ever thank you?" Jessica asked. This was one of the most wonderful, unexpected gifts she'd ever received.

"You can thank me by being true to yourself in all things," Granny told her. And then she'd shooed her out of her tent to go join the other women at the fire.

Several days later they made camp in a grove of trees near Mavington, which was one town closer to Ghren than Tamblin. This was their last stop before turning to the west along the trade route towards the mountains. Normally they would have made their camp closer to Mavington, but Nicolai chose this secondary campsite for two reasons.

First, the closer they got to Ghren the worse the conditions of the people living here became. There was little trade to be had - it was feared the gypsies were next to be under the scrutiny of the king. Second, and most importantly, his wife had gone into labor and would not be able to wait until the next campsite.

They circled the wagons and while the men set up the bachelor's tent, Jessica went to see if she could help with the birth. It wasn't that she knew much about delivering babies, but her healing gift might come in handy and she said as much to Granny Warrick.

Granny looked at her worriedly. "She's losing too much blood."

"Have you any healers?"

"Yes, but I fear this is beyond them." She looked back towards the exhausted woman. "If we cannot stop the bleeding and speed up the delivery, I fear we will lose them both."

"One of my gifts is healing," Jessica told her without hesitation. "If I can be of any help . . ."

"Please!" one of the two healers kneeling by the straining woman's head said. "Our gift is small. Between us we can save either the mother or the babe, but not both."

The other women in the wagon moved aside to make room and Jessica joined the other healers. "I've never done anything like this before," she admitted. "You'll have to tell me what to do."

"If you could add your strength to ours, it may be enough," the second healer suggested.

Jessica stood as near to the head of the bed as she could. Reaching out to either side, she put a hand on the shoulders of the two healers. Closing her eyes, she turned her focus inwards to the multi-colored strand of magic. The healing green was thicker than it had been and she was able to divide it into two, sending a steady stream towards each of the healers.

She didn't attempt to do any healing herself with the woman in labor, it seem like too delicate a job for her to be mucking about with, so she concentrated on feeding healing energy to the two healers instead. There were gasps and mutterings around her, she assumed the energy was manifesting itself in the physical world, and before long there was the sound of a baby crying loudly. Still Jessica fed energy into the healers, so they could take care of the mother.

"Enough," Granny Warrick told her, bravely reaching out to touch her arm. It was a dangerous thing to interrupt a healing.

Jessica came back to herself with a start. "I'm sorry," she said. "Was it enough? Do you need more?" Unlike the other times she'd used her healing magic, this time she felt no fatigue at all.

"No!" both healers answered at once, one of them held up her hands as though to ward her off.

She looked at Granny Warrick in surprise. "I don't get it. Did I do something wrong?"

"No, my dear," Granny said with a chuckle. "But you're far more powerful than you realize. Your gift almost overwhelmed those poor women."

"Oh. I'm sorry."

"No need to be, look."

Jessica looked at the smiling mother holding her newborn son and felt a tug at her heart strings. "What are you going to name him?" she asked.

"Why Nicolai, of course."

She grinned. "Nicolai the third?"

"No," Granny told her, heading for the door. "The seventh." She opened the door and became the focus of every soul in camp. "It's a boy!" she called out.

The entire camp erupted into cheers.

Chapter 34

Later that evening there was a celebration throughout the camp. Jessica sat on a log between Sebastian and Dominic, passing a wine skin back and forth. They were part of the large circle around the fire, watching the dancers that were part of the festivities. Sebastian was taking a break from his turn playing.

"So let me get this straight," she said. "You're telling me that the firstborn son of each generation of his family is called Nicolai? Isn't that kind of confusing?"

Sebastian shrugged. "Not to them. And when each Nicolai reaches maturity, he leaves the caravan and starts one of his own."

She thought about that for a moment. "So what happens to the old Nicolai?"

"He continues as leader until he grows old and dies."

"But what happens to all the people he was leading? Do they just continue on without him? Or get absorbed into the newer Nicolai's band? Or does someone change their name to Nicolai and take over?"

"Here," Dominic passed her the wine skin. "Have another drink. Too much thinking is bad for the celebration."

Having already consumed her fair share, she considered this and then nodded wisely. "You're right. Thinking is overrated anyway." She took a healthy pull.

"Hey!" Sebastian grabbed it away from her. "Save some for me."

She giggled, leaning away from him and into Dominic.

The music changed and Jessica jumped to her feet. "It's a S'veska! I know this one!"

Dominic forgot all about the wine skin as he watched her dance. He wondered if somewhere in her lineage there was gypsy blood. Or maybe it was the elf in her.

"She's pretty good, isn't she?"

He made some non-committal noise, refusing to be distracted.

"You know the gypsies have a saying about people in your situation," Sebastian told him.

"Hmm? What?" He spared a glance for his friend. "What saying?"

"I don't know. They have a saying for everything so I'm pretty sure they have one for your situation."

"What situation would that be?"

"Your feelings for the fair Jessica." He leaned over to speak in a conspiratorial whisper. "You've got it bad, my friend."

Dominic made no reply, just went back to watching Jessica dance. Sebastian sat back with a smug expression on his face.

When the dance ended, the music changed again and Sebastian pulled Dominic up with him as the women left the dance ground and the men took their place. Dominic had had just enough to drink to go along with it. There was something in the air tonight that fired up his blood. He didn't want to stop to examine the feeling too closely, like he said to Jessica earlier, this wasn't a night for too much thinking.

Jessica couldn't seem to tear her eyes away from Dominic. He must have gypsy blood in him somewhere, he looked right at home in the ring of men dancing around the fire. She sighed. He was so beautiful . . .

The last few days had been very frustrating for her. The first couple of nights after her rescue, Dominic had stayed in the wagon with her. Twice she'd awakened from a nightmare and he'd been there, his presence a solid comfort. But since Granny Warrick declared her fully recovered, he'd been spending his nights in the bachelor tent with the other unattached males.

It wasn't as though she had any virtue for him to protect, she thought irritably. And from the stories Sebastian had told her, she didn't believe him to be puritanical either. So maybe it was just her. Maybe he just wasn't attracted to her like she was to him.

But no, that didn't make sense either. She'd seen the way he looked at her when he didn't think she was looking. There was something there, she was sure of it. She just needed to get him alone. She sighed deeply.

"You do not enjoy the dancing?" Granny Warrick, who was sitting beside her, asked.

"No, the dancing is great. I was just wondering . . ." Her eyes focused on Dominic again, his smiling face and graceful moves.

"Yes?" Granny asked with a grin. It hadn't escaped her, where Jessica's attention lay.

"I was just wondering if there were any dances for both men *and* women," she asked with studied casualness.

Granny laughed outright and as the music came to an end called out, "The Rope Dance!"

There was a cheer from many of the unmarried women.

"The Rope Dance?" Jessica asked a little uncertainly.

"Take this," Granny handed her a long green rope, "and just do as the others do. Trust me."

Dubiously, Jessica took the rope and joined the other women who arranged themselves in a loose circle with their backs to the fire. Each of them held a colorful length of rope in their hands; they held onto one end and tossed the other onto the ground in front of them. And then they waited.

The music began with a staccato beat. The unattached men formed a larger ring around the women, well back from the rope ends. They raised their arms and stamped in time to the music, moving clockwise around the inner circle. As the music sped up they began to dip and weave, whirling and changing places.

Jessica could see no pattern to their dance; she hoped she wasn't going to be expected to replicate it. All the other instruments save the drums stopped. The drums were struck five times and then the men and women exchanged places, the women keeping a hold of their ropes. Once the women were in the outer circle and the men the inner, the music started up again, the men moving in tight formation around the fire, spinning and circling counter clockwise.

They dipped down and each picked up an end of a rope.

Stamping and raising their arms above their heads, while firmly grasping the ropes, they streamed outwards between the waiting women, then back towards the fire again and stopped. Now it was the women's turn.

Half the women's circle faced to the left, the other half to the right so they were facing each other in pairs. They raised their arms and clasped hands, then let go and traded ropes and places so each was facing a new partner and held a new rope.

Jessica concentrated on following the steps, finally feeling like she was getting the hang of it when the women stopped and twirled in place. Jessica felt a tug at her middle and looked up in surprise to see the rope had wrapped around her waist and the other end was held by a grinning Dominic. The men stamped and bowed with a flourish and then tugged on the ropes they held. The women made a token resistance and then began to turn again until they fetched up against their male counterparts. A cheer went up from the watchers and the music stopped.

"Now what?" Jessica asked breathlessly, face flushed from both the dance and the amount she'd had to drink.

"Now we dance a different dance," Dominic told her with a grin, and led her towards the trailer by the end of the rope.

A surreptitious glance showed the other couples were similarly disappearing into trailers and Jessica laughed in return. She made a mental note to thank Granny for her choice of dances in the morning.

When Jessica awoke the next morning she was alone in the trailer. But there was a huge smile on her face as she stretched and got up. Compact as the bed might be, she and Dominic had certainly proved it was big enough for two. And if he thought he was going to keep her at arm's length for the sake of propriety after last night, he had another thing coming. Dressing quickly, she left the trailer intending to search him out.

The camp looked like a hurricane had struck it. Obviously the celebrating went on long after they retired for the night. But although she could see several women and even a few children cleaning up, there was no trace of the men.

"Where is everyone?" she asked.

The woman closest to her, more girl than woman to Jessica's mind though she'd been part of the Rope Dance the night before, told her, "There's some be down at the river having a bath and doing the washing while the rest of us work here and look after the children. When they're done we'll switch places. There's too many of us to all go at once."

Jessica looked around. "And the men?"

The girl, Mara was her name if she remembered correctly, made a face. "They be hunting."

"Hunting? All of them?"

Mara laughed. "When there's work in the home to be done, you can be sure they'll find a way to get around it. 'Tis ever been the way."

Granny Warrick emerged from the wagon that held the newest Nicolai and his mother.

"A good morrow to you," she called to Jessica. "And did you find the Rope Dance to your liking last night?"

Jessica grinned. "Very much so, thank you. I—"

"Riders!" A young boy came racing into the camp. "There be riders coming!"

"Easy now, Jonah," Granny put out a hand to steady him. "What direction do they come from?"

"The east."

She nodded. East was the road leading to Ghren. "Take the other children and into the woods with you. Make for the river and tell the others to stay put."

The children were amazingly obedient. Obviously they'd been through this before. Everyone under the age of twelve followed Jonah into the woods, the older ones carrying the younger ones.

"I don't understand," Jessica said. "What's going on?"

The other women had stopped what they were doing and milled about in small groups, many of them picking up the nearest cooking utensil to use a weapon.

"It's a sweep," Mara said, face pale.

"There must have been watchers set on us," Granny said. "They waited until the men were all gone. But we'll not make it easy for them. All you maidens, into the wagons with you."

There were a few protests, but most of the younger women returned to their wagons to wait.

"You as well," Granny told Jessica.

"But I can help," Jessica protested. "I can use my magic—"

"No! That's the last thing we need. You'd doom us all if they thought any of us could work magic."

"But—" Surely Granny was exaggerating.

"You cannot use your magic. Promise me!" The old woman was adamant.

"But—" Though she hadn't had much experience in defensive magicks, she could probably at least stall whoever was approaching until the men could be found.

"Promise!"

Granny spoke so fiercely Jessica felt she had no choice. "I promise," she said reluctantly.

"No matter what happens."

"But—"

"Your word!"

Jessica let out an angry breath. "All right! I swear I will not use my magic in your defense no matter what happens."

"Good." Granny nodded briskly. "Now into the wagon with you as well."

She didn't even try to argue, just climbed back inside and slammed the door. This wasn't right. She couldn't just stand idly by while her new friends faced danger. But she'd given her word, and if using her magic really would put them in more danger . . .

The waiting was agonizing, but it couldn't have been as long as it felt before Jessica heard the pounding of hooves. Riders were encircling the camp. Then she could hear voices. The deep baritone of a man giving orders, followed by Granny's raised in protest. There were voices raised in pain and Jessica had to clench her fists to keep from charging out there.

The choice was taken from her. The door to her wagon was jerked open and a fully armored soldier, wearing Ewan's colors, ordered her to get out. When she didn't move fast enough he grabbed her by the arm and jerked her outside, throwing her to the ground.

Jessica couldn't hold back the cry of pain. He was wearing a metal gauntlet and she knew she was going to be bruised where he'd grabbed her. And her landing on the ground had been anything but soft. He kicked at her but she rolled aside just enough so he missed.

"On your feet," he ordered.

She did as she was told, but there was a pleading look in her eyes as she sought out Granny's gaze. Granny shook her head ever so slightly and Jessica had no other choice but to join the others, herded into a group like cattle. Some of the older ones had angry looks on their faces as they tried to comfort the younger ones, who were weeping.

The one who appeared to be in charge, a big bear of a man on the largest horse Jessica had ever seen, just sat and watched as his men searched the wagons, pulling out the protesting women. Even the chief's wagon was searched, and the chief's wife dragged from her bed.

Jessica couldn't stay silent any longer. "Leave her alone! She's just given birth, you bastards!"

She never saw the blow that knocked her unconscious.

When she came to she was back in her wagon. Her face hurt. Mostly her jaw. She must have moaned or made some other noise of distress, because she heard someone stir.

"Jessica? How are you feeling?"

It was Sebastian's voice and she had a sense of deja vu, having him nearby as she awoke from something unpleasant.

"I feel like I've had my face run over by a horse," she said. "What happened this time?"

He helped her sit up. "You don't remember?"

She thought about it for a minute. "I remember waking up alone," she said peevishly. "And then . . . all you guys had gone somewhere - hunting or something, some excuse for getting out of clean up detail. And then . . ." Her memory came flooding back. "We were raided!"

"Not exactly," he told her, his face uncharacteristically grim. "It was one of Ewan's sweeps."

"Sweeps? Sweeps for what?" She asked in confusion. He didn't answer right away and she took a moment to think out loud. "It wasn't just about rousting some gypsies, otherwise why wait until the men were all gone?" She thought back to the way the soldiers were separating the younger women from the older ones. "Holy Saint Christopher!"

She looked at Sebastian, feeling sick to her stomach. "They were there to kidnap women for Ewan, weren't they?"

The look on Sebastian's face was all the answer she needed. "How many?" she choked out.

"Seven, all under the age of twenty. Two of the matrons were killed trying to protect their daughters."

"Damn her!" She pushed to her feet and then had to sit down again when the blood rushed to her head making her face throb.

"Damn who?" Sebastian asked, holding on to her arm to steady her as she tried again.

"Granny Warrick. When the riders were approaching, she made me promise not to try using my magic. I could have saved them!"

"No you couldn't," he said quietly.

"Yes I could!"

"How, exactly would you have stopped them?"

"I could have conjured up a shower of fireballs or spooked their horses, or—or—" She suddenly realized how very little she knew of defensive magic. Howard had just begun to teach her when the moonstone pendant had been lost.

"There were too many of them and there were bowmen in the woods. All you would have done is get yourself killed."

"All right. Fine. But I can't just sit here doing nothing. You and me and Bandit - where is he anyway?"

Despite the seriousness of the situation his lips twitched. "You really have to stop calling him that."

She made a moue of displeasure. "I know, I know. But I've known him as Bandit longer than I've known him as Dominic. Where is he?"

"He and a group of other hotheads have gone off to rescue the girls."

"What?" She jumped to her feet. "We have to go after them! We can help!"

"Sit down!" Sebastian barked.

Jessica sat.

Sebastian sighed and ran his hand through his hair, sitting down on the bench opposite her. "We can't just go charging in without thinking it through first."

"But—"

"I know you're worried about him; I'm worried about him too," he said gently.

That took the wind out of her sails. "Why didn't he wait until I was awake? He knows I could have helped."

"If you could have seen the look on his face . . ." Sebastian shook his head. "He thought they'd killed you."

"So what happened?"

"After Granny reassured him that you were alive, he carried

you in here, told me to watch over you, and then he and a dozen others went charging off. There was no stopping them."

Jessica just stared at him, appalled. So few against Ewan and his whole army. "They can't possibly hope to succeed! They're riding to their deaths, and how is that going to help anyone?"

"They can't hope to win in a frontal assault, 'tis true. But Dominic grew up in the castle and knows all of its secrets, secrets I doubt even Ewan is aware of."

"So you think they can just sneak in there, rescue the girls who were kidnapped, and sneak out again without anyone the wiser? Are they crazy?"

"I'm sure it will not be as simple as that, but 'tis the only chance they'll have."

"Isn't there anything we can do to help?"

"If, as you said, they had waited for you to awaken, we might have come up with a better plan, utilizing your magic. But . . ." He spread his hands wide. "All we can do now is wait."

"This really sucks."

Sebastian nodded in agreement.

Chapter 35

It was fully dark by the time Dominic and the others reached the outer edge of Ghren lands.

When he and Sebastian were boys, they stumbled across a secret passage that went from the kitchen up to a little used linen closet at the top of the castle. Emboldened, they'd searched the ancient castle records but could find no mention of it. Then Sebastian had the bright idea of sneaking into Thackery's workroom to find a spell that could help them find other passages. They were caught, of course but instead of punishing them, Thackery gave them a stone that gave off a glow when they were near what they sought.

"You never know when you might be in need of a secret passage," he'd told them.

They found several other hidden passages, one of which led from the dungeon to an outcropping of rock far outside the castle walls. It was this passage Dominic sought now.

The white hot rage that filled him when he saw Jessica lying there, struck down casually by one of Ewan's soldiers, was starting to abate, but all it meant was that he was in a better frame of mind for planning. He felt not the slightest bit of guilt for leaving her behind, despite knowing she would have wanted to help. Her powers would have been a definite asset but if they were caught . . . he couldn't risk her falling into Ewan's clutches, especially not after everything they'd gone through to get her away from him.

The landscape had changed in the last ten years, but that was to be expected. It took him too many precious minutes to find the rocks sheltering the tunnel entrance. The gypsies with him began muttering about forgetting stealth and making a direct assault on the dungeon when he found it, a large bush having grown up in front of it.

They entered the tunnel and followed it to the dungeon. As Dominic had hoped, it was unguarded. Obviously Ewan had not stumbled across it, but then the only occasion he'd have to visit the dungeons would be to direct the torture of a prisoner, and his lack of imagination would keep him from exploring.

Dominic had an uneasy feeling, being back in Castle Ghren once more, even if it was more beneath it than in the castle proper. The lack of guards didn't unduly worry him, the dungeons of Ghren were famous for their impregnability so unless there was a prisoner of importance being kept down here, any guards would be in the guardroom at the top of the stairs.

The guardroom was empty, however. Apparently Ewan had no guests in his dungeons. But now came the most dangerous part of the rescue. Using his meager ability to scry, Dominic learned the gypsy women were being held in a storage room opposite the guard room, but to get to it they needed to cross an open courtyard.

Luck was with them. There were only a few torches on the outer wall of the courtyard and though the moon was three quarters of the way to fullness, a cold wind had clouds scudding across the sky to hide it. The heavy lock on the door to the storeroom presented no difficulty for someone who'd made his living as a thief, and Dominic had it open in a matter of seconds.

All seven girls were accounted for - apparently Ewan hadn't started the evening's entertainment yet. Aware that could change any second, Dominic directed the gypsies to move as quickly and quietly as possible back the way they came. His uneasy feeling was almost a scream now. Something wasn't right - this had been too easy.

They were almost to the guardroom when a series of torches flared to life above them.

"A noble attempt," Ewan said from high atop the wall. "But you were doomed to failure. My wizard knew you were coming." He gestured towards the robed figure beside him.

They froze in place at the sound of his voice. A few of the girls began to weep quietly. As well as Ewan and his pet wizard, there were more than two dozen guardsmen, some armed with spears, the rest with bows. The bowsmen had arrows nocked in place aiming downwards.

Dominic's heart sank. They'd been so close! But there was still a chance for the others to get away. He only hoped Jessica would forgive him for what he was about to do.

"What's the matter Ewan, lose your touch with the ladies now that you're not momma's little golden boy?" Dominic taunted, using a name from their childhood. "Now you have to kidnap them and tie them down before they'll have you?"

There was just enough torchlight around Ewan to see the way his face pale and his eyes widen. "No, it can't be . . ."

"What, after all these years you've no greeting for your brother?" Dominic stepped out into the center of the courtyard. The moon chose that moment to show its face, bathing him in its light. "Next time you pay someone to kidnap your brother and kill him, make sure they have the stomach for it and don't sell him into slavery instead."

"Did you not think to warn me?" Ewan turned to his pet wizard.

"I saw no reason to, your highness," the man said, hands open in a placating gesture. "I knew he would be captured with the others."

"You knew nothing, you traitor!" Ewan spat out. Before the man could turn away, Ewan drew his sword and ran him through. The body toppled from the wall, landing with a thud.

Dominic glanced over at it. "I know him," he said. It was Braxton, the wizard who'd hired him to steal Jessica's moonstone. He'd thought it was the source of her power. "He owes me money."

"Bring him to me!" Ewan ordered.

"Yes, sire. And the others?"

"The others don't matter, they're nothing. Just bring me that piece of offal."

Dominic made a gesture to the gypsies, who continued on to the guardroom and disappeared inside. Three of the men lingered but he gave a quick shake of his head and they followed silently.

The guards weren't quite sure what to do when they reached

him. On the one hand, their king had given them an order. But on the other hand, he'd called this man his brother and if he truly was the long lost firstborn son of Randor, then they dare not lay their hands on him.

He solved the problem for them by moving forward to meet them, then leading the way to the stairs they had just descended. Two of the guards hurried ahead while the other two trailed behind so they at least gave the appearance of being in charge. Dominic was stopped from going right up to Ewan by two guards who crossed their spears in front of him.

"No embrace for your long lost brother?" Dominic asked flippantly.

Ewan glared at him. "I had not thought to see you alive again."

"Sorry to disappoint."

"No, I do not think you are sorry in the least. But trust me, brother dear, I will make you sorry you were ever born."

"You always were overly dramatic."

Ewan's eyes narrowed. "Take him to the dungeon. Make sure you put him in the witch's cell. And no need to be gentle with him."

If Jessica thought waiting was difficult, she found it nearly impossible when she learned the gypsies were breaking camp at sunrise. Not even Sebastian could stop her from confronting Nicolai.

"What do you think you're doing?" she demanded. "You can't just leave them behind!"

"Is that what you think we're doing?" he asked, unperturbed by her anger.

"Let's see, you've dowsed the fire, you're packing everything up, and you're hitching the horses to the wagons. So yes, that's exactly what it looks like you're doing!"

"If they succeed in their task, how long do you think it will be before the women are missed?"

"I . . . well . . . not long probably," she admitted.

"And where, think you, is the first place they would look for the women?"

"I guess where they kidnapped them from in the first place," she said, some of the wind going out of her sails.

"Do you not think the wisest course of action would be for us to not be here when the sweep guards return?"

"But why the rush?"

"Because the wagons cannot move as quickly as men on horseback. My people know the rendezvous points - they will find us." He looked at her kindly. "I know you worry for them, I do as well. But I must think of all my people, not just the few who are missing."

"The good of the many outweighs the good of the few," Jessica murmured. One of her favorite Star Trek quotes.

Nicolai shrugged and went back to directing the abandonment of the camp.

They took a well travelled trade route away from the area, back towards the Darkwood Forest, spreading out along the way. Every so often a wagon would peel off and follow a route away from the main one, sometimes two wagons together.

"Why aren't we all sticking together?" Jessica asked.

"To better hide our true destination," Sebastian told her. "One or two wagons leaving the road would not be remarked upon. However, should we leave as a group we would create a trail even a child could follow. This way our numbers are lost in the regular traffic."

When it was their turn to leave the main road, Sebastian took a barely discernible path that led southwards. Jessica counted them lucky - most of the wagons didn't even have that much to go by and she had to trust he knew where they were going.

Under other circumstances she would have enjoyed sitting up on the bench seat of the wagon while Sebastian drove the horses. She might have even lobbied to have him teach her the finer points of driving a wagon, but her mind was too filled with Dominic and what might be happening to him. She had a bad feeling in her gut, and since coming to this world she'd learned to trust her gut feelings.

"He'll be fine," Sebastian said, glancing over at her. "He's already proven he's a survivor, otherwise he wouldn't have made it this far, not after ten years. He'll be fine."

"Do you really believe that?"

He looked back at the horses again. "Not really, no."

"I swear if anything happens to him I'm going to resurrect him so I can kill him," Jessica muttered. "Don't look at me like that," she added when Sebastian shot her a glance. "If I could raise an elf who'd been dead for who knows how many years, I can raise Ba—Dominic if I have to."

"Just so you can kill him again?" Sebastian asked in amusement.

"You betcha."

They travelled in companionable silence until they caught up to the rest of the caravan on the road winding its way towards the mountain passes.

"We have—"

Whatever else she was about to say was drowned out by the sound of approaching riders.

"They're back!"

The caravan moved off of the main road and into a copse of trees where they were able to properly greet the rescue party. The girls were reunited with their families amid much joy and laughter, and the men made their report to Nicolai. It wasn't long before Jessica realized someone was missing.

"Where's Dominic?"

She glanced around and then pushed her way to the front of the crowd around Nicolai. "Where's Dominic?" she repeated. Looking from one sober face to another, she began to get a sick feeling in the pit of her stomach. None of the men would meet her eyes. Sebastian came up behind her and laid a gentle hand on her shoulder.

"Dominic was taken by the king's men," Nicolai told them.

The leader of the rescue party squared his shoulders and stepped forward to face them. "He sacrificed himself so that we might escape," he told them.

"And you just let him?" Jessica's voice rose an octave.

"It was not our choice, but his," the man said stiffly.

"We have to go back!" Jessica demanded. "We can't just leave him there!"

"Of course we won't," Sebastian agreed. "But we cannot just fly off willy-nilly. Such a thing will take careful planning, else all will be for naught."

"Just so long as I'm part of it," she said. "I'm not getting left behind this time."

"No!"

They turned at the forceful sound of voice to see Granny Warrick, leaning heavily on her staff. "He will need you here."

"With all due respect," Jessica said, hanging onto her temper by a thread. "I disagree. They're going to need someone who can work magic. If he'd taken me along in the first place he wouldn't have been left behind at all."

"Perhaps, perhaps not. But I know that if you go with the others to seek his release, you will fail. I have *seen* this."

"But I can't just sit around and wait again, I—"

"No!" The old woman pounded her staff against the ground for emphasis. "You will have your day, but it will not be this one. This is the day you must wait. He will need you here," she repeated.

A shiver went up Jessica's spine as she looked at the old woman. There was something other-worldly about her and as much as she hated to admit it, she knew in her bones the woman spoke the truth.

"The king has angered the gods," Granny said, her eyes losing their focus. "He is a blight on the land. But though there are many who suffer at his hands, there is only one who can mete out justice." She swayed and only her grip on her staff kept her from falling.

"You must learn to trust in others," she said, eyes focused on Jessica once more. "I give you my word they will return him to you. But only if you stay here."

Jessica's shoulders sagged. As much as she wanted to go charging to the rescue, how could she if it meant she was endangering Dominic? Patience had never been one of her long suits, but it looked like she was going to have to learn.

Chapter 36

Dominic paced, limped more like it, within the confines of his cell, clanking with every step. There wasn't a spot on him that didn't hurt. The guards were quite thorough in their pummeling. He was pretty sure at least two of his ribs were cracked, if not broken, and if the pain in his kidneys was anything to go by, he'd be pissing blood for a week.

He was weighted down with heavy chains - a metal collar around his neck and cuffs around both wrists and ankles, all joined together by thick links. Under the circumstances, he thought it was overmuch, but it was obvious his brother was taking no chances.

It was to be hoped an opportunity to get away would present itself before Ewan could decide on what torments he was going to inflict. Unfortunately, Ewan appeared to possess a vivid, if not twisted, imagination and he'd barely had time to explore his cell fully before he heard the guards coming for him again.

It was a different set of guards this time, Ewan's personal guards, well paid to be loyal only to him, instead of just the palace guards who might have had a shred of sympathy for him. There were six of them, burly, taciturn fellows. He was grabbed by his chains and hauled out of the cell, almost losing his footing in the process, but he made no protest and put up no resistance. What would be the point?

He was taken to what in the days before Randor had been the torture chamber. It had never been used in Randor's time, at least not to his knowledge, but it looked like Ewan had made good use of it in the short time he'd been king. It was a large, dank room, well lit by torches set in sconces around the perimeter. There were manacles set in the walls, and the smell of blood and urine permeated the air.

His chains were fixed to a heavy block in the center of the room. From the look of it this was Ewan's favorite place to execute prisoners. Blood stained the wood as well as the floor around it. It was ironwood, from the look of it, but nicked and scratched unlike any ironwood he'd ever known. With great difficulty he suppressed a shudder as the thoughts of what forms of execution would cause so much blood and damage paraded through his mind.

There was a large fireplace off to the side, a roaring fire blazing away. Sticking out of the fire were the handles of several implements, two of them rather large sized. He could only guess what they were but he had no doubt whatsoever as to what they'd be used for. Death by torture. At least Jessica and Sebastian would be spared the sight, and Jessica was safe from Ewan, who appeared to be possessed by some kind of madness.

Dominic's only regret as he faced death in the form of his brother, was that he hadn't had enough time with Jessica, that they'd only had that one spectacular night. It would have been easy to envision a lifetime with her - in her world, his world, it wouldn't have mattered just so long as they were together. But if it was not meant to be in this lifetime, he had every confidence there would be another, and this was the thought that kept him stalwart.

Ewan did not keep him waiting long. There was no fanfare as he arrived, but he entered the chamber as though there was and he was not alone. With him were two men - one dressed in priest's robes, the other in dark blue leather trousers and vest with a black shirt underneath that was heavily embroidered in the eastern fashion. Dominic caught a whiff of patchouli from the handkerchief he had pressed to his nose. Witnesses perhaps?

"I can't tell you what pleasure the thought of your demise has given me," Ewan said, circling around to stand in front of him. "There are so many choices! And each more appealing than the last."

"So you've decided to talk me to death?" Dominic asked. Ewan was probably expecting him to beg for his life. But he'd see him in hell before that was ever going to happen. He intended to give his brother as little satisfaction over his death as possible.

"Ah, bravado. I'd have expected nothing less from you. But put your mind at ease, brother dear, I have decided to let you live."

When Dominic looked at him in confusion, Ewan smirked. "Alive, you represent a threat to my throne. But dead, you represent an even bigger threat - you would become a martyr, a symbol to rally those who would attempt to overthrow me."

Dominic wasn't sure what other choice there could be, but

he was pretty sure he wasn't going to like it.

"Do you know what this block is called?" Ewan ran one fastidious finger along the edge. He stayed just out of his brother's reach as though afraid of being attacked, despite the heavy chains weighing Dominic down. "No? It's called the thieves' block. Would you care to venture a guess as to why?"

"Because it keeps getting stolen?" Dominic asked. He wished Ewan would shut up and get on with it - torture him, kill him, just stop talking and do it!

"It's called the thieves' block because this is where thieves are brought to have their hands removed as a warning to others."

Dominic was unable to suppress the shudder that passed over him. There was an unmistakable glint of satisfaction in Ewan's eyes.

"I could torture you to death, it's true, and I would derive much satisfaction in wringing out every last ounce of pain from you, making you beg for release. But once you are dead, there's no more satisfaction to be had out of you."

He leaned closer to Dominic, though still just out of range. "I want you to live, brother dear, but more than that I want your every waking moment to be filled with suffering."

Pacing away again he went over to the fire to check on the instruments he had heating in there. "I recall you once took great pride in working with your hands. Our father was quite proud of you as well, in fact he never let an opportunity pass by where he wouldn't remind me how much of a disappointment I was to him in that regard."

He turned, giving Dominic a hard stare. "It was just one of the many reasons I hated you."

"If it's any consolation, father never seemed to like me much either," Dominic said with far more bravado than he was feeling at that moment.

"But it doesn't matter," Ewan continued, as though Dominic hadn't spoken. "Father's dead now and I'm king."

There was a glint of pure madness in his eyes. "I could just chop off one of your hands, your sword hand perhaps, but you could quite easily learn to fight with the other and we can't have that. But both hands!" He looked positively gleeful. "You'll never become king without hands, whether I live or die. Not only will you never be king, you'll never hold a sword, never hold a woman . . . yes, it's the perfect solution."

Dominic's mouth went dry. "Just kill me and be done with it," he said, the words slipping out before he could stop them.

"Oh, no, brother dear. I want you to live. And every day you live, your suffering will give me great pleasure."

He nodded to the guards who moved forward, taking hold of him. Dominic made no sound but he struggled with all the strength he had left to him. The guards clamped down on his arms, one to each side, while two more forced him to his knees and held him pressed forward to the block so his arms were stretched out in front of him. Another guard positioned himself on the other side of the block, unlocking the cuffs around his wrists but grasping his hands and pulling them tight.

Ewan pulled a glowing ax from the fire and approached his still struggling brother. There was a distressed noise from the priest and Ewan spared him a glance.

"You will witness my brother become unfit to be king, or you will witness your abbey burn to the ground. The choice is yours, priest."

"What you do here is pointless. By cutting off his hands he will die as his life's blood leaves him."

"On the contrary. The removing of a thief's hand is no fitting punishing if he's allowed to bleed to death. I have experience in this. The ax will burn as it cuts, cauterizing the flesh. And Aremin here," he nodded towards the easterner, "is a physician."

His glance went to the other man. "Remember, your daughter's life depends on my brother's. If he dies, she dies. Although her death will not be as easy, once my guards and I are done with her."

"I hear and obey, majesty," the healer said.

"You're completely mad," Dominic said in a strangled voice, chest heaving from his struggle with the guards. "I promise you this, if you let me live I *will* find a way to kill you."

"Oh, I don't think so, brother dear. You'll be too busy trying to survive without your hands," Ewan said with a smirk. "Hold him steady," he told the guards.

He raised the ax high above his head. Dominic clamped his jaws shut, trying to brace himself, but he was unable to stop the scream of agony that escaped as the ax came down on his wrists. The stench of burning flesh filled his nostrils before sweet oblivion claimed him.

Ewan stared down dispassionately at his brother's limp body. "Toss those into the fire," he told the guard who'd been holding on to Dominic's hands to keep them still. With a barely discernible shudder, the guard did as he was told.

Handing the ax to one of the other guards, he said, "There are more irons in the fire if you need them to stop the bleeding," he told the healer. Ignoring the body draped over the block he told the sergeant of the guards, "I want a woman awaiting my pleasure in my chambers. Blond, I think, this time. And tell the cook I'll be wanting dinner waiting for me after I bathe."

"Yes, your highness," the guard said. "What should we do with your bro—the prisoner?"

Ewan glanced back at Dominic's body. "Once he's no longer in danger of dying, toss him out the gate. Let the rest of Ghren see what has become of their hope for freedom."

He sauntered from the room, obviously in high spirits. The healer moved towards the limp form, the priest moving with him to offer assistance. The guards unlocked the remaining chains and then left.

"I never believed in true evil, until now," the healer said, looking over at the priest.

"The devil wears many shapes," the priest replied. "But I think this is one of his worst."

Chapter 37

Nicolai deemed they had travelled far enough for safety's sake and they made camp in the copse of trees where they had stopped. Jessica shut herself up in the wagon while Sebastian and those who were going to accompany him planned out Dominic's rescue. It was determined that a smaller party than the previous one would have a better chance of success.

It was to their credit that every man among them wished to be part of the rescue operation. Sebastian, although he was not as skilled a fighter as the others, was adamant he lead the party. His knowledge of the castle would be invaluable. Unlike the women, Dominic would be heavily guarded and despite the fact the king did not appear to know of the secret passages, this would be no simple task.

As much as it pained Jessica to admit it, there was nothing she could contribute to their plans. Her knowledge of the castle was pretty much limited to her room in the wizard's tower and her cell in the dungeon, neither of which were helpful. She had no knowledge of fighting, other than what little she knew of swordplay and the martial arts she picked up hanging around the dojo her friend Ellen's family owned. And it wasn't as though she could lend them her magic to use, though she would if she could.

Howard could probably figure out how. Hell, with Howard's help they could probably just magic Dominic right out of his cell. She missed Howard. And she missed Ellen. If there was ever a time she needed her friends, this was it. Aracelia had said something about a scrying spell . . . why hadn't she taken advantage of the elf's willingness to help?

Maybe there was an easy scrying spell in those spell books she brought away from Ghren. Of course as far as she knew they were still sitting in her room in the inn the witchguard and kidnapped her from. At least she hoped they were still there. And her horse. She hated to admit it, but she missed that sorry bag of bones.

With a sigh she flopped down on the bed. She could focus on other things as much as she wanted, but it wasn't preventing her thoughts from circling back to Dominic. They were going to rescue him - there was no other option in her mind. But what kind of shape was he going to be in when they did?

Howard took her to Medieval Times, the historically themed dinner theatre, for her birthday one year. It had been great watching the jousting and sword fighting while eating a genuine medieval feast, but the evening had included a tour of a medieval dungeon filled with torture devices. Now all she could think about were those devices and how Ewan could be using them on Dominic.

He could be slowly dislocating all of his joints on the rack, or using the crocodile shears to maim him, or the scold's bridle or the iron maiden. There was no doubt in her mind Dominic was still alive. Ewan would be like a cat with a mouse - he was going to play with his victim before killing him.

There was a rap on the door to the wagon and Sebastian poked his head inside.

"We're getting ready to leave," he told her.

She nodded silently.

"I just thought you should know."

"I wish I was going with you," she said softly.

He sighed. "I know. But Granny's warnings aside, Dominic would never forgive me if you came with us and something happened to you."

"Just make sure you bring him back to me."

"You have my word as a bard on it."

She followed him out and stood silently with the others near the central fire, watching them leave. As the party rode off, the others drifted away to attend to other things, but Jessica stayed where she was, watching until the riders faded from view.

At last she gave herself a shake, and then went back inside the wagon to wait.

It was crazy, she told herself. She didn't believe in love at first sight or soul mates, but those were the things that kept flitting through her mind. It was insane! She barely knew anything about the man, other than the fact that he made a great dog. He took care of her when she was weak and vulnerable; he rescued her from the witchguard. They had one amazing night together - this was not enough to build a relationship on.

With these thoughts spinning through her mind, despite herself she fell asleep.

Jessica had no idea how long she slept but it was a great commotion outside that woke her up. For a moment she didn't know what was going on, but then her memory returned and she hurried outside. One of the lookouts had spotted the approaching riders - the whole camp was turned out by the time the riders reached them.

She scanned the faces anxiously. The men looked grim and it took her a moment to realize that Sebastian was riding double, Dominic slumped over in the saddle in front of him. He was wrapped in a blanket so she wasn't able to tell how much damage was done to him.

Sebastian handed him down to waiting hands.

"Take him to our wagon," Jessica demanded.

"Jessica—" Sebastian started.

"It won't be the first time I've healed him," she said, starting after the men carrying Dominic.

He jumped down out of the saddle and hurried after her, grabbing her by the arm. "Jessica, wait."

She sent a tiny spark of fire into his hand and he jerked it away. "I'm done waiting."

The men laid Dominic on the wider bed at the back of the wagon and after one look at Jessica's face, swiftly filed out again. She approached the bed slowly. Dominic's face was pale beneath the bruises and covered in a fine sheen of sweat. Biting her lip, she gently pulled the blanket away.

Tears clouded her vision so at first she didn't realize what she was seeing. His clothing was dirty and torn, and there were blood stains, but there didn't seem to be any indication of the kind of torture he must have undergone.

A puzzled frown creased her brow as she stared at the dirty rags covering the ends of his arms. She took a step closer. Comprehension dawned.

"Holy Saint Christopher!" She took an involuntary step backwards, bumping into Sebastian who took her gently by the shoulders to steady her.

"It turned out we didn't have to rescue him after all," he said quietly. "We found him like this, just outside the gates to the castle. There was a priest . . . he said . . ." He choked up, cleared his throat, and continued. "He said the king wielded the ax himself."

"No," Jessica whispered, sinking to her knees beside the bed. She laid one arm across Dominic's chest and laid her head on his shoulder, weeping quietly. After a few minutes she sniffled, then raised her head.

"No," she said in a more determined voice. "I'm not going to let that bastard win."

"Jessica—"

"No!"

She swiped a hand across her face, wiping the tears away, then sat up on the bed beside Dominic. Gingerly she took the stubs of his hands in hers. "I'll make you better," she whispered. "I promise."

Reaching deep within herself she sought out the green healing thread of magic and pulled, then sent her consciousness coursing through Dominic's body. There was so much damage! She tried to go straight to the place where his hands should be, but the magic seemed to have a mind of its own. First she repaired the damage to his kidneys, then knitted three of his ribs back together. There was a fracture to one of his legs and a lot of tissue damage. Only when all of this was mended did the magic allow her to work on his wrists.

It was here that she met her match. Infection had set in and it took everything she had left to combat it and seal the nerve endings that would have been causing him incredible pain, had he been awake. Rather than regenerating his hands, the most she was able to do was smooth over the raw stumps. Even that much left her spent.

"No," she moaned, eyes filling with tears once more. Sebastian caught her as she would have slipped to the floor.

"I can't do it," she said, tears streaming down her face as she looked at him. "I'm not strong enough."

"You did what you could," he said in a soothing voice. "It's all anyone can do. The rest will be up to him."

"It's not enough," she said through her tears. She turned in Sebastian's arms and he held her as she cried, leading her over to the bench. He sat down, still holding her, and she cried on his shoulder.

He stroked her back and made soothing noises, all the while watching Dominic's chest rise and fall. Jessica had done what she could, but would Dominic be grateful? He doubted it. To lose a single limb in this world would make life difficult, but to lose both one's hands? It didn't bear thinking of. The kind of life Dominic led depended on him being able to use his hands. It was worse than being blind.

Jessica's tears began to ease and she hiccupped, trying to catch her breath.

"You're exhausted," he told her. "You need to get some rest.

Dominic's not going anywhere and neither am I. I'll watch over you both."

She nodded and reluctantly loosened her hold on him. He got up and turned her slightly, meeting no resistance as he pushed gently until she was lying on the narrow bench. There were dark shadows under her eyes and they fluttered closed. He found a blanket at the foot of the bench and covered her up. She was going to need all the rest she could get. There were hard days ahead for all concerned, and they'd start as soon as Dominic regained consciousness.

Chapter 38

When Jessica awoke, Sebastian had some bread, cheese, and fruit waiting for her. She looked over at Dominic, who was still unconscious, and shook her head. "I can't."

Unmoved, Sebastian held the plate under her nose. "You're not going to do him any good if you make yourself sick by not eating."

"Apparently I'm not any good to him as I am, either," she said bitterly, but she did take the plate.

There was nothing he could say in reply to that, so he didn't even try, just watched carefully as she managed a few bites of her food.

"Should he still be unconscious like that?" she asked. "I don't have any experience with torture victims."

Sebastian shrugged. "He's suffered a great trauma, that alone will take him some time to recover from."

"I healed as much as I could," she said in a small voice.

"I know." He sat down beside her and gave her a careful hug. "Sometimes the healing can be as hard on the one who is being healed as on the healer."

"Every time I just start getting used to this world, something like this happens and I realize how out of place I am here."

Dominic stirred restlessly and they looked over at him, but he didn't awaken.

Jessica finished the bread and cheese in silence, Sebastian stealing a bite or two for appearances. He passed her a wine skin filled with watered wine, a drink she was getting used to.

"I find I have no delicate way of asking this, but I must know. Does this . . . deformity . . . change the way you feel about him?"

"Of course not!" Her eyes were drawn back towards the man on the bed, to the arms that ended in stumps of flesh. Jessica flashed back to those arms holding her, those hands caressing her. Had it only been two nights ago? And now they'd never caress her again.

"Excuse me," she mumbled, pushing past Sebastian and out of the wagon where she promptly lost everything she'd just eaten.

"For a moment there I thought she actually believed her own words," came a whisper from the bed as the door shut.

"I think you need to give her the benefit of the doubt," Sebastian said, not surprised that Dominic was awake. "How are you feeling?"

"All things considered, surprisingly well. She did a healing on me, didn't she?"

"Would you have expected her to do any less?"

"I would have had you both just let me die," he said bitterly.

Sebastian moved over so he was sitting on the edge of the bed. "You almost did, despite her healing. She healed you to exhaustion, and now suffers guilt from not being able to do more. You would throw away such a gift?"

"This is no gift, Sebastian," Dominic retorted. "He took my hands!"

"But he spared your life. You—"

"Life? You call this a life?" He struggled to sit up and Sebastian helped him without conscious thought. "What kind of a life will I have without hands?"

"You can still lead a full life," Sebastian protested. "Jessica—"

"You think Jessica needs to be saddled with a cripple? A freak? I can't even hold a sword to defend her should we be attacked."

"Why don't you let Jessica decide what she needs," she said from the doorway to which she'd just returned.

"I won't have it," Dominic said stubbornly. "I won't let you throw your life away on some useless cripple."

"You're *not* useless," she said, anger overriding concern.

"I know this is going to take some adjustment," Sebastian put in. "But—"

"Adjustment!" Dominic stared at them, dumb-founded. "This is not something that can be adjusted to. My hands are gone. Gone! I can do nothing for myself. I will need a keeper for the rest of my days." He lay back down again. "You should never have tried healing me."

"I wasn't able to regenerate your hands," Jessica told him. "But maybe I could create prosthetic ones for you. I'm not sure what kind of range of motion you'd have with them, but I'm sure I could get them to look normal. I—"

"Get out!" Dominic shouted, ignoring the stricken look on Jessica's face. "Both of you just get out and leave me be!"

Jessica made as if to protest, but Sebastian took her by the arm and gently pulled her away. Her eyes were swimming in tears.

"I'll be back later to check on you," he said quietly. "Maybe you'll feel up to eating something."

His words were met with a stony silence. Tugging Jessica in his wake, he left the wagon. Only when they were outside did he realize they'd drawn a small crowd.

"Well, he's awake," he said, with false cheerfulness.

Jessica pulled away from his grasp and headed down towards the river. Sebastian braced himself for questions he didn't have the answers to as the gypsies surrounded him.

Jessica swiped the tears as she went, needing to get away from the well-meaning gypsies and just be alone with her thoughts. Her path ended at the river - this one was just a narrow band of slowly moving water - and she followed along the edge to a spill of large rocks shaded by several tall, leafy trees. The perfect spot for thinking.

It would be different if they were in her world. People adjusted to all kinds of disabilities back home, but they had doctors, hospitals, and support groups. Here there was . . . her and Sebastian. Even if she wasn't experiencing the first stirrings of romance with Dominic, there was no way she was going to abandon him. And she knew Sebastian wasn't about to either.

The thing was, Dominic came from a long line of kings, and she doubted his pride would allow him to ever be content with such an arrangement. But what if she was able to take him back to her world with her? They could take him to the wizards in the south, whether he wanted to go or not, and she could get him the medical attention he needed in order to cope with his loss.

Hands or no hands, would he actually be able to live in her world? She tried to picture him in her tiny apartment, or hanging out at the mall . . . and failed miserably. He just had too much presence. He'd be a man out of time and place.

Just for practice, she tried conjuring up a fire ball, frowning when it sputtered and died before it was fully formed. Closing her eyes, she reached inside for the magic. It was still there, but she had to delve deeply for it.

Obviously she needed to recharge her magical batteries, and then try healing Dominic again. Or better yet, tap into a Well and draw a continuous feed from it, like the spell that created the army of illusions that kept everyone out of Ghren.

She dismissed the niggling little voice in her head that tried to remind her that Aracelia had warned her it was dangerous to use too much magic too often. Something about a cost in personal strength. She felt fine, stronger than she'd ever been. And if it took her a day or two to recover, so what?

There was new purpose in her stride as she headed back to the camp. Surely someone knew where the closest Well was.

She arrived just as Sebastian was carrying a tray towards the wagon, which lightened her mood considerably.

"He's ready to eat something? That's great! Here," she tried to take the tray from him. "Let me help."

He swung the tray out of her reach. "I don't think that's a good idea . . ."

She tried again. "Are you kidding? After the amount of time he spent looking after me, it's the least I can do."

"Jessica stop!" Wide-eyed, she let her hands drop to her side and stared at him. "Look, I'm sorry Jessica, but you can't help."

"Why not?"

"Because he said so."

"What do you mean?" Her bewilderment turned to a stricken look. "He said he doesn't want me?" she asked in a small voice.

He sighed gustily. "I'm sure that's not what he meant. He just doesn't want you around when he's eating. Think about it," he urged. "He's not a man used to feeling helpless, and having to be fed is just going to reinforce those feelings. The last thing he's going to want is to look weak and helpless in front of you."

"I suppose you're right," she said, only slightly mollified. "It's just . . ." she looked towards the door of the wagon and her shoulders slumped in defeat. "Tell him I'll be by later."

"I'll make sure he knows."

She watched as he turned and entered the wagon, staring at the closed door. Giving herself a shake she turned around and headed towards Granny's wagon. It didn't matter, she was still going to try and restore Dominic's hands.

Full of resolve, she rapped sharply on the door of Granny's wagon. It opened and a dark haired, dark eyed boy answered.

"I'd like to . . . I'm here to . . ." She let out a breath and tried again. "I need to speak with Granny, please."

Without a word the boy opened the door wide, inviting her in. Granny was sitting in a comfortable looking wooden chair, a colorful blanket spread across her lap.

"I've been expecting you," she said gravely.

"You said I could help him!" To Jessica's embarrassment, she burst into tears.

Granny opened her arms and Jessica sank down to the floor beside her, burying her face in her lap. The old woman put her arms around her, stroking her hair as she cried herself out.

"There now, do you feel better?" she asked when Jessica was done.

"Not really," Jessica said, sniffling. "You said he needed me here. That's why I didn't help rescue him."

"Did you not heal him of his hurts?" Granny asked.

"It wasn't enough!" she burst out.

Granny eyed her for a moment, then gestured to the boy. "Have you met my grandson Davron? Davron, be so good as to fetch us a cup of tea."

The boy ducked his head in acknowledgment and left the wagon. Jessica bit back an angry retort about not needing any damn tea, but it took a great deal of effort.

"You are young in the use of magic, yet so powerful." She looked at Jessica shrewdly. "You think to restore his hands to him."

Jessica raised her chin. "Yes."

"There is not one in a thousand with the healing gift who would be able to do so."

"I have to try," she said, spreading her hands wide.

"Yes, I see that."

Davron returned carrying a tray with two cups of tea on it. He set the tray on the table beside Granny, then handed her one cup and Jessica the other. It was on the tip of Jessica's tongue to refuse, but for some reason she didn't.

"What I need—"

"No." Granny held up a hand. "First we drink the tea."

Chaffing at the delay, she took a sip of the tea. It was hot and strong and it had leaves floating in it. She held back a grimace. It was a little on the bitter side as well. But it had a strangely soothing effect and warmed her up. She hadn't even realized she was feeling chilled.

When she was down to the dregs she was feeling calmer, and even managed a smile at Davron when he took her cup from her. But instead of getting rid of it, he gave it to Granny who swirled it around in a clockwise motion and then quickly slammed it upside down on the tray. Jessica jumped.

Granny picked up the cup again and peered inside. Jessica felt her mouth hanging open and quickly shut it again.

"What do you see?" she said in a hushed voice after a few minutes ticked by and Granny kept staring into the cup.

"What you wish to do is dangerous," Granny said at last. "Both for you and for him."

Jessica bit her lip. "I kinda figured it might be dangerous for me, but how so for Dominic?"

"If you are unable to finish what you start his life may be forfeit."

"Isn't there any way to make sure that doesn't happen?"

"Yes. You could sacrifice your life instead."

Jessica sat back. This was crazy. Could she really give up her own life to save Dominic's hands? She thought about the way he'd taken care of her, of how full of life he seemed. She pictured him dancing with the gypsies, and what happened afterwards.

"But there's a chance I might succeed, right?"

Granny shrugged. "Of course. I only warn you of the dangers involved."

"What happens if I don't try?"

"I do not need the leaves to tell me that. Nor, I think, do you."

No, she had a pretty good idea what would happen.

"Well then," Jessica said with a false cheerfulness. "The only thing left is to point me to the nearest Well."

Chapter 39

"I do not believe there are any Wells nearby," Granny told her.

Jessica jumped to her feet. "Then this whole conversation has been pointless! Without a Well I can't stock up on power, and without power I—"

"Sit!" Granny ordered.

Jessica's mouth snapped closed and she sat.

"How have you survived for so long, capable of wielding the power you can, yet having so little knowledge?"

"I'm not from around here," Jessica mumbled.

"Indeed." Granny pinned her with a stare. "Have you no knowledge of the Fae roads then?"

"Well . . ." she squirmed a little. "No."

"The Fae roads are lines of power that take their own path throughout the land. They are invisible to mundane sight, you can only see them with the inner eye."

"Oh," she said. "You mean ley lines. I've heard of them, yes. My friend Howard is always going on about ley lines and convergences."

"I am unfamiliar with that name. Where two roads cross there is a knot of power, where many cross there is a Well. You can follow the Fae road to a knot."

"And I can draw power from one of these knots?" Jessica asked eagerly.

"It is a most dangerous endeavor," Granny said. "But yes, it is possible."

Tapping into the energy from a ley line, or in this case a Fae road, was easier said than done. Granny had her hold the charm she'd given her to use as a focus, which seemed odd considering it was meant to mask her magic. Once she achieved a meditative state, she was to open her senses to the magic around her. She would feel a pull and was to let the pull carry her to the source, like a leaf following the current of the river.

Every time Jessica reached that stage, she lost her focus.

"Close eyes," Davron suggested.

Jessica gave a start. She'd forgotten the boy was in the wagon with them. This was the first time she'd heard him speak. "What did you say?" she asked.

He ducked behind his grandmother. "Close eyes to see with inner eye," he said.

Granny nodded. "Yes. It will better help you concentrate."

Taking a deep breath, Jessica tried again. She focused on the charm and felt the pull of the Fae road, then she closed her eyes to follow it. It *was* more like a river than a road. She followed it with her inner eye, a frown creasing her brow.

"There's something in the road," she said. "It's like a big, silver rock."

"Good, good," Granny said. "That is the knot."

"Okay, so how do I tap into it?"

"Submerse yourself in it. Think of yourself as a vessel and let it fill you."

Dubiously, Jessica did as she was told and found it easier than she imagined. The magic consumed her, a heady rush of power that tingled as it filled all the empty places inside her. Until this moment the magic had been there whether she wanted it or not. This was the first time she'd actually sought it out. What a rush!

Her eyes suddenly snapped open and she lost her connection to the road as she felt a sharp pain in her arm.

"Did you just pinch me?" she asked in shock.

"There is such a thing as too much," Granny told her, unrepentant. When it appeared that Jessica didn't understand what she was talking about she said, "You were beginning to glow."

"Really?" Jessica held out her arms to look at them, a little disappointed they looked normal again.

"Now that you know the way, you will be able to travel the Fae roads whenever you have the need. But beware you do not become lost upon them."

"I'll be careful," Jessica said absently, still examining her arms for traces of glow. Finally, she looked up. "I know this is a lot to ask, but I have one more favor—"

Granny Warrick held out a small, green glass bottle with a cork in it. "Just a drop or two in a cup of wine should be sufficient," she said.

"How did you know?"

The old lady shrugged. "I know men, and men's pride.

Davron," she motioned to the boy. "Go to Nicolai and ask him for a bottle of the summer wine."

Davron nodded and slipped out the door.

"Summer wine?" Jessica asked.

"One of the bard's favorites."

A few minutes later Jessica approached the trailer she and Dominic had been staying in. She hesitated outside the door for a moment, telling herself she could do this but somehow unable to take that next step forward. Giving herself a shake she reached out and rapped sharply on the door.

Sebastian opened it up, looking rather harried. "I'm sorry, Jessica."

She heard Dominic's voice, but couldn't quite make out what he was saying.

"He's barely tolerating me at the moment, I don't think—"

"It's okay." She smiled wanly up at him. "I just thought . . . maybe . . ." She sighed and held up the bottle of wine. "Here. No sense in this going to waste. Maybe you guys can share a cup or two to deaden the pain."

Sebastian's eyes lit up as he recognized the markings on the bottle. "That's very generous of you. Are you sure you don't want to save it for yourself?"

Jessica shook her head. "I don't like to drink alone." She turned and left before he could see the tears forming in her eyes. This had to work. But at least this way neither of them would be a witness if she failed again.

She walked down to the river and back, judging that to be sufficient time for the two men to share a drink and for the doctored wine to take effect. Granny had promised it was fast acting. This time she was quieter as she approached the wagon. Glancing surreptitiously around to make sure no one was watching, she pressed her ear to the door. She couldn't hear any voices, but they could be speaking quietly.

Knocking softly, she waited a moment, knocked a second time, this time a little louder, then carefully eased the door open. No angry voices greeted her so she poked her head inside. Dominic was lying on the bed at the back with his eyes closed, and Sebastian was slumped over the table off to the side. He was going to have a terrible crick in his neck when he woke up.

Jessica climbed up into the wagon, closing the door behind her. Grabbing a pillow from the narrow bench, she eased it under Sebastian's head. It was the least she could do.

Turning her back on the bard she went over to the bed and sat down on the edge, blinking hard to keep the tears at bay. Dominic looked so pale and weak. He wasn't a man made to look so weak. She brushed a lock of black hair from his forehead, her fingers trailing down his cheek. There was no other option. This had to work.

Taking a deep breath, she unwrapped the stumps at the end of his arms, unable to hold back the shudder as she did so. They were still raw looking, despite her earlier healing, but there was no sign of infection and there was no danger of the bleeding starting again. She'd done that much for him, anyway.

Closing her eyes, she reached inside for the healing magic, focusing on what she wanted to do. She sent the healing green energy into the place where Dominic's hands should be, willing it to do her bidding. Using her inner eye she was able to see the ghost image of his hands and concentrated on making them solid.

It hurt. She hadn't expected it to hurt. Healing Sebastian hadn't hurt, although he told her afterwards it felt like being touched by fire. She could only imagine what Dominic would be feeling if he were awake and was glad she'd drugged him.

Pushing through the pain, she focused harder. The ghost hands were starting to become more opaque. Slowly, painfully, cell by cell it was working. But they were only halfway corporeal when the magic faltered. It wasn't enough!

"No!" Jessica wasn't even aware she'd spoken out loud, but her denial rang out inside the wagon. Recklessly she drew on the magic from the other strands within her, instinctively converting it to healing green. And when that wasn't enough she reached out and tapped into the Fae road, drinking down the magic and sending it into Dominic without a second thought.

It was working! His hands began forming - bone and muscle, flesh and blood. Still she flooded him with healing energy, glowing so brightly with it the green light could be seen through the cracks in the wagon. The superstitious gypsies outside made the sign against evil and drew back, leaving a wide space around the wagon.

She could feel his hands beneath hers now but they were still cold, dead things and she called the magic to her and sent it into his flesh. Color suffused them, green and then a healthy pink replacing the white. They twitched, an involuntary reflex, and she could feel the warmth returning to them.

If Jessica could have breathed, she would have drawn in a big sigh of relief. No, she would have shouted or laughed with pure joy. She'd done it! She restored Dominic's hands! At this moment there was nothing she couldn't do.

Letting go of Dominic, she sat back and let the magic continue to flow through her. The light in the wagon changed from green to incandescent white. Too late she remembered Granny Warrick's warning about becoming lost on the Fae road. She tried to disengage, to pull back, but couldn't. The road had a firm grip on her as it carried her away.

Chapter 40

Dominic stirred, waiting for the after drinking headache to hit. He didn't think he'd drank that much, but his mouth had that muzzy feeling to it and obviously he'd passed out. At least his stumps allowed him to hold a wine skin. He grimaced at that bitter thought. He'd been down that road before - drinking didn't solve anything, only deadened the pain temporarily.

There was something heavy lying across his lap and he rose up on his elbows to see what it was. Jessica. Of course. He sighed deeply. He'd have to do something about her, she couldn't be allowed to throw her life away out of some misbegotten sense of duty. She—

Suddenly he realized he was brushing the hair off her face with his hand. His perfectly working, fully functional hand. Making a strangled noise in the back of his throat, he sat up properly, holding his hands out in front of him, turning them this way and that. They were real - it was impossible, but true.

He looked down at Jessica and gently tried to shake her awake.

"Jessica, wake up." She didn't stir and he frowned, taking her by the shoulders and shaking a little harder. "Jessica, don't do this to me. It's time to wake up now."

A groan was heard from the table where Sebastian slumped. "That was the most potent summer wine I've ever tasted. Either that or—"

"Sebastian!" Dominic barked. "Go get Granny Warrick. I can't wake Jessica."

The bard got to his feet but then just stood there, staring.

"What?"

"Your hands!" he said, eyes wide. "You—you—have them again!"

"Never mind my damn hands! Go get help for Jessica!"

Sebastian swallowed his questions. They could wait until later. Quickly he left the wagon to find Granny Warrick.

Jessica stirred, a groan slipping out before she could stop it. Who was it that said 'No good deed ever goes unpunished'? Whoever it was knew what they were talking about. Why was it every time she tried to do something good with her magic she ended up knocked out?

"Perhaps because you are still new to your power and you try too much, too soon," a gentle, unfamiliar woman's voice said.

"Am I dead?" she asked, a little chagrined to realize she'd spoken out loud.

"Not quite, my dear."

Laughter like the sound of crystal bells filled the air. At the sound Jessica took the chance and cracked her eyes open.

Sitting up, she looked at the woman sitting on the grass

beside her and frowned. "I know you from somewhere."

The woman sat there, smiling, while Jessica figured it out. She was slender and beautiful, with dark hair and vivid green eyes. She looked very much like Aracelia . . .

"The painting in the wizard's tower," Jessica exclaimed. "You're the woman in the painting. But how—" She sat up suddenly and stared around them. "Where am I?"

"You are in the space between worlds," the woman told her.

"The space between worlds?" Jessica repeated. "How did I get here? How did you get here, for that matter?"

"You reached too far whilst healing your . . . companion. The Fae road pulled your soul from your body and brought you here."

"So . . . I *am* dead." It was a bitter pill to swallow after all she and Dominic had been through.

"No." The woman shook her head for emphasis, the movement accompanied by the sound of tinkling of bells.

Jessica looked closer at her and realized there were strands of tiny bells wound through her heavy tresses. She was dressed in the same red dress she wore in the painting.

"Am I just dreaming you?" she whispered.

Again the woman smiled a beautiful, serene smile. Jessica felt better just for seeing it. "No, my dear. I am quite real, at least in this place."

"Where is this place?" she asked. She looked around. They appeared to be in a glade of some kind. There were several slender, white barked trees giving them shade, and they were sitting beside a small pool surrounded by exotic flowers. Butterflies danced over the water and the trees were filled with unseen birds, caroling to each other. Or maybe they were just celebrating the beautiful day.

"The space between worlds," the woman repeated. "A place where the living and the dead can meet in harmony."

"Which are you?" Jessica asked.

"I am not living, nor have I been for many years."

"And which am I?" she asked, not really sure she wanted to know the answer.

"Ah. Now that would be up to you."

Jessica sighed. "I think it's only fair to warn you that I'm not the most patient person and I'm not much for riddles."

"Forgive me," the woman said. "I do not mean to be mysterious, truly. But I have been wanting to meet you for a very long time."

"Who are you?"

"Can you not guess?"

Suddenly, Jessica knew. "Mother?"

The woman smiled her oh, so beautiful smile. "If it would make you more comfortable, you may call me Farenalyssia."

"I don't understand," Jessica said, unable to raise her voice above a whisper.

"Then harken unto me as I tell you my story, which is your story as well."

Farenalyssia settled back and began.

"In the city that was once known as Mythago there dwelt two young, but powerful students of magic, Kiranthus and Anakaron, who both loved the same woman."

Farenalyssia went on to tell her about the rivalry between the two, and how Kiranthus won her heart and Anakaron turned to dark magicks which eventually led him to be cast out of the city. Kiranthus and Farena were married and were deliriously happy together. The way she looked as she said so, Jessica knew it to be true.

Several years went by in peace and then one by one members of the magical council began meeting with accidents, most of them quite gruesome. It was suspected someone was practicing the forbidden art of Blood Magic and the most logical culprit was Anakaron.

Kiranthus sent Farena, who had just delivered their first child, to her father's estate in the country, while he stood with the remaining sorcerers to try and stop Anakaron. Somehow, Anakaron was able to drain the magical energy from the Well at the magical university, destroying the university, and most of the city, in the process.

The only thing the survivors could do was flee the city. While Kiranthus was trying to secure passage on a ship and Paranthel, Farena's father, was gathering supplies, the estate was attacked by magical assassins.

"You were sleepy from a tincture I gave you for a fever, and I gave you the moonstone pendant my mother gave me to soothe your fretfulness. I left you with one of the servants in the garden while I investigated the noise from the assassins breaking in. When she heard the screaming start she lowered you into the well, where your grandfather found you when he returned. You were the only thing left alive on the estate. They slaughtered every living creature, right down to the chickens."

Jessica sniffled, not even sure when the tears had started. "That's so unfair," she said. "How did I get from here to my—

the world I grew up on?"

"Ah." Farena gave a heartfelt sigh. "My father was well-meaning, if not misguided, and your father was so grief-stricken he was easily led. They had no way of knowing that Anakaron had exhausted his powers. It would be many years before he would become a threat to anyone. As far as they knew he was still at large, still wanting his revenge."

"I think I see where this is going," Jessica said.

Farena nodded. "Indeed. Father found a world of little magic where he believed you could grow in safety. He found a woman who agreed to take you, never imagining that she would think you her own child brought back to life again, forgetting your true heritage."

"No wonder she was always so vague," Jessica murmured.

"All things considered," Farena said, reaching out and touching the back of Jessica's hand, "I think she did an admirable job raising you."

"For the short time we were together," Jessica said with a sigh. "What happened to my father and grandfather?"

"They decided to separate, and meet later in the Jewel in Jendara's Necklace, the second most powerful magical site in this world. It took many years before they were reunited, and during that time my father was able to check on you using the moonstone pendant as a focus point."

Jessica sat up straight. "That's probably when my nightmares started. Only they weren't nightmares, they were memories."

"Of course they still harbored the fear that Anakaron would be able to harm you should they try contacting you, so they bided their time. At one point your father had a magical protégé whom he thought to send across to retrieve you, but the boy disappeared and your father was forced to flee."

"Wait a minute." The pieces were beginning to fall into place. "Just where is this Jewel in whoever's necklace?"

"In the southlands. It—"

"Holy Saint Christopher!" Jessica got to her feet and started to pace, short angry strides back and forth in front of her erstwhile mother. "Are you telling me that these wizards in the south I'm supposed to be travelling to see are actually my father and grandfather?"

Farena had risen to her feet as well and put a placating hand on her arm. "I'm afraid so, yes." She sighed as Jessica pulled away from her and stood glaring. "You must believe, their hearts are in the right place. They are truly thinking only of your welfare."

Jessica was too angry for words. Then another thought occurred to her. "Did Howard know about this? Is that why he suddenly had this desire to experiment with magic?"

"Please, let us sit down again," Farena said. She gestured to the ground and a picnic blanket appeared spread out before them, a basket anchoring it at one side.

Staring at this woman who claimed to be her mother, Jessica felt her whole world tilting on its axis. Curiosity outweighing her anger, she sat down on the blanket, crossing her legs beneath her.

"Your friend Howard was an innocent pawn. Though he is capable of amazing feats, he would not have been able to send you to this world without the help of your father and grandfather. In fact, it was their combined strength that caused you to end up in Ghren instead of the southlands as they intended."

"I can't believe this," Jessica muttered. "So why didn't dear old dad and gramps come find me themselves? Why this trip south?" She thought about it some more. "And who else knows about all this?"

Farenalyssia began setting out the things from the picnic basket and Jessica had the feeling it was more to give herself time to gather her thoughts than for any great desire to eat. "They believe you would be in grave danger, should Anakaron learn of your presence and did not wish to draw attention to you by seeking you out. They were able to contact your friend Howard on your world—"

"I knew it!"

"—and convinced him to help them, keeping your true identity a secret for your own safety."

"Let me guess, they bribed him with magic lessons or something like that to get him to help," she said in disgust.

Farena's laughter sounded like bells. "How well you know your friend. They were able to speak with him through the moonstone pendant, just as he was able to speak with you, and later they used a scrying bowl."

Jessica rubbed her forehead between her eyes. "Okay, so Howard knew, and from the way he and Sebastian got so chatty when Sebastian was holding the pendant for me I'm assuming he knows. What about the elf lady, Ara—" Her eyes widened. "Aracelia looks too much like you for it to be a co-incidence. What is she, my aunt or something?"

Again Farena's laughter tinkled merrily. "For truth she would be most flattered to hear that. No, my child. She is your grandmother."

"Wow, she must have been pretty young when she had you. Hey! That means I have elf blood in me." She looked rather pleased at the notion, but then sobered right up again. "But why didn't she tell me?" She couldn't keep the hurt out of her voice.

"In truth I am not sure how your father and grandfather were able to persuade her to keep their secret, but she vowed she would. However, her co-operation came with a price. They were not able to watch thy movements whilst you were in the Elven Realm, nor are they now thanks to the blood tear she gifted you with."

"What do you mean, watch my movements? You mean they were spying on me?"

Farena nodded. "Through the art of scrying they were able to trace your movements, but the blood tear prevents this."

"This is almost too much," Jessica said. She sifted through all the information she'd been given when something else occurred to her. "So Kiranthus, my father, changed his name to Thackery, and ended up in Ghren as a teacher for the king's sons, have I got that right?"

Farena nodded.

"So that would make Dominic the apprentice he was going to send to find me . . ."

"I believe so, yes."

The wheels began turning in Jessica's brain and she didn't like where they were taking her. "So what's his part in all of this? Did he just hook up with me to make sure I wind up in the south where I'm supposed to go?" Was their time together premeditated and their whole relationship a lie?

"Be at peace, daughter mine. Your meeting with Dominic

was chance, or perhaps fate. He had no knowledge of your true origins, although I imagine he suspects somewhat of it from over-hearing conversations between your grandparents."

"Grandparents," Jessica mused. "I always wanted grandparents . . . But why hasn't Dominic said anything to me about it?"

"Perhaps he is still working it out himself." Farena shrugged. "You have not had many opportunities to speak, and it is not something to bring up in an offhand manner."

Jessica sighed, still trying to wrap her brain around everything she'd been told. "I'm taking this very well, aren't I?" she asked with a wan smile.

"That is one of the properties of this place on the living," her mother explained. "It has a calming effect on the spirit."

"The space between worlds," Jessica mused. "How exactly did I get here? Is this where the Fae roads lead?"

"Yes," Farena replied, obviously happy she was able to put it together herself. "But only in special cases."

She thought about that for a moment or two. "Special cases . . . like someone's soul leaving their body when they're following a Fae road?"

"Exactly so."

"Granny Warrick warned me to be careful not to become lost . . . is that what I've done? Am I going to be able to get back?"

"That will be entirely up to you."

Chapter 41

Dominic was fully dressed and had lifted Jessica up on the bed in his place by the time Sebastian returned with Granny Warrick in tow.

"I don't think she's breathing," he said frantically. "I don't know what's wrong with her."

Granny, who did not look at all surprised to see him with his hands fully re-formed, shooed him off to the side.

"I warned her, I did," she said, sitting down beside her.

"Warned her about what?"

"About how easy it is to become lost on the Fae road."

"Fae road? What's that? Why isn't she breathing?"

"Fae road . . ." Sebastian mused. "I know that name. But it's nothing but a myth . . . isn't it?"

"Isn't what?" Dominic exploded. "*What* is the Fae road?"

Sebastian glanced over at Granny, who appeared to be absorbed in examining Jessica, and then tried to explain. "I first came across the name in the Bardic University, it was in a book of ancient ballads. The name intrigued me so I did some independent study. It's said," he went on quickly when it looked like Dominic's temper was about to desert him completely, "that the Fae roads are the source of all magic. The elven race once used them to travel from Well to Well."

"So it's a power source, like the Wells. But if that's the case, how could Jessica be lost on one? Her body is still here."

"Her body is still here," Granny put in, looking up finally, "but her soul has become lost upon one of the Fae roads."

"Lost? What do you mean, lost? Which Fae road? How do we get her back?"

"She reached too far in her quest for the magic to heal you and her soul became separated from her body." She looked at Dominic shrewdly. "You have the talent, boy. You can see the Fae roads if you try."

Dominic looked at her, startled. His ability to work magic was one of his most well-kept secrets. Even Jessica didn't know. Not that he was trying to keep the knowledge from her, they just hadn't had the opportunity to talk about it yet. They hadn't had the chance to talk about much of anything yet. Now it was starting to look like they never would.

He searched his memory and recalled Thackery teaching him about the inner eye, and how it could be used to see into the supernatural realm. To witness things the untrained eye missed. Closing his mundane eyes, he opened his inner one.

Granny appeared as an iridescent glow, her own magic shining through, Sebastian was a far dimmer blue/green. Dominic 'looked' beyond the confines of the wagon. The Fae roads appeared to be all around them. It was like a net over the land, lines of pure white energy criss-crossing. They pulsed and glowed and he could feel the pull. There was absolutely no way of figuring out which one Jessica might have followed.

Closing his inner eye, he opened his mundane eyes, a faint after-image fading away. He looked at Granny in despair. "How do we get her back?"

"We do not. It's all up to her."

Time took on a surreal quality for Jessica. She was sitting here talking to a mother who, until just a few months ago, she never even suspected existed. Although technically she didn't exist. She was dead and had been that way since Jessica was a baby.

"Did you have something to do with why I ended up here?" she asked.

"I may have exerted some small influence on that particular road," Farena admitted.

"Why?"

"Is it not obvious? I wished for us to meet."

Jessica studied her carefully. "This is a lot of trouble to go to, especially when you couldn't have been sure of your reception."

"But worth it, I believe." Farena tilted her head. "You are very much like your father. I think, should you meet, you will surprise him greatly."

"Should we meet?" Jessica pounced on the phrase. "You mean I might not make it to the southlands?"

"This is more than just a mother's desire to meet her child." Farena sighed. "Even though I am not among the living, I am still able to wield considerable power. Enough to send you to your home, if that is what you truly wish."

"You can?" For some reason, and in spite of everything she'd been through, the idea wasn't as appealing as it had been a few weeks ago. "But if everything you told me is true, it's not really my home, is it?"

"No, it is not. But I fear there are dark times ahead for this world. Anakaron has awakened, and he gathers his power and his dark minions."

"Anakaron . . . the man who murdered you."

Farena nodded. "The blood mage who has slain hundreds, if not thousands, of innocent souls."

"Where has he been all this time?"

"Sleeping, regaining his strength."

"And when he finishes gathering his power and minions?" Farena, she had a hard time thinking of her as mother, didn't answer her question so Jessica hazarded a guess. "He's going to go after my father and grandfather, isn't he?"

"Yes. He blames Kiranthus for all of his misfortunes. His sole purpose has become exacting his revenge."

"So . . . it'll only be a matter of time before Anakaron tracks Thackery, Kiranthus, whoever, to the southlands."

"Yes, and he will lay waste to everything in his path until he reaches him."

"This magic I've got," Jessica said slowly. "Just how powerful am I?"

Farena hesitated, and to Jessica that hesitation spoke volumes.

"I mean, everyone keeps talking about my potential, and how important it is that I receive the proper training, but what happens after I am fully trained? Could I help Kiranthus defend himself against Anakaron?"

"Should you stay and receive the proper training," Farena said slowly, "You are likely to become the greatest sorcerer this world has ever known. But—" she held up her hand to stop Jessica when she would have spoken. "That's what makes it so dangerous for you to stay here."

"You think Anakaron will come after me?"

"My dear child, I *know* he will. The moment your power becomes known he will seek you out, if for no other reason than to drain you dry. And should he learn that the child of Kiranthus and Farenalyssia survived?" She gave a delicate shudder. "Oh, my daughter. I fear for your very soul. That is the reason your father and grandfather did not make themselves known to you - to keep your identity a secret from Anakaron."

The light around them dimmed slightly, as though a cloud passed over the sun. But here, in this place, there was no sun, only light. Jessica shivered.

"Your time here is at an end," Farena said sadly. She got to her feet and extended her hand to help Jessica up.

"No, it's too soon!" Jessica's hand tightened on hers. "I don't want to go yet, I've only just met you."

Farena hugged her, then kissed her on the forehead. "I will always be with you, in spirit. Now, first we must retrieve your body, then you will need to picture in your mind where in your homeland you wish to go."

Jessica was already shaking her head. "No, I don't think so."

"If I do not have a clear idea of where to send you, you could end up anywhere."

"Just leave my body where it is and send my soul back into it."

"But . . . I do not understand. You do not wish to return to your home?"

"I just . . . it doesn't seem right somehow," Jessica said with a sigh. "I mean, yeah, it'd be easier, but I'd always wonder what happened to my friends here, if they were still alive, if I could have made a difference . . ." She shook her head. "And knowing what I know, having all this power inside me . . . how can I not stay?"

Farena gathered her to her again, tears in her eyes. "I do not know whether to be proud of you or afraid for you."

"Maybe a little of both?" Jessica suggested with a crooked grin.

"Indeed." Farena gave her one final hug and then let her go again.

"There is one last thing. This false king who plagues the land you now travel . . ."

Jessica frowned. "Granny Warrick said something about him displeasing the gods."

"Indeed. And nothing would please the gods more than for someone to put a stop to him. Say, someone new to their power."

"Me?" The word was startled out of her. "I don't know if I could kill anyone, even Ewan, in cold blood."

"It will not come to that. There is another way . . ." She reached out and touched Jessica on the temple and she felt a burst of heat. "But you will need to face him alone to use this incantation."

Jessica sifted through the information her mother had just zapped her with and her eyes widened in appreciation. "Wow!"

"It is subtle rather than a direct confrontation, but I think it will be all the more effective for all of that."

"No kidding!"

They shared a look of complete understanding.

"There's just one more thing . . ." Jessica said hesitantly. "Kiranthus, my father . . ."

"Yes?"

"Do you, do you think he'll like me?"

"Oh my dear," Farena said with a broad smile. "How could he not?"

Chapter 42

Dominic alternated pacing and looming over the bed with his fists clenched. Granny Warrick had long since gone back to her wagon after reassuring him Jessica wasn't dead and telling him he'd just have to be patient. She wished good fortune to Sebastian on her way out.

"Why would she do such a stupid thing?" he asked.

"You mean giving you back your hands?"

"I mean putting herself at death's door to give me back my hands. I'd have been happy with just my sword hand."

Sebastian shot him a disbelieving look.

"All right, maybe not happy," he amended. "But I could have been content. And she wouldn't be lying here dying."

"She's not dying. Granny said—"

"This . . ." he waved a hand at Jessica's supine body. "Is an unnatural state of being. And it cannot last forever. There is a limit to how long a body can survive without its soul, and I fear time is running out."

"I admit I have had little experience in such—" Sebastian

broke off what he was saying and stared towards the bed. "Did you see that?"

Dominic quickly turned. "See what?"

"It was like a shimmer. I think something's happening."

"Jessica?"

Jessica's body convulsed and she suddenly took a large, gasping breath.

"Jessica?" Dominic was beside her in an instant.

Her breathing evened out and her eyelids flickered, then opened. "Bandit?"

He laughed and gathered up in his arms, kissing her soundly. "Don't call me that," he admonished, holding her at arm's length, eyes searching her face before hugging her close again.

"You had us worried, milady," Sebastian said, grinning like a madman.

Jessica took a moment to relax in Dominic's arms, a little confused after everything she'd gone through. Suddenly she remembered what had started all of this and pulled away from him, taking his hands in hers.

"It worked!" she said happily. "I wasn't entirely sure it would. And then I got pulled away on the Fae road before I knew if I'd finished properly."

"You took a terrible risk," he told her.

"It was worth it," she assured him.

"That wasn't meant as a compliment!"

"Well don't fall all over yourself thanking me or anything."

"Promise me you'll never do anything so stupid again."

"Stupid! You think giving you back your hands was stupid?"

"Yes! When you just about killed yourself doing so. Promise

me you won't do it again."

His voice had been steadily rising until he was shouting.

"Only if you promise not to get your hands chopped off again - that way I won't *need* to regenerate them!" She yelled back.

They sat there glaring at each other and Sebastian looked from one to the other, still grinning. He wasn't sure whether to interrupt them or just sit back and enjoy the show. The decision was made for him when a knock sounded on the wagon door. Being the closest, he answered it to find Davron standing there.

"You come, eat," the boy said, then turned and practically ran.

"Well," he said, a little nonplussed. "Looks like we've been invited to dinner."

Despite what they'd been through, both Dominic and Jessica were steady on their feet, although Sebastian noticed they took great care in helping each other up. He hoped there was room for him to sleep in the men's tent tonight - he suspected his friends would appreciate some time alone together.

Although his companions seemed to be too wrapped up in each other to pay attention to much else, he couldn't help but notice that their gypsy friends seemed a little on the quiet side. And it may have been just his imagination, but they seemed to be giving all three of them a wide berth. After the third time catching sight of someone making a warding sign against evil while looking in their direction, Sebastian had enough.

"If you two could hold off on the billing and cooing for a moment, I'd like a word, if you please."

Jessica blushed while Dominic grinned. "You're just jealous you don't have anyone to bill and coo with."

Sebastian snorted. "I'm a bard. We're well known for our foot-loose and fancy-free ways. But that is neither here nor there. Have you noticed our gypsy friends seem a little . . . distant?"

Dominic looked around, eyes narrowing.

"Maybe they're just getting antsy from being so close to Ghren still," Jessica suggested.

"No, Sebastian's right. Something's going on, although I'm not sure what."

"I guess it's up to me to find out," Sebastian said. Putting his plate down, he went over to talk with Nicolai.

The other two watched the conversation, which appeared to involve much hand gesturing and ducking of heads. The two men finally nodded in agreement before griping each other's shoulders, almost in a farewell gesture.

"Well?" Dominic asked when Sebastian returned.

"It is as I feared. Though as a people they are more used to the ways of magic than most, the miracle of you regaining your hands and Jessica's ability to restore them, are too much for them to be comfortable with."

Dominic nodded in understanding. "I should have guessed."

"I don't understand," Jessica said. "They have healers and people like Granny Warrick living with them."

"Reading the tea leaves to tell someone's fortune is a far cry from using magic to restore someone's hands," Sebastian said dryly.

"How long have we got?" Dominic asked.

"They're leaving at first light. But on the bright side, they're leaving us the wagon."

Jessica brightened considerably at that news. "This is so much better than camping out," she said. "I don't know why you didn't set me up with one of these things in the first place."

Dominic smothered a grin, but Sebastian outright snorted. "You can barely ride a horse, do you really think you could manage driving a team? Little say hitching and unhitching the wagon."

"I learned how to—what was that?" Jessica held out her hand and looked up at the sky. "Was that a raindrop?"

More drops followed and the gypsies began removing the pots and kettles from the fires and dismantling the trestle table the food had been laid out on.

"Looks like everyone's taking cover," Jessica said. "I guess we'd better get inside too."

"I'll just see if there's an extra bed roll," Sebastian ventured.

"Don't be daft," Dominic told him. "There's plenty of room in the wagon for all three of us."

"But—"

"Besides," Jessica pointed out. "They're dismantling the bachelor tent. And you don't really want to sleep out in the rain, do you? Been there, done that, and believe me, it's not much fun."

"But—"

Thunder cracked overhead as if to punctuate Jessica's statement. The heavens opened up and they raced for the wagon. It appeared that Nicolai had resupplied their wagon while they were at supper, there were several bottles of the summer wine along with enough foodstuffs to last them a week.

The three spent an enjoyable evening sharing one of the bottles of wine and a great many stories. Sebastian entertained

Jessica with stories of Dominic as a youth, while Dominic reciprocated with stories of Sebastian. Jessica expounded on the virtues of Dominic as a dog, and Dominic told the tale of the flaming chicken.

The rain had ended by the time they awoke in the morning, and they exited the wagon to find themselves alone in the clearing. There was no trace of the gypsies or where they might have gone.

"They left without saying goodbye," Jessica said, a little hurt.

"It is the belief of the travelling folk that saying goodbye means an end to things," Sebastian told her. "By not saying it they've left fate open to friends meeting again."

"Oh. That's kind of a nice custom," she admitted. "What's the matter?"

This last was directed towards Dominic who was staring off into the distance, a look of concentration on his face.

"It's probably nothing, but perhaps this would be a good time to take the horses down to the river for a drink."

The wagon was too big to hide and in any case it would only slow them down. Jessica led the horses away while Sebastian and Dominic quickly dismantled one of the wheels to make it look as though the wagon had been abandoned, then followed her into the woods. When they reached the river, Dominic handed her a bundle of clothing.

"Not that I'm expecting trouble, but perhaps you'd like to change into some travelling clothes."

She bit her lip, but took the bundle without question, and while he stashed the rest of what he and Sebastian had brought with them in the pile of boulders by the river's edge, she ducked behind them to change. When she reappeared she was wearing a nondescript brown skirt and white blouse with a darker brown leather bodice laced over top of it. Her hair, still dyed black, was confined in a neat braid.

Dominic and Sebastian had also undergone a transformation, looking more like farmers or peasants than gypsies. Somewhere Dominic had found a broad-brimmed, floppy hat, while Sebastian had adopted a stooped posture and was relying on a staff to keep him upright. They looked at Jessica critically, and exchanged a glance.

Hearing the sound of someone, or maybe several someones, approaching, Sebastian quickly stripped off his jacket, putting it around Jessica and effectively rendering her shapeless. As an added precaution, he scooped up a handful of dirt, smearing it through her hair and streaking her face with it.

Jessica caught something of their apprehension and made no protest. Two uniformed men mounted on warhorses approached and she needed no encouragement to move so she was half-hidden behind Dominic.

"Where are the gypsies?" one of the soldiers asked without preamble.

"Don't know sor," Sebastian said with a heavy country accent. "We done stayed close to the river to keep away from 'em."

"There's an empty wagon in a clearing back there," he jerked his head in the direction. "What do you know about it?"

"Don't know nothing sor."

The second soldier circled them, moving his horse closer to Jessica. She strove to look as harmless as possible. "You there," he said to Dominic. "Show me your hands."

He seemed to cringe and shrink back on himself, but slowly raised his hands. They were scratched and dirty, and he held the fingers of one hand close to its palm.

"What's the matter with your hand?" the soldier demanded.

Dominic stared up at him, slack jawed.

"Beggin' yer pardon, sor," Sebastian said ingratiatingly, "Him was thrown by 'is horse. Got knocked on the head. Horse stepped on 'is hand."

"Leave off, Benton," the first soldier said. "We won't get any work outta them."

"Horses can be dangerous creatures," the soldier named Benton said. He circled them one more time, ending up where they'd tied the horses from the wagon. "We'll just be taking these to keep you from getting hurt again."

"But we need 'em to get to the city," Sebastian whined.

"Be grateful we're after gypsies, not dirty peasants," the first soldier snarled. Taking the horses with them, they rode off.

After a few more minutes had passed, Sebastian slowly straightened. Dominic took off his hat and swore.

"All things considered," Sebastian said mildly, "We got off lucky."

"What just happened?" Jessica asked, a little bewildered. It had all happened so quickly.

"We've just had confirmation that the rumors we've been hearing are true," Dominic told her, an inscrutable look on his face. "Ewan isn't content with kidnapping women for his pleasure, he's also taking able-bodied men to force them into his army or to use as laborers."

"This land is dying a slow death," Sebastian said.

Dominic glanced up at the sky. "I think it prudent to return to the wagon."

"What for?" Sebastian asked. "Without horses to pull it . . ."

"We do not need horses to shelter from a storm," Dominic told him, leading the way back to the clearing.

Jessica and Sebastian glanced up at the sky and hurried after him, dark clouds chasing after them. When they caught up to him, Dominic was cursing vehemently. The soldiers had set fire to the wagon - it was already half gone. At that moment the sky opened up and the rain came down in torrents. In seconds they were soaked through.

"This just keeps getting better and better," Jessica muttered. "Now what? Do you think there might be a cave in the rocks by the river?"

Sebastian was already shaking his head. "Not likely. And even if there were, we have no idea how long the rain will last - we wouldn't want to be trapped in a cave if the water in the river began to rise."

"Come on," Dominic said. "The rain has snuffed out the fire. We can shelter from the worst of it underneath the wagon."

It was a tight fit, but the three managed to find space under the wagon. Although it did indeed keep the worst of the rain off of them, it did nothing to impede the rivulets of water flowing along the ground.

Dominic put his arm around Jessica and she rested her head on his shoulder. Sebastian sat on her other side. Despite everything, Dominic had a smile on his face.

"Why are you so happy?" Sebastian asked sourly.

Jessica lifted her head to look at him too.

"We're alive. We're in good health, more or less, and we've overcome every obstacle thrown at us. Were the wagon intact and we were dry, life would be good at this moment."

Jessica smiled and laid her head back down. Sebastian couldn't help grinning back. Time enough for reality once the rain stopped.

Chapter 43

After spending an uncomfortable night under the wagon, they decided to start back the way they'd come. They couldn't get much wetter than they already were, and there was always the possibility of finding better shelter.

It took them three days to back track to Helsenberg, during which time it continued to rain intermittently. To be on the safe side they kept their peasant disguises, although they didn't have much choice, the fire having taken care of all their supplies. Unsurprisingly, they met no one on the road.

They stuck to the back alleys as much as possible, avoiding the main thoroughfares. Sebastian left Dominic and Jessica at the inn they had stayed in previously while he sought out an old friend he thought might help them. The innkeeper took one look at them and declared the inn full to overnight guests, but dinner could be had for a few coppers.

There were several other dinner guests already enjoying a meal as they sat at a corner table near the door. The crowd was neither loud nor boisterous as was usual in a tavern such as this.

The customers at the other tables talked quietly amongst themselves, paying no attention to the newcomers.

"This place kind of gives me the creeps," Jessica said quietly to Dominic.

"Sebastian was right," he said, just as quietly. "Ewan is truly sucking the life out of this land."

"I don't understand why people stay here. Why not just move someplace . . . friendlier?"

Dominic shook his head. "They could try, I suppose, but they would have to travel quickly to outpace Ewan's soldiers. And to do that they would have to leave everything behind. It's not so easy, starting over with nothing in some place new. Plus those with families would have no choice but to stay."

"And to raise enough funds to even attempt to leave they'd have to sell off most of their possessions, and to do that they'd have to find someone willing to give them a fair price in the face of repercussions from the king's men," Jessica finished for him.

"Exactly."

A very nervous barmaid delivered their dinners, two bowls of an unappetizing looking stew served with a plate of bread and cheese. She scuttled away as soon as she set the dishes down, as though afraid they'd ask her for something else.

Sebastian joined them, before they were done, helping himself to the bread and cheese but turning down their offer to order up more stew.

"The houses of pleasure have been temporarily closed to the general public," he said, keeping his voice low. "The ladies are to make themselves available to the king's men only. The public houses are limited to the number of guests they are allowed, the king's men are to be given priority - for free, of course. If you're finished, I've found a room for us but we need to hurry. It's almost curfew."

The sun was barely starting to set, but the few people they passed were hurrying to get off the streets before it was gone. Sebastian took them on a path that twisted and turned through the back streets, finally halting at a wooden door reinforced with iron bars. He knocked sharply twice, paused, rapped once and then three times.

The door opened and the woman who met them held a finger to her lips for silence and motioned them to follow her. She led them to the kitchen where they were ignored by the cooks who were in the midst of meal preparations. There were two large hearths, one at either end of the room but only one with a fire in it. The woman led them towards the cold hearth and tugged downwards on one of the iron fittings. The stone slid aside revealing a staircase at the back.

"The common room is full of soldiers tonight, but you should be safe enough for now. Follow this to the top," she told them. "We don't usually use this fireplace, but we will tonight, so you'll have to wait up there until someone fetches you in the morning. I'm sorry I couldn't do more."

"Thank you," Sebastian told her. "What you're doing—"

She cut him off with a gesture. "Is little enough for my brother's life. Now hurry."

Sebastian led the way up the stairs with Jessica following and Dominic taking up the rear. The way led to the top of the three story house and an attic-like crawl space at the very top. Though it lacked in headroom, it was a large enough room, and someone had been thoughtful enough to leave a tray with a loaf of freshly baked bread, a pat of butter, soft yellow cheese, and some fruit on it. There were also several bottles of wine.

"Ah, they know me well," Sebastian said with a grin, examining one of the bottles carefully.

There were a couple of straw-filled mattresses on the floor, with blankets folded up neatly at one end. The room was lit by candles placed on matching low tables, and there were heavy draperies at either end of the room, behind which were presumably windows.

"I have the sneaking suspicion we're not the first to hide away up here," Jessica said. She hesitated, then couldn't help asking, "Is this place what I think it is?"

"Welcome to Madam Divinity's House of Eternal Delights," Sebastian said with a grin.

"And the woman who let us in?"

"Ah, yes," he said, opening up one of the bottles. "The fair Bethany. One of Madam Divinity's most popular girls."

"She said something about you saving her brother's life?" Dominic asked, passing over three goblets.

Sebastian nodded as he poured. "I evened the odds somewhat when he was set upon by a pack of ruffians. What?" he asked, catching sight of the grin on Jessica's face.

"I have this vision of you travelling the land doing good deeds in return for unnamed favors," she said.

"Which is fortunate for us," Dominic said. "A toast to good deeds."

They drank to his toast and then sat in comfortable silence for a time. It was Sebastian who said what they were all thinking.

"Something is going to have to be done about Ewan."

"I know," Dominic said heavily.

"We need to come up with a plan," Jessica said tentatively. Somehow she didn't think this was the right time to tell the others about her meeting with her mother and her assurance that only Jessica could put an end to Ewan.

"*We* don't," Dominic stated emphatically. "Ewan is my brother, that makes him my responsibility."

Sebastian and Jessica looked at each other.

"I could always turn him back into a dog," Jessica said. "Maybe get him a muzzle as well as a leash."

"Maybe something a little smaller this time," Sebastian suggested. "How do you feel about cats?"

"Look," Dominic said impatiently, "I'm not saying I won't need help, but I don't want either of you anywhere near the castle - it's too dangerous."

"And it's not dangerous for you?" Jessica snapped. "Last time he took your hands. This time he may very well kill you."

"And what do you think he'd do to you?" he snapped back. "Maybe we should get Bethany up here to tell you what he's been doing to the women he uses. Once he strips you of your magic you'll be at his mercy."

"You both need to lower your voices," Sebastian hissed. They grudgingly did so and he continued. "Helsenberg is all but under siege by the king's men. Although it was suspected Jessica drowned, they never recovered her body and Ewan is becoming increasingly wary."

"I knew this was my fault," Jessica muttered.

"It's no one's fault," Sebastian said irritably. "Ewan has

surrounded himself with witchguards, even though the ones he sent after you fled the town rather than face his wrath."

"That's because they didn't want it to be discovered they were frauds," Jessica said with a sniff.

"I don't think so," Dominic said. "I've seen it myself. Magic slides right off of them."

"Sure it does. It'd slide right off you too if you were wearing clothing lined with witch binding."

The two men goggled at her. "Are you sure about this?"

"Yes, I'm sure."

"Well I'll be damned," Dominc said. "I wonder if Ewan knows about this?"

"Doubtful," Sebastian said. "The witchguard came from his friends in the east, and I'm sure he paid dearly for them. He wouldn't need to do that if he knew, he'd just need to pick the biggest, burliest men from his own guard and outfit them in the proper clothes."

"Even those without magic would be terrified of them, just because of their sheer size," Dominic mused. "But how does this information help us? It's not like we'd ever get close enough to strip them of their robes."

"Set fire to them," Jessica suggested. "What?" she asked as both me turned to stare at her. "Other than being lined with the witch binding, which I'm sure is just as flammable as any other kind of binding, there's nothing special about them. Natural fibers burn quite easily."

"I'm glad you're on our side," Dominic said with a slight shudder.

Jessica effectively ended the conversation with a huge yawn.

"Perhaps we should get a good night's sleep and strategize in the morning," Sebastian suggested, not quite able to hide his grin.

"No offense to our hostess," Jessica said, after Bethany delivered a breakfast tray to them the next morning, "But how long are we going to have to stay here?"

"Just long enough to figure out our next move," Dominic assured her.

"Which is coming up with a way to get rid of Ewan," she said. "And then what?"

"Then we continue on our way south."

"But what about Ghren?"

Dominic looked puzzled. "Ghren will be free of his tyranny."

"I think I know what you mean," Sebastian said. "And you're right. Ghren's location and size make it a prize worth fighting for. With Ewan gone there will be anarchy as the wolves close in from all sides."

"As badly as the people are suffering under Ewan's rule, what if someone even worse takes over?" Jessica asked.

Dominic thought about that for a moment. "I suppose we shall have to find someone else for the throne."

"You are his brother," Sebastian pointed out. "It would be a simple matter to raise enough support to put you on the throne where you rightfully belong. The only ones loyal to Ewan are the ones he's paying, and that loyalty will only last until the treasury runs dry."

Jessica held her breath but Dominic was already shaking his head in denial. "I never wanted the throne, even when I was heir.

And I think deep down my father knew it, which is why we locked horns so often."

"I didn't think so," Sebastian said with a sigh. "Although I think you'd make an excellent king."

"So do I," Jessica put in, greatly relieved.

"We need to find one of Randor's bastards." Dominic told them, ignoring the remark about him being king. "That's supposing Ewan let any of them live."

Sebastian glanced at him in surprise.

Dominic snorted. "You think it was a secret, that my father was a womanizer? Where do you think Ewan gets it from?"

"You never said anything to me about it. Ever."

"It was too dangerous. Randor's offspring had way of . . . disappearing."

"Disappearing?" Jessica asked. "You mean someone was killing them off?"

"Thackery suspected Ewan's mother was quietly getting rid of anyone who might be a threat to Ewan," Dominic said.

"You think she might have missed one or two?"

"I don't know," Dominic replied, "But it would be our best chance."

"I believe she did," Sebastian said slowly. A sudden grin lit up his face. "I know just the lad," he said. "Young enough to be fair, experienced enough to rule wisely. And he's newly married as well - his lady is a kind and sensible woman who will make a perfect queen."

"Excellent," Dominic said. "Who is this paragon?"

Sebastian turned to Jessica. "You can vouch for him as well. He is none other than our good friend Gareth."

Chapter 44

With Bethany's help, Sebastian was able to send a message to Gareth bidding him come to Ghren on a matter most urgent.

"I know a man who raises messenger birds who owes me a favor," he told them.

"Of course you do," Dominic said wryly.

"So how come Ewan doesn't know Gareth is his half-brother?" Jessica asked as they prepared to spend another long day hiding in the attic.

"It happened after Ewan's mother died, when he was off in the Eastern lands receiving his education. Randor enjoyed his drink and when he was in his cups, he was not particularly choosy as far as bed partners went. Gareth's mother was a maid in the castle, actually. I'm not sure how she contrived to be in a position to catch his notice, but it was her intent to become pregnant with the king's child in the hope he would marry her."

"How sad," Jessica said.

"It happened more often than you might think," Dominic put it.

"So what happened?"

"I don't recall her myself," Sebastian continued, "But she was either pretty enough or good enough in bed to keep the king's attention, until she announced she was carrying his child."

"What did the king do?"

"He put her out," Sebastian said.

"He did what?" Surely she couldn't have heard that right.

"Actually, he told her he already had two useless sons, he didn't need any more. And then he gave her a few coins to get rid of it." Dominic vaguely remembered the incident. "He sent his seneschal with her to make sure the deed was done."

"That's horrible! How did she get away?"

"She gave the seneschal the slip, and ended up in my mother's quarters," Sebastian said. "Mother took care of her until the baby was born. The maid died once the babe was born and mother placed the child with a couple of minor nobility, telling them only that it was the child of a noble, not who the noble was."

"Wow, that's some story," Jessica said. "Wait a minute. Are you telling me that Gareth doesn't know that he's Randor's son either?"

"That's the beauty of choosing him as heir," Dominic said.

Despite everything that had been happening, Jessica awoke with a smile on her face the next morning. There was a warmth at her back that she could really get used to, and a heavy arm draped over her torso. Sebastian was snoring quietly on the mattress on the other side of the room.

She must have stirred involuntarily because the arm around her tightened. Dominic's lips grazed her ear.

"As much as I love Sebastian as a brother, I could wish he were somewhere else at this moment," he whispered in her ear.

Her smile broadened and she gave an experimental wiggle that made him groan. "On my world we could give him a few dollars and send him to the movies for a couple of hours."

"I think I must visit this world of yours."

Jessica felt a warmth infusing her. "I think I'd like that," she whispered back.

"If you two are quite done over there," Sebastian said, "We need to break our fast and then figure out how we're getting to Ghren."

Jessica stifled a giggle as the arm around her tightened fractionally. "Maybe you could turn *him* into a dog," Dominic whispered.

"I heard that!"

Laughing, Jessica wriggled her way out from beneath Dominic's arm. By the time they'd finished taking turns behind the privacy screen at the end of the room, changing their clothing and taking care of other, more pressing needs, there was the sound of someone on the stairs. Bethany arrived, carrying a tray with fresh food for them. She was closely followed by two of the other ladies, one carrying a small chest, the other an armful of clothing.

All three looked rather tired.

"Is everything all right?" Sebastian asked.

Bethany smiled wanly. "It will be well once the soldiers are gone from our town - they seem to have taken a liking to our house."

"I'm sor—"

She shook her head quickly. "Don't be. 'Tis our own fault for being so good at what we do," she added with a cheeky grin. "I do not wish to alarm you, but there is a reward for three peasants who were seen headed towards Helsenberg."

"A reward," said Dominic, honestly shocked. "Whatever for?"

"It is believed you were in league with a band of gypsies who escaped the troops."

"Why were they after the gypsies?" Jessica asked.

The other woman shrugged. "Since when do the king's men need a reason?"

The other two women had been busy moving one of the tables closer to the window, pulling the heavy drapery aside to give them light to work by. "We're ready over here," one of them said.

"Ready for what?" Jessica asked.

Bethany smiled. "New disguises. Your current ones will no long suffice - the innkeeper where you had your dinner when you arrived remembered you."

"Damn," Sebastian swore. "I knew we should have at least changed our clothing before entering the town ."

"Who's first?" the second woman asked.

Dominic volunteered. He sat on a stool and the women circled him like vultures, conferring in low tones. One of them reached out and rubbed a lock of his hair between her fingers and they consulted again before getting to work.

"Once you are outfitted properly you will be able to move freely through the town. There will be a horse and cart waiting for you."

"It's very generous of you to help us," Jessica said.

Bethany hesitated a moment, then said, "It is not entirely unselfish on our part. Should you be found within our walls, we will all suffer. And . . ." She hesitated again.

"What is it?" Jessica coaxed.

"One of the ladies . . . she possesses the sight. And she has seen that the three of you are our best hope for putting an end to the evil in this land."

"Did she say whether or not we will succeed?" Dominic asked dryly.

She smiled wanly. "That she could not see."

Jessica wandered over to where Dominic had been sitting and found him transformed. Gone was the somewhat cocky looking gypsy and the peasant with the floppy hat. Instead there appeared an old man leaning heavily on a cane. His hair was liberally streaked with grey and he was sporting a beard that was more grey than black.

"You're next," the woman said to Jessica with a grin.

Jessica's disguise involved a great deal of padding in the shabby, but neatly mended skirt and smock she was given to wear. Her hair was lightened to a mousey brown and stuffed beneath a mob cap.

"I look pregnant," she said with a frown, turning this way and that in front of the full length mirror. "Really pregnant."

"That's the idea," the woman said with a grin.

"People don't travel towards Ghren without a very good reason," Bethany explained. "Your reason is that you're with child and there is a problem that only the midwife in Ghren can help with. You are travelling with your crippled father," she nodded towards Dominic, "and your husband." This time she swept her hand to indicate Sebastian.

Sebastian's hair had been swept back off his face and held in place by a cord. There was a very realistic looking scar running up his cheek to underneath an eye patch. He was dressed as a shabby farmer, complete with straw hat.

"Lost me eye in a threshing accident," he said, adopting a country accent.

"Thank you for everything you've done," Jessica said to Bethany.

"Thank me by doing what needs to be done," Bethany told her. "Godspeed to you all."

Just outside the back door they found a mule waiting patiently, already hitched to a cart for them. Sebastian poked through the supplies in the cart.

"Food, water, bedrolls . . . aw, look at this," he held up a baby dress. "Have you ever seen anything more precious?"

"They thought of everything," Dominic said in admiration. "And none of it worth stealing."

Jessica eyed the mule dubiously. "This guy's pretty scruffy looking, you don't really expect him to pull this cart, do you?"

Dominic chuckled. "You really *aren't* used to travelling by horse or cart, are you?"

"Not only will this beastie pull the cart, he'll pull it with us in it," Sebastian assured her.

The cart was basically a wooden box with a place at the front for the driver to sit. She still had reservations, but allowed Dominic to help her up into it. Sebastian took the driver's seat.

"You know," she said. "As your wife maybe I should sit up front with you."

"Not in your condition dear," he said with a grin. "Besides, you need to look after your poor old father."

"And I need a lot of looking after," Dominic said, wriggling his eyebrows at her.

Sebastian guided the mule along a narrow street until they met up with the main road that went to the bridge. There they queued up in line with the others waiting to cross. There was no laughter or chatter from the crowd, they were in fact quite sober. In silence they watched the guards poking and prodding their way through people's belongings, confiscating whatever they wished.

Twice they watched as the hoods were pulled from women travelers so the soldiers could get a better look at them, and once a woman was separated from her travelling companions completely. Jessica wasn't conscious of her hands curling into fists until Dominic touched her arm to get her attention and shook his head slightly. She looked down to see she'd inadvertently been giving off sparks between her clenched fingers.

At last it was their turn. Sebastian got down from his seat to lead the cart forward. The soldiers barely gave them a passing glance until one of them poked through their belongings and found several bottles of wine that Madam Divinity had gifted to Sebastian, hidden under the cart's seat.

"Now what would a farmer be doin' wit such fine wine?" one of the soldiers asked.

"And so much of it," his partner added, drawing the attention of the others. Soon the cart was surrounded.

As Sebastian, who clearly hadn't considered that something

as innocuous as a few bottles of wine would be cause for concern, fumbled for an answer that would placate them, Jessica let all the frustration that had built up over the last few days come through as she acted the part of the put-upon wife.

"Wretch!" she shrieked in an imitation of his country accent. "You promised you gave up the drink!"

"I—"

"Is that where the profit from the sale of the farm went?"

"I—" Sebastian was somehow able to look both contrite and panicky, both at the same time.

"Is this why I'm having to ride in this misbegotten cart instead of a proper wagon?"

Her voice continued to rise as she stood up in the cart and Sebastian shrank back, much to the soldiers' entertainment.

"Sit down, please my love," Sebastian pleaded. "I've no wish for you to injure yourself or the babe."

"Don't you 'my love' me!" she yelled. "You promised!"

"All right, all right," the soldier in charge said. "That's enough of that. You," he pointed at Jessica. "Sit down and shut up."

Jessica's mouth snapped shut on a caustic reply and she sat down with a huff, arms crossed over her chest, glaring at Sebastian.

"And you," he turned to Sebastian, "We'll just be relieving you of that there wine."

Sebastian stood aside, a mournful expression on his face that was only half-feigned, as the soldiers helped themselves to all six bottles. The leader glanced at Jessica's angry face that boded no good for her supposed husband, and then tucked one of the bottles back under the cart seat.

"If'n I were married to a shrew like that, I'd be driven to drink too," he said with a wink at Sebastian.

He straightened up and waved them on. "We're done here, get moving."

"Thank 'e sirs," Sebastian said with a bob of his head. He clambered up onto his seat again and shook the reins, moving them forward.

They moved at an unhurried pace across the bridge and then through the town itself. It wasn't until they were on the open road beyond the town that they breathed a sigh of relief.

"You were magnificent back there," Sebastian told Jessica.

"I agree," Dominic said, giving her a hug. "I admit to being worried that our disguises would not stand up to close scrutiny, but you distracted the bridge guards nicely."

"We were lucky," Jessica said soberly. Images of all the people who weren't so lucky filled her mind.

As if he knew what she was thinking, Dominic rested his hand on her arm. "You aren't responsible for the actions of the soldiers towards the others, none of us are. And our best chance of saving them is to cut the head off the serpent."

"I know," she said with a sigh. "But I'm just not used to such . . . blatant injustice."

"There's no injustice in your land?" Sebastian asked from the front of the cart.

"Of course there is. It's just not . . ." she thought about it for a moment. "I guess I'm just not used to having to deal with it on such a personal level. I'm starting to feel like I've led a very sheltered life. Or a shallow one."

"I think it's the same all over," Dominic said. "Injustice is everywhere, it's only when faced with it directly that we are aware of it and feel the need to do something about it."

"Perhaps when you are back in your own land you will see your world through new eyes," Sebastian said.

"Maybe," she agreed, and then lapsed into silence.

Chapter 45

Jessica spent the rest of the day deep in thought. She knew Dominic was growing concerned by her silence, he kept shooting little looks her way and a couple of times he looked like he was going to say something, then changed his mind, as though realizing she needed some time to think.

Things had been happening pretty fast since they'd been with the gypsies. She still couldn't believe she'd actually been able to re-generate his hands. Her! Jessica Jane O'Connell, the most boringly normal person she knew.

She stole a glance at him - he was sitting opposite to her in the cart and appeared to be dozing. Even in his disguise he was good looking. Without it he was almost too attractive. Not polished, like Ewan, Dominic was more ruggedly handsome. More . . . regal. She couldn't believe he was giving up the throne.

"You're thinking too hard," he said, opening his eyes. "I can hear you from over here. What's wrong?"

Flushing at being caught staring, she said, "I was just trying to see the resemblance between you and Ewan and I'm not finding any. You two are so totally different, it's hard to believe you're brothers."

He sat up in a more comfortable position and shrugged. "We did have different mothers . . ."

Squinting, she took that as an excuse to study him further. "I only saw your father briefly - he didn't much like me - but there were a couple of portraits of him. I do see some resemblance to him - the eyes, the dark hair. I guess Ewan must take after his mother."

"Not so's you'd notice," Sebastian put in from the driver's seat. "Cassandra was somewhat stout, with flaming red hair."

"Hmm," Jessica pondered. "How did she end up with the king after your mother died?"

"She was actually one of my mother's ladies in waiting," Dominic said, a trace of bitterness in his tone. "There were rumors that she was already carrying Ewan before mother died."

"I wonder . . ."

"What?" he prompted when her voice trailed off.

She looked a little discomfited. "I just . . . well, there seemed to be nothing of his father in him, and Sebastian said he didn't take after his mother either, I just wondered if maybe Randor wasn't his father after all."

"Huh." Dominic sat back for a moment. "I suppose it's possible. As I recall, the one character trait she and Ewan did share was their ability to plot."

She sighed and shut her eyes. All this thinking was getting to be a habit, a bad one. She was already working so far out of her comfort zone it wasn't even funny. Thinking just put another nail in her carefree coffin. She was in serious danger of turning downright responsible.

They kept to their leisurely pace and reached Wodenville, a town just a few hours from Castle Ghren, in three days. Unlike Helsenberg, Wodenville was not overrun with Ewan's soldiers. Perhaps because of its proximity to Ghren it was believed an extra military presence was unnecessary, or more likely it was because there was a distinct lack of entertainment in Wodenville. But whatever reason, they had no problems securing rooms in the town's single inn.

They were, in fact, somewhat reassured when the innkeeper's wife, upon learning their intended final destination, did her best to dissuade them.

"There be plenty of midwives in Antogin," she told them. "'Tis a short journey if ye take the river. There's still boats be leaving from the harbor in Tamblin."

"That's very kind of you," Jessica said gently, "But we've another reason to seek out the midwife in Ghren. My sister was apprenticed to her . . ." she let her voice trail off, as though unable to go on.

Sebastian, ever the concerned husband, placed his hand over hers. "We haven't heard from Tessa in several months."

"Oh, you poor dears," the woman sympathized. She looked like she was about to go on, but the door to the inn opened and she hurried off to see to the new customer.

"Nice touch," Dominic murmured.

"Thank you," Sebastian said. "I—what is it?" he asked as Jessica sat up straight, a broad grin on her face."

"Look! It's Gare—ow! What was that for?" she asked as Sebastian kicked her under the table.

"Quiet!" he hissed. "We don't want to draw attention to ourselves, or to him."

"Fine. But you didn't have to kick me so hard," she grumbled, reaching down to rub her leg.

The innkeeper's wife chose that moment to pass by with Gareth in tow, leading him to a table in the back of the room. He glanced at them but obviously the disguises were effective because there was no hint of recognition.

The trio finished their meal and headed up to their rooms, Jessica solicitously helping her "father" along. Sebastian stumbled when they were abreast of Gareth's table, jostling him slightly.

"Sorry, sorry," he mumbled in his country accent. "Not too steady on me feet since getting kicked by the mule," he added.

"No harm was done, good man," Gareth said amiably. "Good even' to you."

"And to you, sir."

"So if we're not supposed to talk to him," Jessica said, once they were up in the room she and Dominic were sharing, it being the bigger of the two, "How are we supposed to let him know we're here?"

"Already done," Sebastian said smugly. "When I jostled him I left a note on his table."

"Sneaky," she said in admiration.

"You're very quiet, my friend," Sebastian said to Dominic. "Is something amiss?"

"I've been thinking . . . Perhaps it might be wise to keep the truth of young Gareth's parentage from him until Ewan has been dealt with."

Sebastian nodded. "Aye, I can see the logic in that."

"Well I don't," Jessica said. "Doesn't he deserve to know?"

"I doubt he'll take the news well," Dominic told her. "And should the truth become known . . ."

"If Ewan doesn't kill him, then I'm sure there's a rebel group or two out there that would love to use him for a figurehead," Jessica finished for him. "Okay, I get that. But you guys sent for him. What are you going to tell him when he asks why?"

The two men looked at each other.

"We tell him a partial truth," Dominic said finally. "We tell him we're going to overthrow Ewan and we need his help."

"Sounds a little thin to me," she said doubtfully.

"You forget," Sebastian told her. "He does not yet realize Dominic has returned. Once he does, he'll be too dazzled by his presence to question our motives."

He ducked and laughed as Dominic threw a boot at him.

With perfect timing, there was a tentative knock on the door. Jessica, being the closest, answered it, pulling an astonished Gareth into a big hug. "Gareth! It's so good to see you! Come in, come in. Don't just stand there gawking."

"Forgive me, my good woman," said Gareth, trying to resist as she pulled him into the room. "But do I . . ." He squinted at her. "My lady Jessica?"

"Cool disguise, isn't it? And you remember my husband, Sebastian?" she said, waved a hand in his direction.

"I . . . but . . . "He looked from Jessica to Sebastian and back again, then his eyes widened as he took in her protruding belly.

"What . . . how . . .?"

Jessica smacked him in the arm. "It's part of the disguise, you nit."

"But—but—but married?"

"Jessica, I think you need to let the poor lad sit down," Dominic said, gently pulling her away.

Gareth's gaze swung over to him. He stared, obviously trying to see through the disguise, then his eyes widened. "I know you," he said. "But this can't be! I was but a child when it was rumored you were dead!"

"As you can see, I am quite alive," Dominic said dryly.

"My Lord!" Gareth went to one knee. "I know not why thou hast summoned me, but I am in thy service."

"See?" Sebastian said with a smirk to Jessica.

Dominic sighed. "Oh, get up. This floor is filthy. And stop talking like a history tome."

"Why don't you sit here," Jessica said, offering the chair she'd vacated.

Dazed, Gareth followed her suggestion.

"Maybe a glass of wine?" Sebastian offered.

Gareth nodded and a goblet was pressed into his hand. He took a big gulp. "It would be the death of any one of you should Ewan discover your presence in Ghren."

"That's why we're hiding our true selves," Sebastian said.

"When last I heard you, friend bard were safely beyond reach and you, my lady, were presumed drowned. Why return?"

"We're here to get rid of Ewan." Jessica told him. "And we need your help."

Gareth choked on his wine.

Chapter 46

Jessica was fuming as she perused what passed for a market in Wodenville, trying to find the herbs on the list Sebastian had given her. Apparently it was his recipe for a potion that would knock the guards out cold. She wasn't stupid, she knew they kept finding reasons to send her out of the room so they could talk about their plans without her overhearing.

She still hadn't told them about her encounter with her mother, though she couldn't say why. It wasn't as though she was deliberately trying to keep it a secret, it was more that she didn't quite know how to broach the subject without them thinking she was crazy.

"Oh, hey guys. Yeah, I know you're making these big plans and all, but my dead mother says I'm the only one who can stop Ewan. So you boys just relax and I'll take care of everything."

Oh, yeah. She could see that going over well. They'd probably find a store room somewhere to lock her in. And there wouldn't be anything she could do about it because her magic was still pretty weak, although Farenalyssia assured her she didn't

350

need it for the task at hand. What was it she said?

"The summoning is made through determination and a call for justice."

She also said to wait for the light of the full moon. Jessica had been keeping an eye on the moon, and it would be full in two days. It was time to start making her own plans.

Accidentally stepping on her skirt, she stumbled, nearly losing her basket. For sure her plans were not going to include wearing this stupid costume; the novelty had long since worn off. She was tired of tripping over her skirts - why did women put up with it? But she didn't dare be seen wearing pants. According to Gareth, a woman wearing anything but skirts was cause to be arrested.

The marketplace was pretty picked over, and she was only able to find a few of the herbs Sebastian had requested. Tucked away in a corner was a stall run by an old woman, who looked like a light breeze could blow her away, who questioned her closely about why she wanted these particular herbs and her knowledge of herbs in general. Jessica apparently passed some kind of test because the old woman directed her to an apothecary for the rest.

The apothecary's shop was down a narrow alley, the door almost hidden unless you knew where to look. It seemed as though it wasn't just magic workers who were persecuted in Ghren these days.

The apothecary was younger than she expected, a tall, thin man in his mid-thirties from the look of him. He squinted at the list and then silently began filling her order. When he was finished he gave her a speculative look and then reached up on a shelf for a small vial.

"This will accomplish much the same thing, only it's easier on the system and you don't need to mix it up."

Jessica took the small vial and held it up to the light. It was filled with a clear, red liquid. She looked at the apothecary. "How do you know what I want these herbs for?"

He snorted. "You think you're the first expectant woman looking for a respite from her husband?"

Though there was no reason for it, she couldn't prevent the blush that suffused her cheeks. "I'll take it as well," she mumbled, an idea forming in her mind even as he wrapped up her purchase.

"No more than two drops in a glass of wine," he cautioned her. "This is highly concentrated."

"Is it dangerous?" she asked.

"It will not cause lasting harm, if that's what you fear, but at the same time you wouldn't want your husband to sleep for a week."

She thanked him and hurried back to the inn, tucking the vial in her pocket.

Two days later, just after Gareth left to see about arranging for mounts, Jessica entered the room in the inn carrying a tray with refreshments on it.

"You've been refining your plan for hours," she told them. "You need to take a break."

They looked at her, a little bleary-eyed, and made room for her to set the tray on the table between them. There was bread, cheese, and fruit as well as a bottle of wine and three goblets.

"You are kindness personified," Sebastian said.

"Yes, very kind," Dominic agreed, a hint of suspicion in his tone.

"What?" she asked, pouring the wine.

"I find your acquiescence to our plan a little surprising."

The plan included her staying behind, a plan which she had argued vociferously with at first, then gradually accepted.

She shrugged. "I finally realized you were right. I don't have the fighting skills to be of any real help if you run into trouble, and my magic hasn't returned - even if I could use it properly. This is too important to let my ego get in the way. I hate to admit it, but whether I like it or not I'd be more of a hindrance than any help."

He looked at her searchingly, but she wore her sincerest expression.

"I'd like to propose a toast," she said, picking up one of the goblets. "To the success of the mission and the end of Ewan's reign of terror."

"To success," they echoed.

Since she was the one who poured the wine, they never saw the drops of the apothecary's drug in the bottom of each of their goblets. She watched in satisfaction as they drank heartily.

"So," she said as they sat their goblets down again. "Have you decided when you're going to make your move?"

"Yes," Sebastian said. "We . . ." His voice trailed off and he swayed in his seat.

Dominic was fighting to keep his eyes open. His gaze swung around to Jessica. "What—"

She winced in sympathy as his head hit the table with a thunk.

"Huh," she said. "I didn't expect it to be so fast acting." She shrugged. "Just so long as it doesn't wear off as quickly." The apothecary had told her to use only a drop or two, and she'd used five, just to be on the safe side.

The door to the room rattled and Gareth entered.

"I have secured mounts for us, and—my lady Jessica?" He looked past her to the unconscious men and his eyes widened. "My lady, what has happened?"

"Oh, Gareth. Good timing. Help me get them over to the bed, they'll be more comfortable there."

"My lady?"

"Don't worry, they're just sleeping. I'll explain everything once we get them settled." She grabbed Dominic by the arm. "Come help me with him."

Gareth finally moved away from the door to do as she asked and she breathed a sigh of relief. He'd had a bit of a crush on her when they first met and she was counting on it holding true now to convince him to help her with her plan.

The two men were heavier than they looked, but with Gareth's help she managed to wrestle them onto the bed. And if Dominic's head accidentally hit the frame, well, it served him right for making plans that didn't include her.

"Okay," she said, once she and Gareth were sitting down at the table where Dominic and Sebastian had been. "First of all, do you trust me Gareth?"

He opened his mouth immediately but she held up her hand to stop him. "I want you to really think about it for a minute and be completely honest. I promise it won't affect our friendship in the least."

He studied her carefully and then said, "Yes, I trust you."

"Good. Because what I'm about to tell you is going to be a little unbelievable, but I swear to you it's true."

She then proceeded to tell him about being carried away by the Fae road and meeting the spirit of her mother. He listened attentively, not interrupting, until she was finished. Then he was quiet for a few moments.

"Well?" she asked when she couldn't stand it any longer. "What do you think?"

"I think were it anyone else but you, I would say you have the makings of a fine story-teller. But I do not understand why you did not share this tale with my lord Dominic or the bard."

She sighed. "At first it was because I could hardly believe it myself. Then things started happening so fast I never had the chance. And now . . . well, you've watched him and Sebastian making plans, and he's gone out of his way to keep me out of them. Do you really think he's going to listen if I tried to tell him my dead mother insists I'm the only one who can stop Ewan?"

"Nay," he said, shaking his head. "I cannot."

"And as much as he doesn't want to put me at risk, we can't put him at risk either," she continued, happy now that they'd decided against telling Gareth who his true father was until after Ewan was dealt with.

"My lady?"

"Once Ewan is dealt with, Ghren will need a new king," she said. "Who better than a brother? Do we really want to take the chance of something happening that would leave the way open for someone even worse than Ewan to take over the kingdom?"

It wasn't exactly a lie, she just didn't specify which brother would be declared king.

"I find it difficult to believe there could be worse," he murmured. "But I see your point."

Thank god he appeared to be reasonable about this. She almost breathed a sigh of relief but there was still the matter of him helping her.

"With your help," she said, "The risk to me should be minimal." At least she hoped that would be the case. "I heard you telling Dominic that Ewan takes a nightly walk along the battlements. Do you think he still does that?"

"Aye, it was his habit to survey his domain from a great height."

"Now, I know you know more about the castle than anyone, so you have to know a way to get up there, right?"

He hesitated. "I know of one, yes," he admitted reluctantly, "Other than the direct path."

"Great! As I see it, our only problem will be making sure he's alone up there."

"The castle will be heavily guarded, and he has protections in place to keep him safe from magic. You cannot mean to confront him thus?"

"I'm not going to confront him exactly," Jessica hastened to reassure him. "And I'm not going to work magic, but perform a summoning."

"But the risk—"

"Is mine to take," she said firmly. "Now, are you going to help me, or am I going to have to do this on my own?"

"I know not how I will face his highness," he nodded towards

Dominic, "should anything happen to you."

"Well, we'll just have to keep our fingers crossed that nothing does, won't we?"

Chapter 47

Jessica frowned at herself in the mirror and used the faintest of magic spells to remove the remaining dye from her hair. The spell worked a little too well and she was left with an off-center streak of white. Tilting her head to one side, then the other, she decided she liked the effect and left it alone.

Once again she was dressed in pants, thanks to Gareth. She had no idea where he'd managed to find the clothes, but she wasn't going to be giving them up again without a fight. The pants were made of a supple leather, as was the vest that laced up over a fine linen shirt, all in black of course. He'd also found a pair of well broken in boots that were only slightly too big for her, but better too big than too small. All in all, she felt quite dashing and wished Dominic could see her.

Then again, Dominic would probably tie her to a chair to keep her from going anywhere.

She confined her hair in a tight braid and then donned a short, hooded cloak. Gareth looked at her critically, then nodded. "You won't be fooling anyone up close, but from a distance you may pass for a lad."

"Good enough," Jessica told him.

She handed him a goblet. "A drink for good luck," she said.

Smiling, he tipped it back, not noticing how closely she was watching. He swayed in place, eyes widening as he realized what she'd done.

"Sorry," she said as he slid bonelessly to the ground. "It's just as important to keep you safe as Dominic."

If it had not been for the seriousness of the situation, Jessica might have almost enjoyed sneaking around Ghren at night. Once Gareth explained to her, using the maps of the secret passages that Dominic had drawn, how to get from the kitchen to the secret passage that led upwards, she really didn't need his help.

She was tempted to create a light but she didn't. There was no way of telling if using magic would trigger a warning in the protection wards, and she couldn't be sure that the light might somehow be seen.

The dirt covering the stone floor made it easier to step quietly and she breathed a sigh of relief when she peered cautiously around a bend in the passage to see that although every third torch was lit, there were no guards. She held her breath as she tip-toed past the cells. There was weeping coming from several of them, moaning from two others. It was heartbreaking and she had to remind herself that the best thing she could do for the poor souls within was to finish her mission.

She could hear the snoring of the guards before she reached the guardroom at the end of the hall. Still, she kept as close to the wall as possible, avoiding the torchlight whenever possible. Just past the guardroom was the passage up to the kitchen and she had to pass through the kitchen to get to the storeroom where the passage up to the battlement lay.

There were bodies laying on the floor of the kitchen in front of the dying fire, just as Gareth had warned her there'd be. Scullery maids and spit turners, and . . . there was a heap of blankets at the far end indicating there should be at least one more. Where was he? If she were caught now . . .

A faint noise caught her attention and she tracked it to the corner of the room furthest from the fire. Squinting in the dim light she could just make out two figures, moving in tandem. A puzzled frown crossed her face, and then morphed into a grin as she realized what they were doing.

She reached the storeroom without incident and slipped inside. It took her longer than she'd anticipated to find the secret panel hiding the stairs, but she made sure it was shut firmly behind her when she was inside. She was just as glad she couldn't see the staircase she was ascending - it felt rickety under foot and although she was guided by her right hand moving over the wall beside her, she waved her left hand outwards and felt nothing. Hopefully she wouldn't have to leave by this passage.

The stairs went back and forth, zigzagging upwards with a narrow landing on each turn. It felt like she was climbing forever; her legs were beginning to ache. At last she caught a whiff of fresh air and came to the wall that marked the top. She pressed her ear to it and listened, but either it was too thick for sound to penetrate, or there was nothing to hear.

Finding the small stud, she pressed it and eased the hidden

door opened a crack. It was too hard to tell if anything was out there or not, so she opened it a little further and came face to face with a pair of swords.

"Did you really think I would be such easy prey, assassin?" Ewan's voice had a definite sneer to it. "I had the wizard ward the secret passage, before I killed him. I knew you were coming the moment you entered the storeroom."

The two guards reached in and pulled her forward, dragging her over to stand in front of Ewan. He looked down at her in contempt. "Think you you're the first to attempt this? Though I must say, I would have expected someone . . . larger. Well, let's have a look at you."

He reached down and yanked her hood back, then stepped back in shock. "You!"

"Hey, Ewan," Jessica said. "What happened to your fancy accent?"

"You are supposed to be dead."

"Sorry to disappoint."

"Search her!"

Jessica withstood the guards' search stoically. "I'm not armed."

One of the guards shook his head to indicate they found no weapons and Ewan motioned for them to release her.

"Think not to kill me with your magic," he told her. "I have protections against such."

She rolled her eyes. "I didn't come here to kill you."

"Indeed. Then for what reason are you here?"

"I came to give you a chance to repent of your sins lest you be judged." Or something like that anyway. All she remembered was that her mother said she had to give him a chance to change before invoking the incantation.

Ewan stared at her for a moment then burst out laughing.

"You are dismissed," he said to the guards.

"But your highness—"

"Begone! I have nothing to fear from a lone woman."

The guards saluted and left. Jessica watched them curiously, there was something odd about the way they moved, like they weren't entirely sure of their actions.

"I see you're still wearing the Amulet of Athelon," she said. "With a few modifications, I take it?"

"There was a wizard who was able to expand the amulet's power. I found it necessary to ensure the loyalty of my men."

"So not everyone is enjoying your rule," she murmured. "Imagine that." A slight breeze lifted a stray lock of her hair as she looked out over the half wall around the top of the tower. "Quite the view from up here."

"So tell me, my lady Jessica," he said mockingly. "If you have not come to kill me, why have you come? Surely you do not wish to try and regain my favor, although the thought does have some appeal. I think you could beg for my mercy quite prettily."

She suppressed a shudder. "I meant what I said. I'm here to offer you a chance to repent before you're judged."

"Repent? What have I to repent for?"

"How about for all the lives you've ruined? Or the women you've murdered?" She started to get angry as he stood there smirking at her. "How about for abusing your power and authority?"

He reached out suddenly and grabbed her by the arm, pulling

her in and kissing her hard on the lips. "Oh, yes," he said, releasing her again. "I will find it most enjoyable indeed, breaking you. After I've had you stripped of your magic of course. Perhaps I will even let you live afterwards."

"You had your chance," she said angrily, taking a step backwards. "Now you get to face the consequences of your actions."

She raised her hands to the light of the full moon overhead and began to chant.

"*I call upon A'flania, Fae goddess of the moon, the first mother and mother to us all.*

I call upon A'flania, Fae goddess of the moon, to lift the veil between worlds."

He adopted a bored pose. "You're wasting your time, you know."

"*I call upon A'flania, so that justice may be served.*

By the Fae blood that runs through me, heed my words."

Ewan shook his head in mock disappointment. "I've already told you, your magic won't work here, you stupid woman."

"*I call upon the innocents made to suffer.*

I call upon the spirits in torment."

He rolled his eyes and then crossed his arms over his chest. "You don't believe me? Very well. Do your worst."

"*I call upon my sisters from the aether*

Come, and make things right."

A mist began to form between them. Ewan stepped back with a frown, drawing his sword. "Whatever you're doing, cease this now. Your spells cannot work here."

"It's not a spell," Jessica said, lowering her arms.

Chapter 48

The mist began taking shape, that of a woman.

"It was an incantation, a summoning of the wrongful dead."

More shapes began forming and Ewan backed away another step, brandishing his sword. "What do you mean, a summoning. Who, exactly, have you summoned?"

"I've summoned the spirits of the women you've murdered, the victims of your perversions."

He paled and backed away another step as more figures began forming. "You're mad. I have nothing to fear from spirits."

"No? Then why do you look so afraid?"

"Stop this right now and I'll let you live. I swear on my honor."

"You have no honor!" She glared at him. "You had your chance, now it's time to pay the piper."

He took a step towards her, swiping at the still forming figures. "Then perhaps I'll just kill you instead."

"You'll have to get through us first," said a voice behind her.

"You!" Already pale, the color leached completely from

Ewan's face. The sword in his hand wavered as Dominic and Sebastian stepped forward.

More and more figures began forming and Ewan backed away again. As the first ones gained corporeal shape they began whispering.

"You took my life even as you took my maidenhead."

"You took pleasure in torturing me in unspeakable ways."

"I was to take my vows in the abbey."

The spirits of all the women he'd wronged had him backed into the corner of the battlement.

"Stop this!" There was a raw edge of panic to Ewan's voice. "I swear I will pardon you all if you send them away."

The figures drew back as the last one began to form.

"No," Ewan whispered.

"Lady Cassandra," Sebastian said in awe.

The crowd parted to let her approach. "I gave you life. I plotted and schemed to see that you advanced. And how did you repay me? Poison in my wine."

"Mother. I—"

"Though I am not without sin, thy crimes are too heinous to be imagined. I curse the day I birthed thee."

As he looked on in dawning horror, the ghosts of his victims began changing, their appearance becoming more corpse-like.

"What's happening?" he whispered.

"Come, my son." She held her arms open. "Embrace thy mother."

She moved closer, the image of her flesh melting away.

"No! Stay back!" Ewan swung his sword back and forth. It passed harmlessly through the ghostly shape.

Her form had become that of a skeleton with ragged bits of flesh attached. She reached for him. "Give mother a kiss."

"No!" He backed away, stumbling as he hit the edge of the parapet. Arms pin wheeling for balance, he hung on the edge for a second, then plunged over the side, his mother's spirit following.

"Be at peace," Jessica told the remaining spirits.

One by one they began to fade until Jessica, Dominic, and Sebastian were the only ones left on the battlement. They looked at each other, unable to believe it was over.

"Well, that was creepier than I thought it would be," Jessica said to break the silence.

Sebastian moved over to the edge of the battlement and peered over the edge. Dominic and Jessica joined him. There was no question that Ewan was dead, but they needed to see his broken body on the rocks below for themselves.

"What happens now?" Jessica asked.

"Now," Sebastian said with a degree of satisfaction, "We see to the crowning of a new king."

. . . two weeks later.

"That was a beautiful ceremony," Jessica said with a sigh. She kicked off her shoes and flopped down on the bed in her room in the wizard's tower in Ghren's castle. "I've never been to a coronation before."

"I could almost feel sorry for poor Gareth. I don't think it's quite sunk in yet that he's Ghren's new king," Dominic said. He

LUCKY DOG

and Sebastian sprawled in the chairs in front of the fireplace.

Jessica raised herself up on her elbows to look at him. "Are you having second thoughts about giving up the crown?"

"Gods no!" He shuddered.

"I think Gareth will find a good helpmate in Lynette," Sebastian said. "She seems a most sensible girl."

"And anyone can see she and Gareth are crazy in love." Jessica struggled to sit up. The corset she'd been forced to wear so she could fit into her dress was starting to dig into places it had no business digging into. "As much as I'm having fun playing dress up," she said, "I'm starting to have a little trouble breathing. Excuse me while I change into something more comfortable."

"Need any help?" Dominic offered as she disappeared behind the screen at the far end of the room.

"Somehow I don't think you'd end up being much help," she called back.

He and Sebastian were both in their court clothes as well, although all it took to make them more comfortable was removing their jackets and the sashes from around their waists. Sebastian uncorked one of the bottles of wine he'd brought upstairs with them and poured them each a drink.

Jessica returned in an admirably short time, dressed in a pair of hose and a voluminous shirt, a leather vest over it and the shirt tails hanging out. At their surprised looks, she shrugged. "I said I wanted to be more comfortable."

"I find I am beginning to get used to seeing you in men's garb," Dominic said. "It is truly most fetching."

"Thanks, I think." She picked up one of the goblets of wine. "So what are we drinking to?"

"How about to happy endings?" Sebastian suggested.

"Or new beginnings," said Dominic.

"Or how about to King Gareth, long may he reign." Jessica raised her cup.

"To the King," the two men echoed.

"And now I must take my leave," Sebastian said, getting to his feet. "I have promised to meet with an old acquaintance. I will see you both in the morning."

They wished him a pleasant evening and he was gone.

"I have a gift for you," Dominic said as the door shut behind the bard.

"For me? Really?" Jessica was touched.

He produced a cloth-wrapped object and placed it in her hands.

Mystified, she unwrapped it and looked at him in surprise. "A mirror?" It was a finely wrought mirror, made of glass instead of the more common burnished metal.

"Not just a mirror, a scrying mirror," he told her. "You may recall I was once the apprentice of the wizard who dwelt in this tower."

"Yes, I remember."

"Though much of the magic I once learned has been forgotten over the years, I still remember how to scry with a mirror and thought to teach you the spell. You could talk to your friends in the other realm."

"Oh, Dominic!" Tears filled her eyes. "That's the nicest thing anyone's ever done for me."

Thank you just didn't seem like enough so she went over to give him a hug. Dominic tugged her by her wrist until she fell onto his lap and then he kissed her soundly. She kissed him back at first but after a moment or two she wriggled free.

"Hey! We'll have plenty of time for that later. First, teach me the scrying spell."

He let her go with a grin. "It's simple really, just focus on whatever it is you want to see in the mirror and the recite the incantation. Your image will appear in nearest reflective surface."

After repeating the incantation in her head several times, Jessica said it out loud. She tried to focus on both Howard and Ellen, but she kept getting distracted so she concentrated solely on Ellen.

The mirror went dark and at first she thought the spell had failed, but then she realized what was going on. "Ellen . . . wakey, wakey."

There was no reply.

"Hey! Ellen, wake up sleepyhead!"

"Five more minutes," came the sleepy response.

Jessica grinned. "No, not five more minutes. Now."

"Jessica?" The voice was only slightly less sleepy. "I must be dreaming. Go away, dream, and let me sleep."

"Ellen!" She was becoming a little exasperated. "This isn't a dream. So get your sorry butt out of bed right now! I don't know how long I can hold this."

"Jessica?" There was a rustling noise and the sound of bedsprings creaking. A sleepy-eyed Ellen, complete with a nasty case of bed-head, moved into view. "Jessica? What are you doing in the mirror on my dresser?"

"I'm not actually *in* your mirror," Jessica told her, grinning like a fool. "It's just my image, like a video chat. I'm learning to scry."

"You mean like Howard was doing?"

"No," Dominic said, shaking his head. "Howard's scrying was different. It . . . it's complicated."

"Who's that?" Ellen demanded, craning her neck as though she could change the view.

"That's Dominic," Jessica said smugly. She angled the mirror so show him lounging in his chair by the fireplace.

"Wow!" Ellen said.

"I know, right?" Jessica turned the mirror back facing her. "You will not believe what's been happening over here . . ."

Dominic settled back in his chair for a nice long wait as she proceeded to recap everything that had happened since they met.

"I'm not trying to stir up trouble or anything," Ellen said. She leaned closer to the mirror and whispered, "Are you sure you can trust him? After all, he *is* Ewan's brother."

Jessica opened her mouth to reply, then snapped it shut and turned to Dominic. "Would you be a dear and find us another bottle of wine? And maybe some bread and cheese to go with it?"

"If you wanted to talk in private, all you had to do is ask," he grumbled, pulling his boots back on.

"I need a moment with Ellen," she replied. "But I could also use a snack. That banquet seemed like it was hours ago."

"It was." He came over and dropped a kiss on the top of her head. "Will an hour be sufficient?"

"More than enough," she assured him.

When Dominic returned in the allotted time, Jessica was staring pensively into the fire, the mirror laying face down on the table beside her. Her eyes looked suspiciously damp and were slightly red-rimmed.

"Is everything all right?" he asked, concerned.

"It's fine," she waved a dismissive hand. "It's just seems like a really long time since I've seen my friends. I miss them."

She would have said more, but there was a commotion outside of the castle. They got up and went to the window. Jessica was surprised to see fireworks going off in the courtyard.

Dominic smiled. "It appears the whole kingdom is celebrating."

"Do you have any regrets?" she asked, searching his eyes.

"Regrets?"

"Coming back to Ghren, giving up the throne . . . any of it?"

He leaned back against the window casement and looked at her seriously. "I had returned to Ghren to make my brother pay for what he'd done to me, so that part I certainly don't regret. And giving up the throne? It was never my intention to sit upon it."

"But—"

"But most of all, I do not regret having taken the commission to rob an innocent witch of her amulet. Had I not, I might never have met you."

"One might even say you were quite the lucky dog," Jessica said with a smirk.

Her laughter filled the tower room as he tackled her to the bed.

THE END

About the Author

Carol R. Ward has always had a love of writing. She grew up reading old copies of Edgar Rice Burroughs and Robert E. Howard so it's no wonder her first love is fantasy and science fiction.

She always believed she was meant to be a writer of short stories, however her stories tended to be rather long. They also tended to have a romantic thread running through them. Finally caving in to the inevitable, she embraced her genre and began writing novels of fantasy/science fiction adventure with a dash of romance thrown into the mix. She has never regretted it.

Today she lives with her husband and four cats in Ontario, Canada and writes a variety of prose: non-fiction, flash fiction, short stories, and novels – in a variety of genres: humour, horror, contemporary, romance, science fiction, and fantasy. She's also a prolific poet.

Carol loves to hear from her fans and you can email her directly at: crward.author@gmail.com

You can also visit her blog at:
http://www.randomwriterlythoughts.blogpot.com or look her up on Facebook (Carol R Ward, Author) or Twitter (CarolRWard).

Other Books by the Author

The Moonstone Chronicles
Magical Misfire

The Ardraci Elementals
An Elemental Wind
An Elemental Fire
An Elemental Water

www.ingramcontent.com/pod-product-compliance
Lightning Source LLC
Chambersburg PA
CBHW030248270626
47156CB00021B/204